THE DIARY

OF

HENRY FITZWILLIAM DARCY

as fantasized by
Marjorie Fasman

NEW
LEAF
PRESS

New Leaf Press
P.O. Box 361240
Los Angeles, CA 90036-9440

Paperback First Edition

Set in Caslon typefaces.
Printed on 70# Finch Opaque Vellum Text
Printed by Ventura Printing, Ventura, California
(using the waterless process)
Printed and bound in the United States of America

Cataloging-in-Publication Data

Fasman, Marjorie.
    The diary of Henry Fitzwilliam Darcy /as fantasized by Marjorie Fasman. - 1st pbk. ed.
        p.   cm.
    1. England - Social life and customs - 19th century - Fiction.
    2. Young men - England - Fiction.
    3. Courtship - England - Fiction
    I. Austen, Jane, 1775-1817. Pride and Prejudice. II. Title.

PS3556.A7788D53 1998

ISBN 0-9660778-1-4

To be opened and read only by myself   . . . H.F.D.

17 SEPTEMBER, 1795

Hello, Diary!

It is I: Henry Fitzwilliam Darcy. I am supposed to write in you most regularly. Of course, you cannot talk back, and that gives me a great advantage.

So Hello!

Hello?

I am ten today. You are my birthday present. You, and a long list of properties I am to inherit when my father is dead. I do not consider that a happy thought! And, quite frankly, nor do I much welcome you, although I have promised to keep you faithfully.

In truth, what I truly most desire for my birthday is a puppy. There is a new family at one of the tenants' homes. I was taken to see the litter when they were first borned, and again two days ago. They were a marvel. I told my parents I would like one for my birthday. (Although, in truth, I would like them all!) My father told me that dogs are for the Hunt. (They live outside, and until I learn to ride properly they are no part of my life.)

Nurse Elise tells me not to despair, that she will think of something. What?

No puppy for the heir to Pemberley. Instead he gets YOU, Mr. Diary. Are you warm and soft and squirmy? Are you funny and playful? I think not. Actually, I must confess that for a book you are quite handsome. Fine leather, with a nice aroma. Real gold embossing on your cover. My name in gold. And a fine, heavy key. I shall lock you every night, and I shall never lose the key.

Someone by the name of Peeps (I think) wrote a very famous diary. Everyone quotes what he says at the end of the day, so I shall say it to you, "And so to bed."

&

18 SEPTEMBER, 1795

The puppy! He came today! Nurse Elise and Cook went off before the sun was up and returned with a basket which they carried into the nursery. ("Nursery!" A fine mockery at my age.)

I was at breakfast. I never could eat another thing.

He is round and fat and soft and has little teeth like needles.

(Excuse the blotches, Diary. I am learning to use a quill and it sputters and catches. I have ink all over my hands and the desk.)

We played all day. Except he gets sleepy, so when he did I lay on the floor with him and closed my eyes too.

He is white with brown spots. He has bright eyes, like buttons. They say he will turn into a fine hunter. His nose is wet and it wiggles at everything. He chews at everything too, even my nose and fingers and toes. He has already destroyed a slipper. I have named him Sultan (from a book I am reading).

Good afternoon, sir. My parents will be here shortly. They are coming to tea.

&

19 SEPTEMBER, 1795

I have not cared to write, or to do anything. Sultan was taken away, and my heart is broken. It will never be mended.

After I wrote you, my mother came to tea. I had invited my father too, but he is away. That disappointed me, but I would not show it. Nurse Elise had me all dressed up for the visit. She made me sit still so she could put to rights my hair where the pup had been tugging at it.

When my mother arrived I did not hear her approach and she discovered me huddled on the floor all wrapped around Sultan.

"STAND UP! THIS IS NO POSITION FOR AN ENGLISH GENTLEMAN! MAY I ASK FROM WHERE THIS CREATURE HAS COME?!"

Hubbub upstairs! Downstairs! Sultan was snatched up and taken away. I cried and that made things worse. Nurse Elise is in disgrace and every one of our staff is acting most strange. If Nurse Elise is sent away I shall not survive.

But so far she is here, and tonight she patted me when she put me to bed, and told me to be a brave little English gentleman and to take my disappointments with a stiff upper lip.

She promised that later we would go to visit Sultan and his brothers and sisters. That consoled me somewhat, but not a lot. I had been sure that he would have been in my bed this night.

After she closed the door I relit the candle, made a shield of my covers and turned to you. I need to tell you all. I hope I do not burn the house down!

※

20 SEPTEMBER, 1795

I did not see Nurse Elise this morning. A new man by the name of Keith brought me my breakfast. I heard the carriage wheels outside and heard my father returning. I heard doors opening and shutting, and the sound of my mother's light tread going down the staircase.

I *slipped* out of my room, crept to the banister and peered down. Mother went into Father's study. I saw Nurse E. go in.

After not very long she came out. She was crying. I knew something bad had happened to her, and therefore to me. I started to cry and could not stop, although I heard my mother coming up the stairs. She heard me and came to where I was crouched.

"Go to your room! And never let me see you EVER AGAIN spying on people. It is beneath you. You dishonor us. I am thoroughly ashamed of you!"

She hurried away and disappeared into her rooms. I heard the door close. I am bade never to enter a closed door, and I did not dare to enter there.

I am all alone, D. I have only you.

⚜

21 SEPTEMBER, 1795

Now I have Nurse Reynolds. She says she has known me since she came to the downstairs staff when I was but four. Hello – Aren't there a lot of changes here at Pemberley! I feel all hollow without Nurse Elise, but Mrs. Reynolds seems like a good sort.

We two do not change, do we? Well, maybe one of us does. I think I may be getting a little taller. That is the first thing Nurse R. did when she came. No, the second. First, she looked at my books and said nice things about the choices I had made. Then she said we should have a chart to record my height, so we made one, put it on the wall, and she had me stand straight against it, made a mark and put the date on it. She says she will get a measuring tape so we can see just how tall I get.

I like her. I asked permission to go to tell my mother, and I went and did that. She was on her chaise lounge reading, and I wanted most desperately to hug her. I dared assay that, and she did thank me for the hug, but she did not respond overmuch and I felt embarrassed. Am I too rough? I want to hug her hard, and kiss her.

That is all for today. I think things are going to be quite nice after all the awful things that happened. I want you to know this, D. – no matter how dire things seem, it is up to us to be manly and stowic (?) stowick.

Good-bye for now. I have to go to ask about that word.

⚜

28 SEPTEMBER, 1795

Nurse R. stays in my room until I am ready for bed. I kneel down and say my prayers. When I am through she propels me onto the bed, pulls open the covers, shoves me under, and then sits on the edge. She reaches for my hand and holds it. We have a nice chat. I like this. It is truly the best part of the day.

⚜

29 SEPTEMBER, 1795

I have decided that I shall marry Nurse R., but I haven't told her that yet. She will be surprised to learn that she is to be the Mistress of Pemberley.

LATER

I am beginning to think more and more about Nurse R. I believe I am seriously in love with her. It is more than that she holds my hand. I now throw myself into her arms and hug her very tight.

She pats me on the back, ever so kindly and says, "there, there," and then she rises to leave. Before she *dowses* the candle, she blows me a kiss. She shuts the door ever so quietly.

I do not go right to sleep. I think about her a lot. How nice it feels to touch someone and to be touched.

I know I am too young to be wed, but I shall approach my father to get his permission, and then I shall propose to her.

30 SEPTEMBER, 1795

I asked permission to enter my father's study. Permission was granted. I told him of my momentous decision about Nurse R. He actually smiled a little, and said there were several obstacles – my age for one, but most importantly the great gap in social class between us. This, he said, was *impossible* and I must always, always keep that in mind. He made me promise that I would never do anything that would lower our high standing, most particularly always to be in mind that my betrothed must be of my class.

Then, again smiling gently, he said that we must find my mother and tell her of this turn of events. And so we did.

My mother did not receive this news with the same attitude as my father. She was displeased. After saying in a cold voice that she "liked this not" she told me to go back to my room and to stay there.

1 OCTOBER, 1795

My mother is behaving most strangely. She is a lady who rarely shows any emotion. Now when I try to hug or kiss her, she turns her head and pushes me away.

One of our servants became engaged to one of our butlers, and I have seen them hug and kiss and *tousle* one another and I like that. I did ask my father about this. He tells me that people of a lower class are more open about their feelings, but that it is coarse behavior and that we of the upper class must strive to suppress our feelings.

To go on. My mother is behaving strangely. So is Nurse Reynolds. She has told me I must say my prayers by myself. She no longer comes in to tuck me in. I must blow out the candle myself. (I do not, I keep it burning as I fall asleep – the soft light contents me.)

I am angry at Nurse R. I cry under the covers. I have made myself not think about her any more. I shall not marry her! Not ever. And never shall I tell her of the great opportunity she might have had. I had it all planned. My parents would die of the plague and we would be released from the promise I had made to father. We would be in charge of Pemberley together. There would be dogs everywhere in the house. Their home could be in the conservatory. What wonderful times we would have.

I will not think of her, I will not. Not ever again!

❦

2 OCTOBER, 1795

This morning I was called to Father's study. My father announced to me that Mrs. Reynolds was to be transferred to the downstairs staff. It felt like a stone was falling down into my insides. But wait! He then told me that a man was coming to take me in hand and teach me proper attitudes and the proper manner for a gentleman of my "distinction."

Sure enough, GEORGE arrived late the same afternoon. I like him not. I trust him not. I am trying to be civil, but I fear for what is to come.

He started in straightway putting aside the books with which I amuse myself and making a list of what he intends for me to read. The books he put aside are lovely. They are read only in my very own time after my lessons.

I left the room in order to appeal to my father. George was most quick and apprehended me in the hall. He threatened me – never was I to sneak out like "a rat" and go whining to my father. A sharp box on the ear accompanied this threat, and the stinging tears came to my eyes.

"And don't let me ever see you cry."

I am telling you all this from under the covers. I hope I do not set the room afire from my candle! I have made a kind of tent out of my bedclothes, and for a frame I dragged in my old rocking-horse. I miss my pen when I write at night, but a graphite pencil will have to do. I do not think it would be much of a success for the linens if I were to use pen and ink. The pencil comes from Germany. It says "Farber," smells and tastes of glue, sulphur, resin and such. How come I to know of the taste? It writes so *hard* that I have to keep licking it so that the words will show.

Later I will snuff the candle, toss out the horse, and go to sleep. That means you will still be under the covers. Don't get smothered. I think we are going to have a long, wonderful friendship.

This is only between us – I HATE George.

❦

16 OCTOBER, 1795

Diary! I have to hide you away! I came into my sitting room this afternoon and found ugly George sitting at my desk, with you in front of him, searching for your key! Scoundrel! Heathen! Villain!

I am certain he will soon find the key, and I tremble lest he should look into your pages and discover what I have said about him and about my love for R. and about the times I have been angry at mother and said bad things – this troubles me mightily. It is too frightening to think on.

I am plotting as to when I can escape his infernal prying into my doings and can find a safe place to hide you.

I have in mind a fine closet in a faraway room, but I dare not set it down even to you, in the event that the secret could be discovered by my enemy.

I shall miss you. I do not talk to you often, but when I need you it is a comfort indeed to have you near to hand.

Au revoir . . . but never "adieu."

❦

18 OCTOBER, 1795

Dear D.,

I have been confined to quarters. George is not here. A matter of a family tragedy at Southampton. His father has died of "an ailment." Do they think me a child? I have heard whisperings about "gin" (both downstairs and upstairs).

Was George *ever* my age, with a father and mother and maybe a brother or a sister? Hard to imagine. I think he has always been big, mean, and dangerous.

Just as he was leaving early this morning, he looked at me strangely, went for a cloth, wet it from the pitcher, came at me with it and wiped my mouth so hard that he hurt me, grumbling during each swipe about how did I get so dirty. Then left abruptly, slamming the door so hard it must have been heard throughout the vast house.

It did not take long for me to get into trouble, so here I am, confined to chambers. I cannot think that my crime was very grand, but my mother found me hanging on in the kitchen, and was distressed. Now I must await my tutors in my rooms.

I spend much time looking out the window. I like to watch the clouds and the passing procession below – Crowley and his many bemuddied assistants going in all directions with all manner of implements; horses prancing and tossing their heads, sometimes being led, sometimes bearing a stable hand; lumbering wagons filled with hay, sheep, corn, whatever. This morning I saw my father ride off to a fox hunt. He was a colorful sight in his red coat which went well with the red autumn leaves. Yellow leaves, too, and brown.

The other morning the pigs escaped from their pen and it was a grand performance until they were all rounded up. Sorry. I have just ended a sentence with a preposition. Mr. Leigh will not approve, but he will never see it. If he were to see it he would upbraid me, as any good tutor should. OUR secret.

❦

20 OCTOBER, 1795

I awakened to the sound of carriage wheels this morning. The household was in an uproar. I ran to open my door and saw Dr. McPherson rushing toward my mother's room, followed by Rose and Margaret, each carrying towels and a bucket of what was clearly hot water. All this excitement for a bath? I knew this could not be so. Mother must be very ill, thought I. I was frightened, and clung to the door, my heart hammering. Then Reynolds hurried towards me. I was most glad to see her! She led me back into my room, and closed the door.

"Nurse Reynolds! My mother is dying!"

"Not so, Master Darcy. Your mother is bringing a new life into this world."

I was stunned. A new life? Then R. told me that Mother and Dr. McPherson together are working to deliver to me a new baby. She told me to be a good boy and stay in my room, and left hurriedly – Dr. McPh. and my mother – working together? *Deliver to me?*

A baby in the house! This means I am no longer in solitary control as the only son and heir. This means I have to share? My books? My lead soldiers? No one mentioned what this baby is. – A boy? He could well covet Pemberley and become my enemy. A girl? – What can one do with a girl?

After what seemed a very, very long time (I was alone, I was frightened, I was hungry), Reynolds returned to tell me that I have a baby sister.

"Where is she? Isn't she to be delivered to me?"

R. laughed low, put her arms around me and gave me a hug. "You shall meet her very soon."

෯

22 OCTOBER, 1795

Why am I a prisoner? I must inform you that Pemberley is a vast place – all manner of halls and stairs and corridors, some very grand and some only for service. The family suites have a closet-room adjoining, and these are for the servicing of our suites. A narrow staircase leads into the closet room. I find I like exploring and the surprises never stop.

I discovered a straight down wooden staircase with steep steps. Sat me down and went *bump bump* rather fast, but after a few descents my *posterior* felt bruised. I fetched a thick mat from my room, sat on *it* and went into motion *very* fast. *Bully!* OH, OH! At the bottom, *a suddenly opened door,* a butler bearing a huge tray – OH, OH!

Descending Aladdin! Collision! Upended tray! Dishes in the air! Dishes and vittles *raining down*!

CREAM cascading over the butler. Peas bouncing in relentless descent. Butter landing on my head. No one hurt. Darcy laughing out of control. Butler not amused. Commotion throughout the vast home, butler departed in fury. Scion of P. banished to chambers. Even now I want to laugh as I write, sad as I am this day. The memory of bouncing peas rolling down the stairs and into the scullery! (I wager they will go rolling on forever.)

❦

28 OCTOBER, 1795

Today I met my sister. I have been expecting her to be delivered to me for many days. It has been over a week and nothing happened until today. Ug.

Let me tell you about it, D. There is a grand rotation of servants "taking care of the young master." Today it was Reynolds who entered my room. She told me to comb my hair and put on a waistcoat, that I was invited to meet my new sister. I asked would I see my mother. I was reassured on that score, and marched the long distance from my room to my mother's.

What did I visualize? Certainly not the stupid bundle which was held out to me by my mother, a bundle which held a squirmy nonentity, all red and wrinkled and floppy.

Mother said to me, "Good morning, Henry Fitzwilliam. This is your sister. She is to be named Georgiana. Isn't she lovely?"

How was I to answer that? My mother is lovely. She looked lovelier than ever for all the time I had not been able to see her. This baby is not *lovely*. She is UGLY.

Then Mother drew the bundle back tenderly, and did lay it against her shoulder, and kissed the pruney little face. A pang coursed through my body from my throat to my knees. I almost cried out.

Mother observed this not. "Soon you will have a lovely playmate, Fitzwilliam. I know you will always take very, very good care of her."

Then she lay back on the pillow, closed her eyes, and I was granted the privilege of a small kiss on her cheek, being very, very careful (on instruction) not to touch the baby.

She is to be my charge? I cannot imagine anything worse.

❦

30 OCTOBER, 1795

How did this creature come to us? No one will answer me.

We have farms. Many farms. They lie all around us for miles. I visit them frequently, especially when there are babies. I have seen piglets, chicks (by the thousands), colts, puppies – especially puppies. I like them best of all and go to visit them as often as I am permitted. I am getting big, and soon I shall go alone and not wait for permission.

There are, *forever*, new chicks. One can watch them coming out of eggs, a wet bundle with a chipping beak. They become fluffy and pretty in no time. Our baby is not fluffy and pretty at all.

And colts – Once I came into the stable area when there was a great commotion, and before anyone could cover my eyes and lead me away I saw our stallion throw himself upon Dulcie with such a clamor of neighing and shrieking as I cannot describe. I called to Jarrow that Gannymede was trying to *kill* Dulcie but was assured otherwise by him. Later, there was a colt, but it was borned at night, and I did not see how that happened. An egg? I knew that could not be so.

The colt was so sweet. It was already on its feet by the time I got to the stable the next day. Our bundle has feet, but I doubt that they will ever be used. I asked Reynolds, "How are babies born?" She replied that my father would give me this information.

Sure enough, I was bid to come to his study.

"Congratulations, Fitzwilliam! Do you not have a lovely new companion to share your days!"

"Yes Sir. It is nice to see you back at Pemberley."

He muttered something about how it is with a busy person, shuffled some papers, lit up his cigar, then said, "I understand you have inquired as to the circumstances of your sister's arrival."

"Yes sir."

He leaned back, took some time for a coughing fit, then proceeded to relate to me tales of Greek mythology, and also of the Old Testament. This was not news to me, D. I have read many of the tales he related to me, but it was nice to have this time with him, and I like to listen to fine tales as much as I like to read them.

I heard a great deal about Jupiter and his visits, about Venus and Mars, about Cupid and Psyche. These characters certainly were busy with their own affairs, and getting mixed into the affairs of mortals! And the mortals managed to get themselves into the affairs of the Gods.

Everybody, it seems, falls in love, and children get borned.

But how did they GET here? I asked that, and father told me about Adam and Eve. Did he think that "the apple" would put my questions aside? And what did the serpent have to do with my question?

When I was young I did wonder about Leda and the Swan, and went out to the lake to see what I could learn. In the spring I often heard loud trumpeting from that quarter. Later there would be cygnets. What did I ever *really* see? Calm swans, calmly sailing on a quiet lake, their forms reflected in the water, large pairs at first, later large swans and little ones following.

FROM WHERE CAME MY SISTER????????

2 NOVEMBER, 1795

Workmen have started today to prepare a room in my wing of Pemberley, down the long hall. This I am told, will be the nursery for my sister. It is a good distance from my suite, and I thank the fates that there are no connecting doors. It appears, then, that the bundle will not be delivered to me, but to this place.

I watch the workmen with interest. One of them has provided me with some pieces of wood, some pegs, and when he has a moment he shows me how to make two pieces fit together. Crowley has found me some tools, and I am happy when my tutoring schedule allows me time to attend to this new occupation. I am in mind to create a stable for my toy horses.

The "bundle" is growing and she is getting a face of sorts. I am most perturbed that she has stolen my mother from me. She has been in a suite next to my mother. I have felt strange about this. I am glad she will be moved.

9 NOVEMBER, 1795

The workmen are gone. Now the decorators have moved in. They bring no pleasure to me. They take themselves very seriously, and it seems my company annoys them. They prefer to be preening and fussing with various materials which they bring in tall piles, and unroll for my mother to see, with a great *snap* and a sweep of the arm and the fabric rippling through the air and floating to the floor.

Momentous decisions are being made as to whether it shall be this or that, and should it be *draped or swagged*. The decorators address the problem with the same seriousness as I have heard father and his friends discuss important matters of the shire. Color is a matter of even graver importance. Pink, yes. But just *which shade of pink?*

I decide to return to my room, even though I am leaving the company of my mother. She seems not to notice.

14 NOVEMBER, 1795

George returned from his leave. Darkness descended. And herewith important tidings: GEORGE IS GONE! I need to tell you all about it. It has been several days since he was *cashiered*, (what a happy new word!) but I have been abed.

That was a bad, bad day, even the beginning was worse than usual. We were on our way out for "sports," a fearsome experience when shared with George. He was propelling me down the hall when I espied my mother. I ran to her, but she told me to go outside with George and to behave myself. When her back was turned, George grabbed my ear and towed me back to our chambers. That *hurt*, but I was so mad at him and at mother that I paid it no mind. I ran into the room and tore down a small portrait of her which I hurled with all my strength against the wall. Where, of course, the glass smashed into a million pieces.

George was a sight to behold. I vow he swelled up to twice his already huge size and lunged at me. I ran – ran – with him in hot pursuit, scattering furniture and books and everything until I fell and my head *thwacked* the floor. There was shattered glass there and my head turned all bloody. I knew it was blood because everything turned all red. George grabbed me and my blood spurted all over him. I was screaming loud enough to wake the dead. Sound of running footsteps! Opening of door! A battalion of servants! Both parents!

We must have presented a fine sight but at that moment I fainted.

When I revived I was safe in my bed with my head all bandaged. Nurse R. was back! I wanted to throw myself into her arms but I dared not. She might be taken away again.

Later when I saw Father there was a lecture about how men of stature do not scream and do not faint.

There is no more dreaming about marriage to Nurse R. She is strangely quiet, does her chores for me, but truly she is almost a phantom.

Good night, D. My brains feel strange. I wish there were someone to hold my hand. I hurt.

18 NOVEMBER, 1795

George is *gone, gone* never to return, and these are splendid days. I told my father I wished to *petition* him. I think he liked the word. However so, he did invite me to his study and listened very solemnly. I stated my case – if I am to grow up and be a proper master of Pemberley to follow his example, I would need to grow up very fast, and a governess or nanny or governor (perish forbid!) did not seem appropriate for me at my advanced age. Several days passed, and then I was summoned, and learned that I had well stated my case, and it was agreed upon. EXCELSIOR! I am a free man. Some one (or ones?) (how many?) of the downstairs staff will be in charge of me when necessary.

20 NOVEMBER, 1796

Mrs. Reynolds has been taking care of Georgiana these days. It is to be hoped that this lady will be allowed to remain with us on the second floor. This morning I crept to the nursery door and heard such nice sounds that I knocked, and was admitted, with much pantomiming that I not let my presence be known. G. was lying on a changing table. It seems they were playing "peek-a-boo." R. bade me play the game with my sister. Too babyish for me, too undignified. Soon, however, I did. Soon I was drawn into the fun of the baby's delight. Her eyes looked at me so roguish! And her laughing was sweet. Like the sound of the brook which runs into our trout stream.

⸙

24 November, 1796

No, not to be. Reynolds down, new Nanny in charge. Her name is Miss Behmer. Stolid, stern, dour. I am now paroled; but it seems that my sister is scuttled.

Today I heard her crying so piteously that I *rode* to her rescue. (I imagined myself as a knight in armor, bearing high my banner.) Georgiana was in her chair with the dinner tray in front. Nurse B., it seemed, was trying to train her to use her 'fine silver fork.' From the looks of it, G. had grabbed the peas and squashed them in her little fist. Smashed green was smeared everywhere – face, front, chair, hair. The *bonny* nanny was furious, and was now mopping her roughly. Such a flood of tears, smearing the green farther and wider. In one hand my sister clutched a piece of bread, and now the tears wet that hand and the bread too, which turned all soggy, but still she clutched it, and the tears ran onto her chubby wrist and hand. And now I felt such a pang and such a sense of *the nip* of it. I wished I were older and bigger. I would have liked to make that huge gorgon cry out in pain, as she was making my sister cry. What could I do?

Words could help! I commenced to declaim, " FACE/ FRONT/ CHAIR/ HAIR/" and chanted it over and over until G., stopped her sobbing and brightened. Then I bethought myself and started on, "Green, green/ the *meanest* green that's ever *beeeen.*" And soon she joined in, picking up the first two words of the rhyme, until she had got it right, and soon we were chanting and laughing. Not for long, you may be sure. I was ordered from the room and told not to return.

Far as I was down the vast hall, I could hear Georgiana's renewed crying.

⸙

27 November, 1796

Last night I fell asleep with the faint sounds of weeping in my ears. I went under the covers as deep as I could get, hoping to make the sound go away. What could I do? How ever would we manage to banish the dragon from our midst?

Well, D., the pigs saved us. Let me tell you about it. There is a new litter in the sty near the sheep shed. I went out early to watch the activities. There are eleven babies, and such climbings over and under one another to get to 'their breakfast'! Finally they settled down, save for one rowdy. Many of the farm hands stopped by, some stayed to watch. What I did not know was that baby Georgiana had toddled out of the house after me. She must have spent much time getting down the staircase. And how did she manage it? AND WHERE WAS MISS B.? Or anyone else of the staff?

I was watching intently a pig drama – all piglings were now asleep in the shade, curled up next to the huge sow. Except for Mr. Rowdy. *He* was awake and wanted to suckle. *Mum* grunted . . . he persisted . . . more grunts . . . more mischief. Of a sudden the sow let out a *roar*, swung her huge head and gave him such a swat with her snout that sent him screeching and cartwheeling across the pen. It was then that I espied the advancing Georgiana and realized that she was in direct line of the hurling pig. I *dived* through the air and averted the collision. Held her high, did a neat step, and saw the animal sail by. I remember thinking that I might like to be a matador.

It seems she had managed to squeeze through the slightly opened gate, so begrimed that one could scarce recognize her. I had to hold her tight, as she was squirming and calling "Down!" I let her touch one of the babies and carried her back to the house. Was accosted by a furious Miss Behmer, who snatched my burden and stormed away, holding the child well away from her starched front.

Later when she had been scrubbed clean, when Miss B. was napping away her lunch, I *kidnapped* my sister to the top of the grand staircase and watched her performance. She turned around, lay on her stomach, felt for the next step, and plumped herself down to it – and thus continued until I scooped her up and carried her back to her crib, (never so much as disturbing the snoring nanny).

30 NOVEMBER, 1796

When Father returned from London, I was summoned into his study. He requested an explanation. I asked, "And what had Miss B. to say for herself?"

He only wanted to know of *my* role. He listened intently, I was dismissed. Miss Behmer was summoned. As were the several farm hands who had been present. In the afternoon a carriage took Nurse Behmer away. When Father saw me later he gave me a light cuff, saying "Stout lad."

Eureka!

❦

9 JULY, 1797

I was doing my studies in History this morning when there was a knock on my door. "Enter."

An unknown butler did so. "Good morning, sir. I have a request from your father that you attend him in the study."

"Who are you? Are you not new here?"

"I am new, sir. The name is Bailey. And I fear that your father is impatient for your presence."

"Welcome to Pemberley, Bailey. Please tell my father that I shall come immediately."

He withdrew, thanking me. I carefully marked my place in my book. (I am reading *Herodotus*. Not easy to read, but I like it.)

My father looked up as I entered and bade me good morning. As we shook hands he announced, "It has finally arrived! Come over here, Fitzwilliam."

"Good morning, sir. What is it that has arrived?"

"Take a look, and you will know."

I approached him, he held out a parchment with a grand flourish, which I studied without becoming any the wiser. I asked, "What is this, Sir?"

"You do not understand the meaning of this? Look at it! Use the good eyes that God has given you!"

I studied it as hard as ever I could. He asked me what did I perceive. I told him that it seemed to be a tree.

"And that is all you understand?!" So saying, he took it from me and said in a hard voice that in his hand he was holding the recently completed family tree of the Darcy family; that he had had it traced back for many generations, all the way to France and Italy (and heaven knows where else. Greece perhaps? Might we be descendants of Herodotus? I would like that.)

There were so many names, and in such a fine spider web of print, but soon I found my own, "Henry Fitzwilliam, son of etcetera, b.1785. My sister's name, Georgiana, b.1795." The manuscript was divided down the middle. On my father's side I encountered my Uncle Darcy, Lord _ _ _ _ with his children swinging from a limb beneath his name (do not take this image literally, D.!) Anyway, *voilà* my first cousin Fitzwilliam, the younger son. My father did comment that if he (father) should die before I come of age, and if something dire should happen to me, and if the older brother were to die, that cousin Fitzwilliam would undoubtedly inherit Pemberley, – unless I were to have a brother. Dreadful thought, a *brother!* Maybe several? As for my cousin, fond as I am of him, I felt a rush of resentment that he could take my place. I asked my father what would happen to Pemberley if cousin Fitzwilliam were to die prematurely, and he replied that such was *too unpleasant* to think on, as if contemplating father's death *or my own* is *not* unpleasant!

On the opposite side of the document I found my mother's name, Lady Anne Darcy and that of her sister, my Aunt Catherine, now the very haughty Lady de Bourgh. Daughter – Anne. b. 1790.

Not many children yet, but room on the bough for a *scamperful*. My mother's noble family went high on the page, having been traced even farther back than Father's side. His side is traced to France. The records are not so good in France, says he. The name there was most assuredly "D'Arcy."

Now my father asked me for my opinion. I replied, "There are certainly many of us, are there not?"

"You must be careful, Henry, not to speak in platitudes. Indeed there are many, and many generations ahead, and I can only hope you will come to realize the weight of such lineage, and prove to be fully worthy. I pray that ultimately you will realize your significance in this succession and how much depends upon you and your choice of a suitable wife."

He dismissed me and I returned to my rooms wondering about that word 'platitude' and how had I offended, and about that 'suitable wife' business – A wife! I do not yet know any girls except my sister and one tenant daughter and she has crossed eyes. I was feeling strangely flat. Did Herodotus,

I wonder, have such matters as family trees and family responsibilities to worry him? And if he had, how would there have been time to chronicle those 'great and wonderful deeds' about which I am reading, and which are so exciting.

As I opened my book, I heard a bird call from the tree outside my window. I looked out, saw a rustling on the branch, but could not see the creature. Nevertheless I called to it. (Could it see me?) "I say, hello there! I sit on a tree too!"

Bird did not respond.

⁂

17 SEPTEMBER, 1797

Last night I thought that I was doomed and would die a most humiliating and dreadful death, and this in my twelfth year! I am glad I have you, D. I need someone to talk to.

I went to bed last night in apparent good health, but awoke in the middle of the night soaking wet. My gown was soaked, the sheet was soaked. No ablutions would be in the room until dawn. What was I to do? I took my candle, the horror of my clothes and linens, and my polluted self, crept down the stairs and outside to bury the shameful mess. I was aware there was a chance that Mr. Crowley might hear me, but he did not.

I knew where I would find his shovel and went to the shed. Reynolds must have heard the door open and close, and descended to find me in my despair. The shock of being discovered, the horror of my plight, and my fear of dying overwhelmed me. I sank to my knees and to my further horror began to cry. I know that boys of my station do not cry. I cried.

Reynolds knelt and took me in her arms. She rocked me, and this made it even worse. I cried so hard that my hair and my face got all wet. She pushed back my hair and then she saw my scar. She put her lips on it, and that made me burst wide open and bawl like a dumb little baby. It felt funny to be held and to be kissed, but it quieted me. Then I could speak and told her how ill I was and that I was afraid I was to die.

Murmuring softly, she gave me reason to hope and to have faith in my future. I was not ill. I was not to die. I was to be welcomed into manhood. I would experience this again and again until someday when I would find a happy union which would end my horror. What would that rescue be? She was vague and only said that she hoped that my "rescuer" would be worthy of me. I have been thinking about those words ever since.

And so ended the drama. When I bade R. good night she promised she would be of help to me whenever I needed her. I began to feel better. When we returned to the house she had her arm around my shoulders and that felt nice. She came upstairs with me, went to the linen closet for bedding, and got me fixed up all clean again. I shall be grateful to her for my entire life.

❦

21 MARCH, 1798

Today I was invited by Georgiana's nurse to take tea with my sister. I brought in a book with some nice pictures of alphabet letters which I thought she might like, which I remember studying most hard when I was her age. I liked watching her little hands turning the pages and seeing her smile. She pointed to the apple and I told her to say the word. "APPLE." Her baby voice made it sound delicious.

I looked around, the room looked very pretty and it certainly *is* pink and white!

Then I turned to the book, pointed to the apple and said "red," thence to the cut-open core and said "pink." She looked at me, solemnly turned the pages to "'C' for cat," and said that word over and over. I gave her a pat on her curly pate and thanked the nanny for the nice tea. As I turned at the door to say good-bye, she shouted "PINK!" I applauded her.

❦

1 MAY, 1798

There has been a lot of excitement at Pemberley these days. There was a big ball here. My father was home for several weeks. Georgiana and I were invited to watch my mother's last "fitting" on her party dress. She was so beautiful that I could not take my eyes from her. She even told me (in a lilting voice, so she could not have been offended) to "stop staring" but I could not. I can see her even now in that dress – a cherry color like the fruit in our orchard, soft and filmy with a beautiful ribbon at her waist. She turned to show us how the skirt floated out when she turned.

There were many carriages and many candles and the table was beautiful with flowers and filled with many dishes. And the music! I could not sleep D., and crept down the stairs to watch. I must have fallen asleep where I was crouched, because sometime later, when it was all quiet again, I awakened in my own bed. Some nice butler must have carried me there. I remember watching my mother dance, and what a lovely sight she was. And how she smiled at my father during the dance. When I saw him kiss her hand I felt happy.

The music still stays in my head, and the happiness of the night remains also. Today I was in the garden and heard singing. Such a lovely sound! Found my mother in the flower garden, cutting tall blue flowers. I kneeled behind the hedge and stayed there listening until she went into the house. I followed her to the conservatory and asked if I could watch her whiles't she was putting the flowers into a vase. She agreed. I asked her if she would sing again. She put the flowers down, sat down, pulled me to her, and looking right into my eyes, had just started when a servant brought her a folded note. After she read it, she rose hurriedly (pushing me away) and ran from the room.

☙

5 APRIL, 1799

We have been to a grand party. We have departed the party quite early. My mother has gone to her room and shut the door. Georgiana is crying in her room. And I am writing to you, D. No tutors, sad to say. It is Easter week.

My mother has (*had?* She seems to feel the relationship is wrecked by *the affaire in the garden*) a very exalted friend who is the Mistress of a very special estate in the Midlands. We were invited there for an Easter fortnight. We departed with cases and valises to bow the springs of our best carriage. Flocks of seamstresses and tailors had been summoned to outfit us. For G. white dresses each with a wide sash, which I am given to sport with

– until chided. (She likes the game of "Horsey.") Bonnets with all manner of adornment. I toyed with the idea of bringing in a live frog as an offering to join these adornments. Too good an impulse to resist. Did so. Nurse Alder fainted. To be sure, I was called to the study. This was *a good* time as I could see my father trying to suppress a smile during the lecture, and I was not punished.

As for me, I was bullied into a 'skeleton suit' which forces me to wear jacket, pantaloons and a FRILLED SHIRT. And a childish cap, which I managed to lose out the carriage window.

Arrived at N. Park at the same time as many other families, were taken to our rooms, put into our *costumes* and hurried down for the festivities. First, there were games in the grand salon – Oranges and Limes, Hunt The Slipper, Wind the Jack. Then to the terrace dining hall where a grand buffet was spread for our pleasure. Nurse Alder (why did *she* have to come with us?) avers that she counted sixty different 'presentations,' in groups of fifteen platters at each corner of the large table. I liked the food, I especially liked the sugar village in the middle of the table, set on what appeared to be real lawn, with rabbits, made of a sweet pasty, placed everywhere. We were informed that at the end of the fortnight each child would be gifted with a rabbit and a piece of 'the village.'

Then we were summoned into the large reception room for the opening of birthday gifts for one of the daughters (there are eleven children in this family) and this took a long time and was boring because we had to stay quiet and attentive the whole time of it. Finally a call to the Easter egg hunt. We boys ran out of the house with yells and the thundering of boots, with mothers vainly calling after us, but to no avail. The hunt was organized – babies on the lawn, children in the old-fashioned garden, older boys in the woodland. I was eager for this! We lined up, ready to race for it, when I heard my mother calling my name and had to go to her. Where was Georgiana? Where was Nurse Alder? I knew where to hunt out the big lady. The food table. She was gorging on widgen, preserved ginger, pastries, syllabub and who knows what else had gone on down. 'Georgiana is with her mother.' Not so! I left hurriedly. I ran through all the rooms of the downstairs, a good thousand meters, I would judge. And then I heard sounds which I followed. There, in a far parlor, stood a harpsichord and my sister was sitting there, her feet dangling high above the ground. (How got she onto that stool?) She was picking out notes and chords. I told her she must come with me immediately. "No!" "Then I shall have to carry you." "NO!" Did so, she crying at first, soaking and *chewing* on my frilled collar, and then *screaming*. It was thus that we arrived into the middle of the gathering on the lawn. Orders from the hostess to "get the caterwauling child *out of here!*" Frantic march up the stairs, 'abandonment of ship,' carriage ordered, retreat! I have never seen my mother in such a state. I could not help wondering would she have been thus unstrung if the child had gone to the lake and been lost. My ruined collar also upset her. It seems we are a family *disgraced*. It did not help matters that G. suddenly remembered the promised candies, and wept piteously for that.

⚶

14 APRIL, 1799

When my father returned (why must he be absent so often?) he was surprised to find us back at Pemberley. My mother talked to him in his study for such a long time. I watched from above and saw her emerge, weeping. What is the tragedy? The loss of a friend? I did not find 'Lady Easter Egg' so admirable. She has ugly skin and mouse hair and a fat stomach and hairs on her chin. Her voice is scratchy and unpleasant. Squinty eyes . . . My mother, on the other hand, is perfection, with a lilting voice and a graceful body and everything else so beautiful. Weeps she for the loss of 'the Egg,' or because of the 'outrageousness' of her children? Or both? Why fled my mother in such despair? The Major Domo was sent to protest our departure. It does appear that Lady Egg was banishing *the noise*, not the lot of us.

I do not understand why grown-ups behave so strangely. And such a commotion about titles! Lord, Lady, My Lord, Your Grace. Will it be *the guillotine* if one gets it wrong?

I wonder, if my father receives an elevated title, will my mother be addressed as "Your *Dis*grace?"

⚶

16 AUGUST, 1799

Most of our staff remain here forever (it seems). Except for various

Nurses, that is. Whenever I liked one she got sent away, or so it seemed. Reynolds has held fast through all the various dramas, and she is a source of contentment for me. Now, two new characters enter our scene. Wickham, father and son. The mother??? Never discussed.

The father has been engaged to be Steward of Pemberley. Father says he needs help as the estate gets larger and more and more *complicate.* Fine. But must we have the son? The elder is a fine, upstanding man and most helpful in every way to my father. His son is another story. He is a sorry, loutish, sly, lying blackguard. It seems he cannot look one in the eye, and I do not like that. I do not like it that he is as tall as I am. I do not like him in my life. At first we played together. I was content to be with a boy my age (as long as he played fair.) We were taught together how to hold a fishing pole. How to bait it and cast, and (once in awhile) how to catch a fish and remove it from the hook. Also, how to scale it. (This he would not lower himself to do.) But so many things went strangely wrong. Snarled lines, objects placed under my feet to make me trip, sudden pushes that would send me tumbling. The latest event sent me plunging head first into the stream. (Luckily it was at a deep place.) One of our staff must have seen this, for now we do not play together.

Even so, I know that he sneaks into my room and steals my lead soldiers. So many have disappeared! I avoid him as much as I can, but could not avoid involving myself in an encounter this day, which has ended with my being sent to my rooms in disgrace. And here must I remain until the parents decide I may reenter the good life at Pemberley.

Crowley has been setting about to plant a new fruit tree in the orchard, and he, with assistance, has dug a rather large pit. The tree is to be planted therein tomorrow. Crowley's young son, Clive, was helping as best he could (he is young, smallish, and most diffident.) At lunchtime when the workmen were off, I heard a cry of distress and ran to see the source. I saw two figures struggling on the edge of the pit. One was Wickham Junior, and to my horror I saw him throw young Clive bodily into the pit.

D., I cannot govern my feelings when I see a person maul someone smaller and weaker than hisself. I ran to the scene and in a fit of ungovernable rage, I hit W. square in the eye and then pushed him after his victim straight into the pit. Such a caterwauling you have never heard! It brought every person in the county to the scene of the crime, including my parents. Father wanted to know what had happened. What was I thinking? Why did I do it? I faced him square, explained nothing, and let him assume the worst.

In the meantime both wounded had been brought from their grave distress (sorry, D., call that a play upon words.) Wickham, whose eye was a sight to behold, realized that I was steadfastly refusing to place the blame, and took fine advantage of the situation. The story he manufactured on the spot was quite a performance, and I must give him credit for his sheer genius at falsehood.

I have been sent to my room. I can see that Wickham is playing in the fort that I am building. As I looked out just now I saw him kick at the wall, and some of it fell down. I would like to run out and give him a poke in the other eye, but I dare not.

Why should he not be punished as well as I? It does seem most unfair.

᪻

30 AUGUST, 1799

I am learning to ride! Father has given me a horse, (which I have named Champêtre). For your information, my provincial friend, champêtre means "rustic" in French.

Wickham and I had another fight.

Today I rode Champêtre in the lower field, with my riding master watching. His name is Mr. Jarrow. He makes me ride bareback, says I will get the proper "seat" this way, which when riding correctly will make it appear that I and the horse are as one. Also, it will train me to keep my upper leg muscles tight, so that I cannot be thrown. If I learn to do it correctly, I *cannot be thrown.* He says he has seen a horse shy and seen the rider just slide off as if there were goose grease on the seat.

Off I went at a trot. Since as yet I cannot post without stirrups, I held my legs as tightly as I could, and kept my tongue well inside my teeth so I should not bite it off with all the jolting.

I was following every instruction most impeccably, and the horse was perfection. What no one could count on, (the horse least of all) was that Wickham was hiding in the grasses at the bottom of the field. He rose with a loud shout and tossed a huge clod at us. Champêtre shied. I SLID off.

I was not hurt, but even if I had been I would still have chased this varmint through the field until caught. This time I gave him *a bloody nose.*

Of course, I was punished again. I was sent to my rooms. I did not see my mother, but she sent word that I was not to ride for two weeks. Mr. Jarrow protested the decision to my father, who would not relent. He told my father that I am ready to learn how to do the canter properly. Father sent Jarrow upstairs to tell me about it. (Decent of him. A consolation? A small one, to be sure, and I have something to look forward to.) This is what Jarrow told me –

I will lean forward to the right, pull up on the reins ever so slightly to the right, pulling the horse's head round, give a gentle kick with the right foot, and put Champêtre into a slow canter. I am eager for this advance. The canter is like a rocking chair, it is faster, and surely more comfortable than trotting bareback.

I thanked Jarrow. He withdrew. I dragged out my old rocking horse. (Can it be that there was a time when my feet were above the ground when I was so mounted?) and went to it. Lean to the right, kick with the right foot – came a knock on the door. My father! I jumped off and tried to look unconcerned.

He did not notice anything untoward. He had come to tell me to stop causing my mother so much annoyance. That she is indisposed, and should not have to trouble herself with my continual mischief. MY mischief!

I asked could I not go in to see my mother. Denied. I fear she must be ill. I have seen Dr. McPherson enter the house on several occasions, and go to her room. I am worried.

I wish I could be a better son so she could be happier with me.

❦

4 SEPTEMBER, 1799

I do not tell you much about Wickham, the Nemesis, because I prefer to think of him as not being. But I needs must detail the events of this day.

It has been damp and drizzly all the day. The ground was still slick after my tea, but at least the rain had quit, so I went outside to finish my fort. It is a fine piece of work. I have a plot of ground behind the kitchen gardens, a most satisfactory place to dig the clayey soil I need for the walls. These walls are now so high, that when I climb through the narrow entrance and stand inside, I can no longer see out.

So I did. Climbed in, stood – but when I did, I did see a despised face somehow on the top of the wall above me. Face only. It seemed to be disembodied, but I knew it was *not* from its odious changes of odious expressions. It was Wickham. I told him to *get out*, he moved not. I dived back through the entrance way and found him perched on a barrel, about to climb over the top. I kicked the barrel out from under him, and left him dangling, trying to pull his knees up to the top. NOT SO! I grabbed him by the boots and pulled him down.

I tried to throw him to the ground, but the ground being slippery, I almost lost my footing. In that moment he broke from me and ran for the house with me in hot pursuit. Oh glory! As his boots hit the polished stone of the scullery, traction was lost altogether. His feet shot out in front of him, he was thrown onto his rear with a most audible thud, and shot like an arrow down the corridor. All the way!

A fast moving object totally out of control – a superb lesson in propulsion! A more wonderful sight I have never beheld. I began to laugh so uproariously that I had to bend over to hold my stomach lest I laugh myself right out of it.

An audience was assembling from out the kitchen, and they too were regaled by the performance. It did look as if the hurling Wickham would crash right into the whole clot of them, but his momentum slowed in time to avoid collision.

Advancing through the group in full sail came my mother, with a furious look. She told Wickham to dust himself off and go to his father. She told me that she would have a word with me in the study. I followed her there.

I shall not forget what she said, nor her chilling anger. She upbraided me for my hoarse and vulgar laugh. She told me how ugly I looked with my mouth open, braying like a donkey (in fact, she used another word. I like it not and will not repeat it.) This kind of laughter, said she, is for the common folk, who have little else to give a spice to life. It is NOT for the English gentility, and I am charged to remember henceforth that I have a standard to uphold, and that I am failing miserably.

I am humiliated and ashamed. I vow solemnly that I shall yet make her proud of me. I swear it! And I shall pray to God tonight to help me.

10 September, 1799

Well, D., it did not take me long to break my vows to my parents.

A gorgeous summery day. I, fairly bursting with good feelings all over, head to toe (*cap à pied* do they call it?). I was eager to be done with lessons, and out in the sunshine. I wanted the sun to beat all over me, and felt the need to strengthen my arms, my back, my shoulders.

Took the stairs three at a time, ended outside in record time, went to Crowley to fetch a shovel, and so armed went to it at my fort. Now, the moat. The earth is reasonably soft at the site, and in good time I had the beginning of a fine trench. So eager was I to see if the water would hold, that I boosted myself out and brought in several buckets full. Yes, indeed! It held so successfully that it was mirror bright and (miraculously) enabled me to accomplish *legerdemain* so that I could demean Wickham and remain an innocent, all at the same time. Let me describe –

There was I, whistling and shoveling at a great clip, sun beating on my bare back, muscles being brought into full use, when in the 'mirror' at trench bottom I espied *a devil's head* looking over the mounded earth. No question as to the identity. Without turning my head, and with the greatest nonchalance I took a shovel full, aimed it well, up and over my straining back, covering the wretched boy with wonderfully thick mud.

Strangled scream. Astonished oath from Darcy. Feigned surprise upon viewing the mucilaginous onlooker. *How could this have happened? Why did he not let me know that he was watching?*

Wickham père came and hustled off the 'gingerbread' boy to the stream. Not without looking at me keenly, somewhat askance. I assured him that it was totally accidental, all the while being sure to keep my crossed fingers in my pocket. Wickham père assured me that he believed this, telling his protesting son to keep quiet and behave himself.

I laugh when I think on the scene, D. Am I proud? 'Yes and no.' Why 'yes?' Because I am content to know that *anyone* can play the bad games that men play. Why 'no?' Because it is all too easy and because it demeans one. Amen. Now I know I can lie as well as the next fool, and get away with it as well as the next fool. Will I do it again? Never. Amen, Amen.

21 SEPTEMBER, 1799

I know now that my mother likes me not. I am growing very tall and my voice is getting high and squeaky and I often feel uncomfortable in my body. This afternoon we three had tea together (Georgiana? I asked her Nurse to bring her in, but my mother countermanded the invitation.)

My father commented on my height and remarked that I must marry a tall fine lady so there would be many tall fine sons to ensure the continuance of our line. I was embarrassed and turned to my mother, but she looked away. My father went on (does he not observe my discomfiture?) to describe again what this lady's attributes must be, and stressed once more that I must be sure to stay within my own class (or reach higher).

I was relieved to hear him then bestow a word of praise upon my mother. It did seem passing strange that he would define desirability in a woman without referring to her as a model. She accepted the compliment demurely, and then suggested that they retire, as a large group were to attend them at dinner.

Of late I have been dining with them. I asked what would be the appropriate dress. I was informed that I was not included. Instead I was served quite late in my rooms, long after their roast had been served. Cold roast, soggy Yorkshire pudding, coagulated gravy. Is this any kind of feast for the noble young master of Pemberley? I pushed it away, untasted.

When the festive dinner was over and the two groups had adjourned to their respective salons, I crept down the stairs and listened at the mens' salon door. If laughter, as my mother said, is for plebeians and commoners, why were my father and his friends so merry and so loud?

It seems my mother wants me set apart like some pariah and I hate her, hate her, hate her and I never want to see her again!

❧

14 OCTOBER, 1799 HARROW

Here we are at Harrow, D., banished, exiled, set atop a precipice to be devoured by vultures. (In your case it will be worms.)

One minute I was living peacefully (or so I thought) at home, the next minute I was packed off and deposited here. I feel whirled about like a top.

I do believe this is a direct result of my wicked thoughts after the day my mother rebuked me about my smiling and I said "I hate her and I never want to see her again."

God heard me, D., and here I am. I pray every night that God must understand that I love my mother to distraction – Hate her??? I adore her hopelessly, and I not only want to see her, but see her all day every day without interruption, and also at night when I fancy that she will sit on the edge of my bed and read to me as Reynolds has done.

Why can I never do that which pleases her?
WHY?

※

28 October, 1799 Harrow

I am not the only one, but I am the one I care most about, and I am in great despond. There must be a term for what I am feeling. I have no appetite, I feel sad all the time, I keep thinking about home, and I want to be there and not *here*. At home "school" was staying in my handsome chambers and entertaining a colorful parade of tutors, coming, going, talking, lecturing, reciting, listening to me recite. It was a jolly good routine.

Here, "school" is a sprawl of drafty buildings filled with scuttling students of various sizes and shapes, taught by frozen professors of various sizes and shapes (but not various colors. It seems to me that they are all *grey*.) They, of various hauteur and docility, teach in various classrooms of a deadly sameness. The weather is as grey as the professors. Even when the infrequent sun is supposedly shining, it does so through a miasma of coal dust and other swimming, ugly particles.

Unlike school at Pemberley, here there is competition for attention, for marks, and for status. I appear to have no problem in any of these categories.

I am sadly remembering the chart at Pemberley which was started for me by Nurse R. My height seems to keep going up and up, causing me a compendium of aches and strange pains. They tell me I have "growing pains" and not a person in the Infirmary has failed to utter, "And small wonder!"

There is not much good company here. I like a good conversation. I try faithfully to speak only when there is something worth saying. Let measlier mortals (nice phrase, that!) mouth the idiocies.

My classmates you ask? One rarely hears an unusual word or an interesting idea from any one of them. In type they range from inane and innocuous to nasty and brutish. Perforce I must be in company with them in class, at meals, and during sports. This, of course, signifies that I am with them most of the endlessly long day. At night, I find their conversational subjects either silly or lewd. The adolescent boasting about sexual conquest is loathsome, and I resent hotly the contempt in which they hold woman-kind. Accordingly, I stay to myself after class and after sports. I read. Books are excellent company. And I can write to you.

Good night, D. Sorry to be such a complainer. "English gentlemen must abide with – etcetera, etcetera." I can hear my father's voice, and I confess that I would trade anything to be back at Pemberley and forced to listen to a long, long lecture. Even that would seem like heaven.

I bid you good night. I shall see in my mind all the images of glori-ous Pemberley as I drift off to sleep.

Why was I sent away??

❧

31 October, 1799 Harrow

Dante must somehow have attended Harrow. I feel as if I am trapped in one of his circles of Hell. I have had no heart to write you, D., until tonight. Now comes the bright side –

Today I struck up a friendship with a chap I like. To be sure he is too cheerful by far, too friendly to one and all, too eager to please, and too optimistic. But he is of fine character, good in the long discourse, bright and conscientious in his studies, well spoken, to the manor born, and best of all, I think he likes me. He is Charles Bingley, and we do well together.

Charles has five sisters. One has already "come out." The next oldest is to come out when she is of age. He wants me to meet her. Her name is Caroline. I look forward to our meeting someday.

Thank heaven for Charles. His bed is not far from mine, and we will be able to talk after lights out, assuming the headmaster is not present. And sure enough, here cometh he now. Off to bed with you, D.!

❧

2 NOVEMBER, 1799 HARROW

The days are only dreadful here. The nights are pure Inferno. The freshman class is fox for the hounds, the latter being the upperclassmen. One fights (I fight like a tiger, and since I am as tall and strong as they, they leave me alone) and some lose. It is appalling to hear the shrieks of pain, and the moans and cries which follow. What breed of creature are we?

Tonight it came closer to home. They went after Charles. What they knew not was that Charles and I are good friends. This night he became a target. He was fighting manfully but it was three to one, and soon he went down. I shouted and dove across the intervening cot straight at the brutes. Two had their heads knocked together and the third soon had my hands on his throat. When he ceased to struggle, I released him, pulled Charles out from the tangle of bodies. I hugged him but a moment as he sagged against me and then I let him go. His only words were, "I shall never forget this, Darcy."

I have written pater beseeching him to let me come home. Response? Negative. "England," saith he, "needs her fine men of good birth and exalted position to be annealed like metal and be prepared to further the forward course of the Empire."

A fine mockery!

20 NOVEMBER, 1800 HARROW

Grace à dieu! I have found a good equestrian center here. I am playing cricket and rugby, and it seems I am splendid at both. I am training in pugilism. This is not for attraction to the sport, but because one needs a means to protect oneself from one's glorious English classmates. Fencing is another matter. I am most attracted to this sport, and apparently excellent in performance. It is nice to daydream about standing on a noble parapet, defending myself with my wicked *saber* against hordes of howling Harrow men, who assail me in constant waves and are beaten back, broken and bleeding.

I like my courses (if not the professors). I am reading voraciously in and out of my subject fields. Reading is my salvation. And talks with Charles.

Recently I have encountered the *Histoire Naturelle* by George L. Buffon, which has sent me, in turn, into the works of Erasmus Darwin and J. B. Lamarck. Such wonders there are in the natural world! And what, indeed, is our relationship to all these creatures? And do any behave as badly as Harrow lads?

Once more am requesting permission to be allowed to come home.

❦

28 November, 1800 Inn at Preston

Went with my parents for two days at the Inn at Preston. I herewith report to you, D. Father had refused permission for me to come home, or even for a visit home, but had agreed that he and mother would come to the school and we would thence go together to the inn in the village of Preston.

When first they arrived, I guided them about the school, introduced them to various teachers and students, showed them the cricket grounds, the stables, the fencing studio. My parents listened to many compliments about my prowess in many fields without comment, saw my dormitory, and then suggested that we leave for Preston.

Conversation in the carriage? I had many questions about Pemberley; I asked about my sister. Seems there is a new nurse. (Logical!)

I wanted to tell my parents how much I miss them, but did not know *how* to tell them. Kept my silence.

We had a long two days together. There were endless moments when I was tempted to confide my reason for despair to my father, but with Mother present I found myself mute. Father attended this same Harrow, and he must have experienced the same dreadful nights in his first year. I would undoubtedly have been treated to the usual advice about "the stiff upper lip." (How does one write that in Latin? It should be emblazoned in marble above the door lintel on every educational edifice in glorious England.)

The weather was unseasonably splendid – clear skies, and surprisingly warm. The inn is a comfortable, sprawling place, with delicious food (on which I *gorged*), which far outclasses the Harrow Commons, and a splendid afternoon tea. We took long walks, seeing such places of interest as were recommended. It is the most time I have ever spent alone with my parents, and I drank it in thirstily. We separated for afternoon rests, and, of course, at night. They were down the hall from me, the closest I have ever been to them. I tried to imagine what it would be like in their private moments, but was not successful.

My mother was most charming the entire time. Warm and friendly, listening to that which I cared to report. Shall I ever encounter her equal among the young women of my acquaintance? I love her so much! My father was also pleasant. There were no lectures, just some interesting talk about my classes. He was ever so nice to my mother. Once, during a walk, I saw him put his arm around her waist. When she turned to him she looked so beautiful! It made me feel warm and good.

When I went to bed I tried to imagine how that would feel when I am old enough to walk out with a woman.

It was wonderful to fall asleep without worrying about invading barbarians, as we must at school. I thought about Miss Caroline Bingley. Will she fit my image of her? Someday I shall meet her. In the meantime she is always in my arms as I fall asleep. Until I awaken in disgust.

***

30 November, 1800 Harrow

I have finally found a professor who pleases.

His name is G _ _ _ _ _. He was late in returning for Michaelmas term, but blessedly has taken the chair of the idiot who preceded him.

His class is English Literature. Here is one who is worth my time. He has a dry, ironic, wicked wit, and presents his material with a fine flourish. He likes my essays, he marks my examinations well, he likes that I can identify the lines which he quotes to us. He is wasted on these jackals, but not on me.

His homework assignments are challenging and downright amusing. For tonight we are to

a.) identify four famous enchantresses of literature.

b.) *smother the same* in alliterative adjectives.

For b.) I have written, "hell-bent Helen of the heliotrope orbs; dreadful Delilah with the dangerous dagger; sidereal Siren with thy sibilant song; jejune Jezebel jeering at Jehovah."

Enough for you, D. It is Professor G. who hands out the marks.

❦

1 December, 1800 Harrow

I have neglected you, D., but I am indeed a busy man. I seem to be racing in all directions, all day. I feel that at any moment I shall meet myself racing from Drama class, while another me is racing from the cricket field, and even a third Darcy is galloping from the study hall.

The drama class is the most demanding (and the most exciting). My "Romeo" was most well received, as have been other readings to which we have progressed. I get along better with the chaps in this class – having a common interest seems to keep things on an even keel.

Class Day is in two weeks, and Professor S. suggested that we perform a piece in the assembly. We settled on Act IV of *King Lear*, and I leave it to you to figure who is to play the title role. No more applause, please, we all do our best. I did not tell my parents about the play when I wrote the invitation to come to Harrow. I did mention that I will have a surprise for them. They have accepted, and I am in a high state of anticipation.

❦

15 December, 1800 Harrow

D., I must write you, although my heart is heavy and I would as leave forget this 'night of nights.' It is late and I would like the blessed comfort of sleep. Why, then, do I write? I have the need. *Entendu?*

Following the last rehearsal, I awaited the arrival of my parents. I waited all afternoon. As the other students went off with their families to the Commons for supper, I confess to having felt much chagrin. Not for the loss of supper. I would not have eaten in any event.

Finally had to go to the theatre. I persuaded the crew to hold the curtain, peering out in vain for a sign of my parents' arrival. We could wait no longer and proceeded without further delay.

There is a tale told about Mme. de Maintenon, the favorite of *Le Roi Soleil*, who received the news of her son's death on the battlefield immediately before her entrance in a court theatrical. She went on nonetheless, performed handsomely, and on the instant when the curtain had fallen, swooned dead away.

Think what a disaster if this had been a comedy! Lear can handle a tragic mortification. As it was, the part very quickly took me over and I performed well, except for one bad moment.

As I was declaiming "Ha! Goneril, with a white beard! They flattered me like a dog," – "They told me I was everything. 'Tis a lie – I am not ague-proof."

Immediately upon speaking these words, my voice *broke* most miserably. Lucky for me – Gloucester's line saved my life, "The trick of that voice I well remember. Is't not the King?"

I improvised on the instant – Holding up my kingly hand for silence, (and in so doing quieting the audience laughter) I proclaimed, "Ay, every inch a King, although my voice is not as it were accustomed."

There was a general gasp from the audience. I heard Professor S. shout, "Bravo!" and then a tumult of applause, all the more vigorous for the potential embarrassment to myself and to the evening.

We proceeded from this point in high form, the audience with us every inch of the way.

My parents? I found a note had been delivered during my absence. Some twaddle about a social function which was most important, apologies, etcetera, etcetera. I tore it in a million pieces and put it in the chamber pot.

Enough said. Good night.

❧

16 December, 1800 Harrow

Congratulations were proffered in class this morning, and there was discussion about our performances, with some suggestions as to how the lines might better be read. I came in for little criticism, actually hearty praise; a grand fuss was made of my *ad libitum* remark; a round of applause from the class, and more laughter.

After class some few crowded around, and some dared ask prying questions about the absence of my parents. I answered them not, save with a withering look (which apparently has more effect since I have gained another inch or two,) turned and strode off to the playing fields.

I want not to think about it for a moment longer. I have resolved that I shall discuss it not with my parents. But I shall not ask them to another Class Day.

Professor George spoke to me after class, most pleased with my role. He suggested that I join in the collation which he serves in his chambers after study hall. I accepted with alacrity.

⁂

12 February, 1801 Harrow

I knocked on Professor G.'s door after study hall, and it opened to reveal a good many people draped in and over chairs, while others were standing about or sitting. There were several Professors, and a few students, all upper classmen. I was by far the youngest person there. I perceived this to be a compliment, and although diffident at first, I soon found myself absorbed into various conversations, all most stimulating and worthwhile. I was most happy to find that I was able to keep up with the various subjects which were being treated, and I was grateful to have studied hard, read widely, and retained it all. To my delight I was invited to return tomorrow night, and have been accepted as a functioning member of the "club." My one disadvantage is that bed-time is earlier for my class, and I am required to leave the proceedings prematurely. I did so with regret, with many handshakes and great claps on the back, and favorable comments about my *Lear*.

There is one enormous advantage to this opportunity, besides the great pleasure of finding such good "heads" with whom to share ideas. Now that I, a freshman, am known to them, I doubt that there will be future invasions of our dormitory.

⁂

19 FEBRUARY, 1801 HARROW

Is there no end to the misery of mankind? What a benighted race we are!

I was again invited to an evening gathering in the chambers of Professor G., and went thither with my usual anticipation. To my surprise there were but the two of us.

He seemed much ill at ease. After serving the usual port he took his chair and we started to discuss the Marvell works which we have been studying in his class. I had just begun to quote, "Had we but world enough, and time," when he let out a groan, flung himself from his chair onto the floor at my feet and commenced to pour out wild expressions of his passion for me, about how little time there was for one in this world – so stunned was I that I recall little else of his rantings.

When first he flung himself at me I had the schoolboy's apprehension that I had misread the lines, but quickly realized that *this* matter had very little relationship to *that* matter, and I had best act quickly.

Thoughts raced through my mind – how could I help save our connection with this new turning? What was to happen to him? To the courses he taught in which I take so much pleasure? Where did this all start? Had I in any way given him encouragement? And, of course, an overriding feeling of shock – dreadful cataclysmic shock.

In the meantime I was trying to extricate myself from his clutching and pathetic hands.

It seems the mere act of my rising to my feet, calmed the storm. I have added several inches to my height in the past months, and indeed tower over most of those at Harrow, professors included. Especially those on their hands and knees on the floor.

I was as tactful as I could manage, but I fear I left him trembling and weeping, and dared not try to console him.

Quo vadis?

❦

26 FEBRUARY, 1801 HARROW

Professor G. has left Harrow quite abruptly, and there is a great deal of conjecture, but luckily no light has been thrown on the matter, except for a bleak announcement that he is in ill health. I keep my counsel. Privately, I grieve. I grieve for him, and yea, for myself. I was leaning heavily on this relationship. His class brightened the day, the homework held me fast in study hall, and I relished the evenings in his rooms – except for the ultimate *soirée!*

Good conversation is very important to me, and conversations at these evenings were capital. I was fortunate to have been invited to share in them, even if much of the time I was silent, drinking it all in.

On occasion I ventured to utter my thoughts, and apparently acquitted myself well. It was heady indeed to have professors and upper classmen listen attentively to my few words.

Now I need to inform you of a happier turn of affairs. Naturally there was a new man in G.'s class, and I lost interest. Sought and gained permission to transfer into an extracurricular drama class. Have been on edge with interest ever since doing so. Currently we are reading and readying for a performance of Shakespeare's *Henry The Fifth*.

I have been assigned the part of the Dauphin, awarded me because of my superior French accent.

The world looks brighter. *Bon soir, mon ami.* I have lines to learn.

❦

15 MARCH, 1801 HARROW

Dear D.,

You are to participate in a drama class with Professor S. Kindly open your books to *Henry The Fifth*, Act III, vii. Mr. Fitzwilliam will kindly read –

And so I do –

Dauphin, "What a long night is this! I will not change my horse with any that treads but on four pasterns . . ." (Interruption – we discuss "pastern.")

To go on "Ca, ha! He bounds from the earth as if his entrails were hairs – le cheval volant, the Pegasus chez les narines de feu! When I bestride him, I soar, I am a hawk. He trots the air. The earth sings when he touches it. The basest horn of his hoof is more musical than the pipe of Hermes."

[Orleans has lines here, and I wait impatiently, I am on a tidal bore, and I care not for interference.]

"And of the heat of the ginger. It is a beast for Perseus – he is pure air and fire, and the dull elements of earth and water never appear in him but only in his patient stillness while his rider mounts him. He is indeed a horse, and all other jades you may call beasts."

We now take this apart most thoroughly; there are suggestions from the class, corrections of timing and pronunciation, but I brook not corrections of my French accent. Professor S. gallantly admits that it is most immaculate.

How like you the drama class, D.? I like it well! I like my role also, although it does make me most nostalgic for our horses at home, and I would ride out this night, home to Pemberley. But I would look back in regret. Who can fill my role? Who indeed? Methinks I turn my steed around and gallop back to Middlesex.

❦

3 June, 1802 Harrow

Father has a private box at Epsom and when I find time, I go to watch the horses run. Sometimes I bring a friend or two, ofttimes I go alone. I do not place bets, but I enjoy watching the action when bets are placed. My passion, however, is the horses. I am racing with them! I feel in my own body the movements of theirs, I feel the excitement of their speed, I feel their energy coursing through me, and above all I love their beauty.

Next to our box there sits a very small man, who is always alone, who bets on all races, and appears to win constantly.

One day he leaned over and whispered the name of a horse to me. Then he introduced himself. I might have known it. He is a descendant of the famous Samuel Chifney – Joseph Chifney, jockey, now infamous for having been ousted from the sport by the Jockey Club. Why? Because of an addiction to drink, yet here he sits, surrounded by the English gentry. He must have a great deal of influence, else he had powerful friends who have made him my neighbor.

Indeed, he smelled powerfully of the stuff. Could one get drunk from the very fumes of his breath I wondered? He asked me did I not want to bet. I told him no. He urged. I told him that I would be expelled from Harrow, if not from my own family, as I am under age. He said I could get away with it if I "wuz clever." I told him indeed I am clever, but I do not break the law.

Now came the race, and we both rose to our feet. His horse was in the lead from the start. He kept pounding on the rail and shouting in my ear, and leaped so high at the finish that I was sure he would be hurt. Soon he went to fetch his winnings. When he returned, he handed me over a wad of pound notes. I dare say there were ten to twelve. I refused politely. In our family we do not discuss money, or deal with it thusly. He waved the lot at me. "Give it to the pater for the window tax, I dare say it must be a vasty one." I refused again.

Now came the waiter and asked would it be the usual, and he said yes, but make it two. He turned to me, "At least let me treat you to a drink, son, a nice rum to whet your whistle?" I told him that I do not drink. "Well then, Mr. Righteous, how about a glass of milk?" This amused him so that he fell to coughing and almost choked. I ran around to his box, but the waiter was already pounding on him. He recovered and told the waiter to bring me a lemonade. He asked me to sit. I did, feeling most ill at ease. Now was I treated to the story of his life, now I felt that I could not leave.

"Do you like girls?" he asked. "I like girls, but I do not know many." "You will, you will, ye are a very handsome lad!" The waiter returned with the drinks. Mine host pulled out a thicket of notes, thrust them upon him, whispered hoarsely "'Mr. Paddington' in the fifth! And give my regards to Windham and Newcastle!"

Now he told me of his descent to "ruination." Caused, he told me, by a certain night when he made "a fatal move" on a woman he was then forced to marry, and who has destroyed his life with her profligacy and debauchery. (These are not his words, they are mine, D. I would not set to paper the words he used.) "Take my advice, young man. Kiss the ladies ye may, but only on the lips. The body? Never! Never kiss a lady anywhere on her body."

"What about the hand, sir? I have been trained to kiss a lady's hand. Is that not part of the body?"

Now he laughed, thwacking his thigh so hard he almost knocked himself from the stool. "The hand! Ain't you the sharp one! Forget the hand. It's just a fancy part of the baggage. You can kiss the hand. But never the wrist. That is part of the body. Yes, lad, never put your lips to the body, not to any part of it! Ye will be doomed, for ye will not be able to stop, and ye will end – ruined – like me!" So saying he tipped forward, and would have crashed had I not steadied him. His tankard flew out of his hand and the rum splashed me full on.

Now I reeked from the strong scent of the rum. Who would listen to my assurances that I had enjoyed only lemonade? I would need a total submersion and fresh clothes. If only our house were not closed! Aha! I would go to the Bingley home, where I knew they would believe me, would arrange a bath, and lend me something of Charles' to wear back to school.

❦

14 July, 1802 Pemberley

The summer, ah, the endless summer. I left Harrow with all manner of plans to have a happy release and felicitous times at Pemberley. Instead I was informed that I was to be put into harness in order to learn the great art of managing a vast estate. Why father insisted that I learn this year, I know not. I confess he looks off the mark to me, but he insists he feels fine.

To see him in action is reassurance enough. He has set a schedule which keeps us busy for the better part of each day. We started with an overview of our holdings – tenancies, fields, farmlands; wood and forest lands, village church and rectory. This took upwards of two weeks. Father then started farm by farm, cottage by cottage, to introduce me to our various tenants. Followed by a comprehensive introduction to laborers of every description from ploughmen to artisans. I am keeping a journal of every detail and every name. When we return we have a quick tea and then he proceeds to instruct me in the art of keeping the complex *books*.

FINALLY I am allowed a respite to go to the lake. I am teaching myself to swim (this is one endeavor for which I have not been assigned a tutor.) This involves self inflicted breathing exercises. Even at this early beginning I can stay underwater for a fast swim from bank to bank at the narrow end of our lake. My ambition, by summer's end, is to make that trip across the vast center, underwater all the way.)

All was going well until this night at dinner. Dinners are usually stiff affairs with desultory conversation of very little import, and long silences. My sister adds nothing to the evening. She is mute at all times, and leaves at the earliest opportunity to be with her music.

This night my mother suddenly threw down her fork with an impatient exclamation. The loud clatter froze us, forks in midair, or chewing, as I was. She demanded of me why I am so withdrawn and unpleasant. I was (and still am) completely shocked. How have I offended? I try to be as polite with her as she would have me, deferential, as she would have me. It seems that the lessons she has taught me have led me to exactly the manner I display for her.

I was not able to answer, and our dinner ended most dismally. I would have thought that my father would try to ease matters, but he remained silent.

I had determined to bury myself immediately in writing of this strange strangeness, D., but my father requested my presence in the gentleman's salon. He poured a round of port, lit the ever present cigar, puffed, blew the heavy smoke upward, wafting the dreadful stench in my direction (I swear, I shall never smoke) then offered me a most generous opportunity. He told me that mother had been strangely moody and restless of late and perhaps it would be best for the family if I were to take a holiday from our "training." He went so far as to suggest a visit to my friend Charles, of whom they both think most highly.

What a happy conclusion! I shall straight off write to Charles and invite myself for a visit. I hope I shall be wanted in his home. Apparently I am not wanted here.

᪥

15 JULY, 1802 PEMBERLEY

Sad, sad news, D. I shall relate in proper order. Downcast as I have been, this is yet another blow, and I suffer it ill.

In my effort to keep my spirits high after the strangeness of my mother at dinner, I joined in a Ride to Hounds this morning. It was good to see old friends and be introduced to new. The morning felt fresh and tonic, and I was glad for the event. Off we went with the usual shouts and the baying of hounds, over broad fields and rolling hills. Came to a narrow valley, thundered down it. Suddenly our leader pulled up. We all came piling in behind him, some horses rearing with the suddenness of the stop. Now ensued a long, earnest discussion about the safety of the obstacle which confronted us. Part fence, part hedgerow, the latter well concealing the fencing, and thus presenting a true hazard. It was decided that we would change our course. Then young Meynell vowed that he was willing to wager "that Darcy could do it." We surveyed the terrain, entered a heated discussion, bets were laid.

Folly! Darcy, it seems, cannot say *"no"* to a challenge.

I do not know why the accident occurred, although, as I look back, there was a second when Champêtre seemed indecisive, and I must have marked that well, because I was prepared for an emergency. Luck would have it, in my case, that always I jump without stirrups.

I talked to Champêtre, leaning in to speak into his alert ear. I told him I knew he would manage it well, rode back into the field, urged him into his gallop, lowered my hands at the proper distance from the fence, leaned into the perfect balance for the two of us, and up we soared. For a moment it was akin to flying, and I wanted to shout for the joy of it. At that moment his back foot caught the fence, and thereafter there was a wild confusion of falling horse, falling rider, shouts from the winners of the wager, shouts from the losers, and a moment of quiet when I was grateful to find that I was not hurt. I had managed a well executed tumble and landed in a clump of thick bushes, luckily not of the spiny hawthorne variety. And then I saw Champêtre, trying to rise from the ground, and unable. I ran to him. The look he gave me almost broke my heart, D. And my heart *is* broken. His foot was hanging at the fetlock. I must have sobbed aloud. All I knew was that I was holding him in my arms, my head buried in his mane, and weeping like a child.

The others approached, some sympathetic, some crowing over their victory. Luckily, the horse was my sole concern, else I would have given these latter knaves a thrashing for their gloating (despite that many of them are elderly. One, I know, is in his fifties.) All agreed that the horse must be done away with. Not so I!

Luckily, Meynell is a decent chap and arranged to send back a dray and several hands. We loaded my friend (such a piteous sight) into the wagon, and somehow got him back to our stables. Our head groom gave the patient a dose to make him quiet and free of pain, bound the foot as best he could. When my companion is somewhat mended (he will never be able to use that leg again) I ordered that he be put out to pasture. I shall never let him feel deserted, I shall always treasure his noble friendship and courageous heart, and I have hopes that he will live a long and peaceful life free of care.

Will I never jump a horse again? Of course I will. Will I ever take a dare again? I much doubt it.

❧

16 July, 1802 Pemberley

I have learned from our local doctor that a new school of veterinary medicine was opened in London some eleven years past. I asked Father if we could apply for help for Champêtre.

He reminded me that I would be going to London and should make arrangements when I get there. In the meantime he would look to the horse during my absence. I thanked him with all the warmth which two proper Englishmen can manage.

⁂

22 July, 1802 Pemberley

Charles' response came in the post last week. In the affirmative. In fact, he is enthusiastic. (As usual, but I confess he does seem especially so. We should have some good fun together in London. I can tend to Champêtre's needs. And I shall be meeting Miss Caroline!)

And so I am to depart in the morning.

Had a session with Father in the library after dinner. Dinner was silent, as usual, my mother most withdrawn.

The sermon tonight was replete with admonishments and strictures as to the correct behavior at all times . . . wheresoever, whensoever, whatsoever, and with whomsoever.

He was most diligent to advise me against the prostitutes in London who, he says, are to be found ready and only too obliging, wherever one walks. Without telling me anything of real substance about what it is that I am *not* to do in regard to these ladies, he did suggest that I had probably heard all I need to know from other Harrow students. How correct he is! Inasmuch as it is such an easy (and most frequently discussed!) topic, I do wonder why he makes it such a difficult subject into which to enter.

Should I tell him of my fiendish nights? What a thought!

⁂

25 July, 1802 Inn at K. en route London

Here we are at the Inn at K. Left Pemberley early this morning. I felt strange at first and took no joy in the journey, but later I came out of my low mood and took some pleasure in the passing scenery. England is splendid in the summer. We are to spend the night here, and I want to record one strange moment which occurred at departure from Pemberley.

Father was at the door to bid me farewell and pleasant journey. I asked for my mother. Father told me that she was still asleep. He turned to supervise the luggage, and at that moment I looked up and espied a movement at a front window of the second story. The curtain was pulled aside, and my mother stood there. I could see that she was weeping. I dwell on this because it is, indeed, passing strange. She wanted me away. Yet she cries when I leave. I do not understand and would put it from my thoughts. You may hold them for me.

***

26 July, 1802 London - Belgravia

Here we are in London, chez Bingley, D. The house is situated in Belgravia. It looks much like our London house, although somewhat smaller. Adam style, good proportions, proper address. I entered with my heart beating fast and myself tense as a drum. Such a thumping. Could it be heard throughout the house? I was about to meet Caroline, the Lorelei of my dreams!

Followed my luggage up the narrow stairs, searching with my eyes for the feminine form to which I have been clinging throughout the many nights. Somewhere above I caught a brief glance of a swirl of skirts and heard the receding tones of a skittering high laugh. She? Charles' smiling face now appeared above me. He was hanging over the balustrade, grinning broadly.

"Hold on!" he cried, mounted the banister and slid down to the second landing, just as I arrived there.

A happy reunion! Was ushered to my room. Narrow, with high ceilings, like all London chambers. Tasteful mahogany furniture, rubbed to a high luster, neoclassic design in all details. Dark blue striped wallpaper, blue fabric. A desk!

I did not meet Miss Caroline or her sisters until tea time. At precisely four o'clock I walked into the large upstairs sitting room in great excitement. There they were, five girls, and Charles, all arrayed prim in a circle, about their attractive mother. Charles held a plate on his lap, a cup and saucer in his hand. He was already dug into a heap of cakes and scones. Nevertheless he tried to rise. I heard Mrs. Bingley softly suggest that one of the girls relieve him of his impedimenta before he destroy part of her tea set and the rug beneath. Charles resumed his place and returned enthusiastically to his repast.

Charles' mouth being stuffed full, his mother made the introductions, each daughter rising and making an awkward curtsy. I bowed to each. I could not look direct at Miss Caroline but spoke my greeting into the floor.

Mrs. B. offered me a place next to her. I sat. The tea cakes were plentiful, but I had doubts that I could enjoy any. My hands were not steady and I was afraid that I would be the one to knock all that china to the floor. I was put off by the giggling and inane small talk of the sisters, and sat silent except when Charles or his mother asked me questions. Finally I dared steal a glance at the enchantress of my dreams. Oh oh – Reed thin, arms too long, legs too long. Skin? O! Perhaps it is her age, but I could not help thinking of the creamy complexion of my sister.

My "dream lady" makes strange gestures, a pathetic imitation of her suave and comely mother . . . She utters insipid remarks, which are all the worse for being punctuated with a series of treble titters.

Tea ended, I went with Charles to his rooms. His window looks out over the area courtyard, beyond which one can see a vast ocean of dingy chimney pots. I looked over his books. Conventional choices. While I was studying the titles, he started an enthusiastic recital of our plans during my visit, a recital of the cricket games being played, a recital of the merits of his sisters. He wanted to know of my impression of sister Caroline, but waited not for the answer (luckily). I told him about the accident to Champêtre, and my plans to find the hospital.

Supper? Mr. B. is a lively gentleman who steadfastly maintained a running monologue, allowing for no interruptions. A great spate about "futures" and markets and trading routes. Etcetera, etcetera, etcetera. He is a handsome fellow of sturdy build, well groomed, very self assured. He is clearly one of the more successful of the new successful merchant class. He and Mrs. Bingley have met my parents at several distinguished homes, and he spoke admiringly of them, commenting especially on the beauty of my mother.

I know not how to repair the dreadful blow to my nightly "visitations." My 'enchantress' has vanished in a searing dose of *reality!*

Phrases run through my mind from G.'s class. "Nattering Neriad," "Nickering Nymph" – (Someday, somewhere, someone should get together a book which will reference words of similar meanings.)

Climbed into my bed. Mrs. Bingley has begged me to consider theirs as "my home away from home." Such a nice thing to say. She patted me on the shoulder, had the servant hand me my candle, asked if I needed aught, and bade me good night.

"Home away from home." I savor the phrase, start to think about Pemberley, and about Champêtre, feel the sorrow well up within me.

❧

27 JULY, 1802 LONDON

Father is indeed accurate in his description of the "good hunting" on London streets. I fully intended to dodge these pathetic predators, but this night I succumbed – not so much to desire, but to the mockery of the group with whom we were consorting. I have never rejected a dare, nor could I this night, despite my vows never to accept another.

Would that I had! Charles gave us all a disapproving look, and disappeared from the scene. Would that I had done the same! Now I needs must settle not only my traducing of the pledge I made to father, but must live with the unwelcome shame and sadness which haunt me.

D., I care not to tell of the details. Nor would you relish the telling. I just will mention that following the animal release which the lady enabled, I made the mistake of wanting to thank her with a warm look and a kiss on her brow. That was my undoing. The saddest and most ravaged visage I have seen, and in one so young! We are supposedly living in a civilized society, and I saw tonight only the opposite! One can only wonder if there are any who find real pleasure in such a travesty of what is ineptly termed "making love."

And what of our so called "Civilization?" How can we allow such misery to go untended?

❧

29 JULY, 1802 LONDON, CHEZ BINGLEY

When first I awoke this morning, memories of a dream resurfaced. I was astride Champêtre, and I could see clear the coppery glints of his sorrel neck, and the blackness of his mane. We were riding, riding, my heart was singing, and I was happy.

Threw back the covers and sprang from the bed. I had work to do!

I was on my way out of the house when Mr. Bingley halted me. "Why so early, young Darcy, and what about a warm breakfast?" I assured him I was not hungry and was eager to get to the Veterinary Hospital.

"Rinderpest is it?"

"Rinderpest?"

"You may know it as 'Cattle plague.' Serious problem throughout India and Asia."

"I do not know it at all. This is a matter to do with my horse."

"Eat first. Horse later. Come in here." I was forced to comply. He inquired as to where was I going, and how did I intend to get there. Upon discovering that none of this had been considered, he graciously offered his driver and the family curricle.

No sooner offered than done. Awaiting me was the carriage, which is pulled by a well matched pair of bays, (the whole equipage rented from a London jobber who had been well recommended). I was informed by my coachman that there was ample equipment available to take the master to his office and not to worry about the inconvenience I had caused.

New as the college is, the only description of its address which I held was to "take the Highgate Road, and to look for the building some-where in the vicinity of Pancras, Camden Town, in the vicinity of Somer's Town." My driver scratched his head, murmured something about "needle in a haystack," but flicked his whip at the horses and we sped off. I yearned to be the driver, but could not dare hope for that.

Soon dense London commenced to give way to increasingly larger fields and small communities, each with its church and steeple. Before a half hour had passed, somewhere near the churchyard of Pancras, I espied a large unstuccoed brick building. The side facing us lacked both windows and portals. It did have three great, tall, *blank* arches, soaring almost to the roof line. Leaped from the carriage, the driver following. The entrance? We had a fine chase to find it. We had to circuit the building, the east side being blocked by the Fleet River which runs between it and the Highgate road. Came to a stone courtyard which ran down to a muddy path. Behind us, at the far end of the courtyard, I espied a tall arched portal, "The London Veterinary College!" The driver raised up his hands, "Holy of holies! I wuz sure, young man, that this was a fool's errand! Even when we got here it looked as if it wuz a fool's errand! I shall wait for ye in the carriage."

I ran up the walk, eager to get to the business at hand. Discovered there is but one person in charge, and wasted grievous minutes before I could chase him down. He is one Edward Coleman, surgeon, who insisted on telling me in measured tones that he had inherited the post in 1794 from the founder, a Frenchman, one Charles Vial de St. Bel. I told Professor Coleman that I come of French ancestry. "Is that the reason for your visit," he asked, "to tell me that?" Feeling foolish, I stammered out my real purpose. Then felt even more foolish and, in fact, wretched, when he told me the impossibility of saving a horse with such an injury. My intense reaction softened his callousness, and after a few puffs on his pipe, and several harrumphs, he asked me what were our facilities at Pemberley. I described to him our splendid fields for pasturing, the number of attendants and grooms, which he took in gravely. Puffing mightily, he stared out the window for many minutes, clouds of smoke billowing around his shaggy head. Then he took up paper and pencil, outlined for me the possibility of an extra strong splint which would help Champêtre to stand, and made several sketches, which he handed over to me. I thanked him profusely, demanded to know how I could recompense him for this unprecedented privilege. "Mend your broken heart, my lad, and tell your father about the work we do here. We are in dire need of funds, and it occurs to me that he might well be able to help us." I was then invited to attend a class he was to conduct for the entire college, apparently consisting of less than a dozen students. I told him I had need to return the carriage to its owner.

He then informed me that there are several students graduated from the college who are now veterinary surgeons including one William Stockley who had graduated in 1794 and gone to the cavalry to be of assistance there. By now, he told me, he might well be mustered out and available to help us.

I thanked him profusely, ran back to the main road, leaped into the carriage, and we returned, I being allowed to handle the reins for some time, and in such exuberant spirits that the horses caught the same and lifted high their elegant hooves as back we sped.

❧

30 JUNE, 1803 HARROW

Get ready to return to Pemberley, D! The Harrow years are ended! We have come through with flying colors – top grades and commendations in all subjects, an award in drama, medals and honors in all sports, with special commendations in fencing and in cricket.

As I advanced to the dais to receive my diploma, I was favored with a cheer from a bloc of my classmates who apparently think better of me than most. Received said diploma, tossed the tassel of the foolish mortar board to the opposite side, then tossed the whole cap into the air, thereby creating a commotion for the retrieval of same.

Joined my parents. My father was beaming, not so my mother. I knew immediately that such abandonment of dignity had caused her embarrassment. Nevertheless we had a pleasant time during the refreshment period, and they both graciously accepted introductions to the many who crowded around. I was proud as a (no! No clichés, Darcy). Several of my classmates commented to me how lucky I am to have such a beautiful and charming mother, and I heartily seconded their praises.

Not many are going on to Cambridge as I shall be, but to those who will be there, I made promises that we shall see one another. And so came the farewells, and at long last it came time to return to Pemberley.

Off we rolled, my luggage (so many books!) piled high atop the carriage. We spoke little. I was embarrassed to find that I kept nodding. Small wonder. There was not much sleep the last few days. But it did seem a breach of etiquette. Ironically, it was both parents who nodded off.

I put my head back, but my thoughts were rolling, rolling, with the humming sound of the carriage wheels, and the pounding of horses' hooves.

How much had transpired since I had left for Harrow! Memories of cricket matches, fencing matches, drama classes, *Beowulf*, classmates, chapel (this, complete with loud chords of organ music, all ringing through my head), memories of the commencement, and my mother smiling and so winsome and delightful. Perhaps I should see to it that she is always surrounded by admiring throngs. She is so different then. What happens to her at Pemberley? Can not I fashion some kind of change for her? Finally, I too must have fallen asleep.

I awakened as we drove through the gates of my dreamland. Paradise regained! In the soft colors of early dawn the grounds appeared even more beautiful than I had remembered. And as the house appeared from behind the parkland, I felt the tears stinging my eyes. I was overcome with affection and pride. Never will I do anything to besmirch the nobility of this corner of heaven. I herewith do pledge it!

My father awoke. I asked for Champêtre.

"I thought you knew, we had to put the horse down."

I could not contain my explosion of shock. My father put his hand on mine. I looked for sympathy from my mother. I knew she was awake. But she kept her eyes closed until the carriage door was opened. As we descended, my father told me that a new horse was being broken for me, and would be in the stables soon. He suggested I name him "Augustus."

I said nothing in reply, but I knew that the name would be "Champêtre." Always, always, my steed would be "Champêtre."

LATER, PEMBERLEY

I had been anticipating eagerly the delights of an entire summer here. Not so. Prepare to travel again, D. It seems that next week we are scheduled to embark on the "finishing touches" for "a proper English gentleman," viz – the Grand Tour of Europe, that which is necessary to complete the proper education of the proper scion of the most proper status. I am to be accompanied by a companion who has been highly recommended to my parents. His name is Hippolyte Acton. The name alone is enough to make me most dim in my anticipation of this next "pleasure."

24 JULY, 1803 GRAND TOUR

My anticipation of Hippolyte has not been proven to be wrong. In every way possible, the man is an ass. I will credit him with knowing his Europe, and which places to visit, and which works of art are to be viewed. In all fairness, I shall return from this regimen with a good knowledge of the high points of civilization. If only he were a mute! He talks, nay *lectures*, endlessly on every last detail of every place and each piece to which we attend. He continues to rave on as we dine, and does not stop until a series of disgusting snores suddenly stand in for his shrill endless voice.

I have not written to you, D. because it takes all the energy I have to write the required letter home to my parents each night. I shall collect these when I return home (ah! Home!) and place them inside your covers, so you can absorb them like butter into a scone. Assuming, that is, that my parents bother to cherish my missives.

France is wonderful – I love the language and am appreciated by all we meet for my care for their *accent*. Paris is a city of dreams. Left it with regret. Traveled south to Nevers, Villefranche, Lyon, Avignon (*formidable*).

Tomorrow we start to explore Arles, noted for its Roman ruins, which include an amphitheatre, a famous twelfth century Romanesque portal and the requisite cathedral, this one being St.Trophime. Hippolyte is an expert on all its several rebuilding phases, and I am certain he will go into detail on each.

We shall then go to Marseille, and sail thence to Italy.

※

8 August, 1803 Italy

A fortnight has passed since we arrived in Italy, and there has been such a prodigious banquet of architecture, sculpture, paintings, and chapels, that my head is spinning. Venice tomorrow, and thence by ship back to England. I am ready for the return, although I must credit my parents with insisting upon this excursion. I have in my possession a large folio of papers which includes passes into the various sites we have visited, engraved cards with replications of some of the works which I have much enjoyed, and a raft of other such mementos. When I return I shall devote myself to putting all of the above mentioned into order as I know I shall be the better for having seen, absorbed, and then stored indelibly these scraps and what recollections they will have for me.

I shall tell you now of my favorites – Giotto, Ucello, Mantegna. They were refreshing, purifying, exciting, and satisfying on all levels – aesthetic, intellectual, and – dare I say – spiritual.

When we began, however, to encounter later works of the Renaissance, there began a disturbance for me. The kaleidoscope of naked ladies, posed most seductively, were troubling to me indeed. By the time we arrived in Rome I was tormented by the question which kept arising (would I had chosen another verb!) – am I seeing Religion depicted or pure carnality? There is an endless offering of such subjects!

My nights are dreadful, and I am mortified lest my roommate hear my thrashings and comment on them.

Who were these artists, and were they, too, prisoners of the flesh, as am I? It could not be! Were they so shackled, they could not have created such images. I curse my fate not to have lived in such times, in such climes, with the blessed release which these men must have enjoyed.

Today we went to the Cornaro Chapel at Santa Maria della Vittoria. Here we find an enormous altar in white marble, depicting the *Agony of Saint Teresa*. I purchased a sketch of this work, D. Exactly what is this lady experiencing, and *how* did Bernini find the model who could so vividly depict that which I conclude *is* depicted? What, one wonders, exactly *went on* in this sculptor's studio?!

To make matters worse for me, we went on to the Altieri Chapel, where we find the same portrayal in the *Death of the Blessed Ludovica Albertoni*, apparently posed by the very same lady with exactly the same instructions.

It was in this place that I caught Hippolyte studying me with a strange expression as I was experiencing these works (and these thoughts). I have noticed him on other occasions exchanging glances with men whom we pass on the streets and in the cafes. It is well that the trip is nearing its close, well that I tower above him – despite my younger years – and could hoist him easily by the scruff of his nasty neck and toss him into the Trevi Fountain.

❦

28 AUGUST, 1803 PEMBERLEY

Arrived home last night. Everyone seemed happy to see me, even my mother. My parents had arranged a welcoming party in my honor which took place this night. Friends and family were invited from far and wide. The house was merry with voices and music, there was an opportunity to dance. I have been sent (forcibly) for lessons in that art, and now take great pleasure in the dance. There were several young ladies present, some of whom were not too difficult to wheel about. My mother accepted my invitation to dance, and that was a grand moment. She is graceful and light, and appeared to enjoy herself. It seems we cut a fine figure, and were watched by many of those present, who then gave us the compliment of loud applause.

I was sorry when the evening ended. I hope there will be evenings to follow when I can show to my parents the many documents I have brought home from my travels.

※

31 AUGUST, 1803 PEMBERLEY

Of a sudden the summer is over, and it is time to ready ourselves for the University. Yes, D., we are off to Cambridge. Prepare thyself.

※

18 SEPTEMBER, 1803 CAMBRIDGE

Well, D., and Hello! How do you like being at England's finest University? (A remark calculated to start a war with Oxford.) I am in King's College, entered into trivium subjects, along with Charles. I have plunged into classes, (philosophy will be my course of study) and into sports with abandon. Sorting it all out takes time, but I like it all. Except for the fact that Wickham is here too. He has located in Christ's College. (What a paradox!) Confound the blackguard! He has blandished my father who believes that he is serious about the Curacy, and has agreed to sponsor his education therein. Father has told me he is "under my wing" to be looked after. Luckily, he is interested in none of my pursuits (nor I in his), so we see little of one another. I have tried to carry out the charge laid upon me, but he avoids and evades me.

※

30 OCTOBER, 1804 CAMBRIDGE

Immediately upon entering the new term I searched down the opportunities for theatre, and as soon as I was allowed to enter elective courses, I enrolled in the drama class. I have done several readings in Shakespeare plays. Have done some of the minor comic parts, which were well received. We are currently casting *Tartuffe*, and I have read for the lead.

Good night, sir. Sleep cannot come soon enough! I am sore tired.

❦

14 December, 1804 Cambridge

Well, D., *Tartuffe* is mine and I am deep in rehearsals and costume fittings, and high with excitement and anticipation. It is a wonderful role, and much applicable to any society. Perhaps my deep scorn for rogues and hypocrites helped me into the part, but one may also look to my excellent French accent, and for that I can thank some of my tutors at Pemberley.

There seems to be more than the usual excitement about the play, partly because the production has been arranged to include parents. I have chosen not to trouble my own, and have not sent them the invitation.

Charles has invited his family and they are coming in full force. I told him that I had not troubled mine with an invitation to attend.

❦

6 January, 1805 Cambridge

It is Friday night, and there is some consternation. I refer not to the play which we are about to present which is frantic enough, God knows. I refer to the fact that Charles, thinking to repair a hurt that was done to me at Harrow, has invited my parents and they are coming! He likewise invited Georgiana, but she declined. Would that *they* had!

Can't dwell with thee any longer. Sleep well. I doubt that I shall.

❦

7 January, 1805 Cambridge

My parents indeed are here. They also brought Wickham the elder. Things started off badly enough, as no one could locate Mr. George Wickham, and I was assigned the blame for having not *landed* him as directed. Accepted the charge, a habit of character well bred into me, although I had tried mightily to locate the fool.

The Bingley family joined us for supper last night at the inn over-looking the Cam. My mother and Mrs. B. get along smashingly. My father and Mr. B. appear to have many subjects in common, and went into deep discussion on the far edge of the terrace.

A lovely evening, fresh after a day of rain. Pleasant for this time of year. The trees were sparkling in the light from the setting sun, and the river bubbled merrily along as if it had taken on an extra draught of energy. Some punts were out, which made for pleasant conversation, thus welding the two family groups into a pleasant convocation. Lucky for me, the Wickham "failure" was let drop. Let us trust that the miscreant's pater was able to locate him at his digs.

Supper was announced and we went inside. I? I could not eat. Was urged to eat. Resisted. And soon came a rising anxiety and nervousness. *On dit* that this is the curse of all actors. I have been told that if one is *not* nervous, especially just before the curtain rises, one will perform poorly. Also the foolish prating of Miss Caroline suited me ill. Whenever we are together she seems to attach herself to me with some sort of infernal muci-lage which she must secrete through her silly pores.

Today arrived soon enough. It developed that my mother had made plans to include me, which had to be abjured for reasons of a rehearsal and a costume fitting. My mother was ill pleased. She had arranged to be with friends whom she had met in London, who have an estate in Cambridgeshire, who, it seems, had heard of her grown son, and that he was "not unhand-some." She was eager to "show off" this prize. I would not – could not – and held my ground. She was icy when she left for the afternoon.

Then, *curtain time!*

When first I entered the stage I was a bit off my stride, but soon forgot that my parents were in the audience, and romped through to gales of laughter and a wonderful ovation at the close, with many curtain calls.

When my group came to 'the green room' we were in a state of great exhilaration. My parents, however, seemed distant. Cool and polite. The others gave me a noisy reception which served to cover my parents' remoteness. But not for long.

It was following the roisterous after-theatre party that I received my sentencing – I am not to act again. Not a fit activity for a gentleman of "my rank and quality." I did not protest. They are training me for the role I must play in life and I must be grateful to them for their standards and example.

How fare I, D.? We shall discuss it nevermore. The matter is closed.
THE MATTER IS CLOSED!

12 April, 1805 Cambridge - London

Shocking news today, D. Charles has received word that his father has died. He must go to his home as soon as the carriage can come for him. I offered to accompany him, and he accepted most gratefully. We left early in the morning, in a cold grey mist, and found London floating in an eerie and vaporous sea that well befitted our mood. How had this come to pass? There had been no warning of any illness. Charles looked haggard, and confessed that he had not slept the night.

Mrs. Bingley was waiting at the door as we drove up. She too – pale, and ravaged by her crying. But still she looked beautiful and when she opened her arms to Charles and took him in, I wanted to be in that embrace. The two stood silently for some time. I stepped away, more moved than I cared to show.

Now she greeted me. I kissed her hand, tried to express my condolences. She thanked me softly for being so good as to come with Charles.

We two entered and were shown into the breakfast room, where hot coffee was awaiting us. So very welcome! Breakfast arrived. Charles, usually ravenous, picked at the food. I fell to with eagerness, although I did wonder if this was appropriate to the occasion.

Now Charles asked for the circumstances, which she detailed for us, with many an interruption to wipe her eyes. (I could not avoid noticing how the tears misted them softly, and clung tremulous to her lashes.)

Such a shocking tale!

It seems that Mr. Bingley was concerned about the supply of sperm oil for his factories. I learned that he is (was? How *does* one refer to the activities of the deceased?) one of the largest suppliers of oil to the candlemakers. In fact, it seems, he had (has!) one of the largest factories for the making of candles in England and is much depended upon for provisioning His Majesty's Navy.

I had been acquainted with the fact that Mr. Bingley was involved in a major business venture and had made his immense fortune therein. Only that. Since Englishmen of rank do not inquire as to the livelihood of a friend, I had never asked. It was interesting to learn of it – but not under such circumstance.

It seems that Mr. Bingley had reason to entertain serious concern about an adequate supply of oil for the oncoming winter. Also, it seems, there had been reports about something amiss on his latest shipment.

"He worried more lest the people be in darkness than for his own safety" cried Mrs. B. bitterly. Charles calmed her, and she continued, "He went to the whaling ship when she came into port and insisted on boarding her, although his foreman has told me that he had been well warned of the dangers. Somehow, in all the activity and confusion, his foot became entangled in a rope which was letting heavy drums down onto the wharf. He was carried to his death."

She could not continue. One hopes that she was not given too many details about this. It is frightful to contemplate. She excused herself, and fled upstairs to her rooms. Charles and I stared at one another, then he bowed his head and buried it in his hands. I went over to him, put my hand on his shoulder, and thus we stood until he had recovered. He excused himself and went to his room.

I knew well my room in "my home away from home" and was on *my* way to solitude when I heard sounds of weeping coming from the salon. Therein I espied Miss Caroline in a wretched condition. Such a sad and lonely figure! I seated myself next to her, held her hand, then took the courage to put my arm around her shoulder. She did not rebuke this, and thus we sat; she, trying to regain control, I, silent until a servant came into the room and informed me that Mrs. Bingley wished to see me. I kissed Miss Caroline's hand, expressed my condolences, and mounted the steep stairs.

A mercer was in Mrs. Bingley's sitting room when I entered, unrolling yards of black cloth. The salesman was dismissed, and I was told to be seated.

Her eyes were red, and she reached for her kerchief often in order to wipe them dry, but I still deemed her one of the most beautiful women I had ever seen. Normally I favor amber colored tresses, but I found myself looking with admiration at her sleek black hair, and deciding that black was even finer.

Now she spoke, "Fitzwilliam, you have been such a fine friend to Charles. I trust your probity and your good sense implicitly. I know not what path he will take without his father to guide him. He is such a guileless young man, so given to sudden enthusiasms, so apt to find a new one and veer suddenly – I am appealing to you to keep an eye on his welfare, to help him make sound decisions, and to take charge when he is in error. May I ask that of you?"

I told her that I was honored beyond expression by her confidence in me, that I would take the charge seriously and never forsake my responsibility. I kissed her hand, and left the room.

The day involved an endless succession of details to be managed. I tried to be helpful, and believe that I proved to be a source of strength to the family. When I learned that Miss Louisa would not leave her room for supper, I am the one who persuaded her to take some nourishment.

Supper was silent and solemn. Mrs. Bingley was staring intently at the tapers burning brightly on the table, then looked up at the chandelier, and over at the wall sconces. She remarked in *such* a doleful voice, "Was this a fair exchange, my dearest?"

There was a dead silence. I broke it by saying, "Is there not something quite *Promethean* about your husband's obsession, Mrs. Bingley?" She looked at me searchingly, and replied, "Thank you, Fitzwilliam, that is a beautiful and consoling thought."

LATER

I will never light a candle again, D., without thoughts of the integrity and passion of this man.

I have arisen to write you a coda to the day. It is deep into the night. I had fallen asleep, but awakened from a dream of such loveliness that I shall dwell on it forevermore. I was with Mrs. Bingley, she held out her arms to me, I embraced her. There was not the usual ending for such a dream. I wanted only to be enfolded. And thus I was.

27 DECEMBER, 1805 LONDON

Another college year, another summer at Pemberley, nose to the grindstone as never before. *Durance vile!* But productive. I enjoyed the proximity and cooperation with my father, and rather suspect that the feeling was mutual.

Back to Cambridge in October. Encountered Professor H. from time to time. One day he invited me to tea in his chambers. I was slightly hesitant, but braved it, and was glad for it. We had a stimulating talk about theatre. Then he turned to me and asked if he might open a subject which has had him most perplexed. I rather suspected it might concern my theatrical career, and indeed I was correct. "What was it, Mr. Darcy? One of the most promising young performers I have yet encountered, such a pleasure to have you for a student; so suddenly removed from the boards. Any explanation?"

"No. No explanation, sir."

He studied me silently. Then shook his head, held out his hand in dismissal, and told me that if I ever reconsidered, to please contact him and he could acquaint me with the more promising of London's theatrical personalities. I thanked him in a flat tone. What was ringing in my head was, "No hope for it, sir. No hope!"

I am spending the Michaelmas season in London with my parents and silent Georgiana. Fencing lessons when I have my way, dancing lessons when my mother prevails. More of the latter than the former, you may be sure of it.

❦

20 January, 1806 Cambridge

We have a splendid opportunity these days to hear one of Britain's finest minds at work – the dazzling Sydney Smith. He is lecturing at the Royal Institution in London, and thither I went today to hear him. I was told to arrive at least an hour early, which I did, (thereby missing my tutorials.) Even so the hall was totally occupied, and I was sent up to the balcony, which has been built expressly for this man's series. (Pungent odor of new wood, which I inhaled with delight.) Stood for an endless time, occupying my mind with scrutiny of the faces about me, and categorizing the shapes of heads below me. When the worthy began to speak, one lost all sense of the discomfort of standing, nay, of the very knowledge of the passage of time. The man is kindly, optimistic, devilishly satiric, and one of the wittiest speakers I have heard to this date. His metaphors are original and vivid, and were delivered to the accompaniment of roars of laughter from the audience.

I have heard him compared to Voltaire, and indeed, to Swift. I found him to be *incomparable*.

Could secure no available conveyance when the lecture concluded, decided to take a canal boat back to Cambridge, entailing a walk of some distance. Once aboard I watched the river sights with some interest, then, as darkness approached I sat me down on an upturned keg and commenced to muse. Vivid images of Venice and the romance of gondola travel came to mind. Venice would be the place to take one's honeymoon! And who would the lady be? Certainly not my cousin Anne (as planned for me!) I concentrated on visualizing a mate. The only image which came to mind was that of Mrs. Bingley.

It was very late when I came to Cambridge. Hopped ashore, stopped at a tavern for my evening meal, reached my destination later than I care to relate.

Worth the effort! A tonic! What a wealth of brilliant minds are to be found in London and environs!

2 February, 1806 Cambridge

Most dreadful news, D. A proctor came into Philosophy lecture this morning, and after a whispered conversation with Professor N. – the latter called out my name and asked me to go with the messenger. I knew this could not bode well, especially when I learned that I was to report to my supervisor. The serious look on that gentleman's face made me fear the worst, and I was not misguided. I was led into his private office and there informed that my father has died, and I am to return to Pemberley at once. So soon after the same event in Charles' life!

I am in great haste, and much distraught. I have started to pack years of accumulation, as word has been sent that I shall not be returning to Cambridge. Books! So many books!! I would not leave a one. Each has marginal notes that represent serious study. I shall put them into the library. *My* library now.

Would it were not so!

Made a round of good-byes, all with the deepest regret. The farewell I cared about the most was that with Professor H. He, who had so boosted my ambitions toward the theatre. He pulled me aside, told me how sorry he was for my bereavement. Now he drew the conclusion that my parents must have known that there would be a tragic loss, and that they ordered me *out* from a consideration for *him*. An amazing reconstruction of the facts, but I did not disabuse him. He gave me a sound thump on the back and said he hoped all would go well with me, and that I will be missed.

I have been sitting here with sad, sad thoughts, but now I must close, and lock you tight, and get on with the packing to depart these hallowed halls. The carriage will be here after 'the last supper.' Charles has offered to accompany me, but 'twill not do, as he must prepare for a disputation and is (of course) not near finished with the preparation for it. I bade him adieu.

And so I am Master of Pemberley, although I want that not. I shall do the best of which I am capable to measure to the kind of man my father was – noble, sincere, well schooled; an example of probity and sound judgement, and of sterling character. I have been blessed to have had such a model. I do solemnly swear that I shall hew to all the values he has set so firmly for me. And I shall miss him!

❦

5 FEBRUARY, 1806 PEMBERLEY

What ho, D. Can you not provide me with a little cheer? It is sad and gloomy here. Hushed voices, visitors coming to express condolences. Such long faces they put on for our benefit. Such doleful tones of voice. I would not be put off by this if I did not chance to glimpse them, when we are not within range, acting quite merry and in good spirits.

Pemberley is not at all the same without Father. He secluded himself a good deal when he was not away on business affairs of his own, but he was a presence nevertheless. I miss him most seriously, and I think Georgiana does too, although she is more than ever an evanescent spirit. As for Mother . . . Mother has taken to her bed, with the door closed. Her grief is hers alone, it appears, and we are not to be taken into consideration as needing her. Which we both do – most desperately.

I am trying manfully to shoulder the burden of what must be accomplished here, day to day. Mr. Wickham is most helpful. There is the matter of a bequest to his undeserving son, but the terms of it do not appeal to same, and we are trying to come to a fair dispensation. Young Wickham is too much around, adding grievously to my discomfort. I have found him reading my letters (those which arrive for me, those which I am in the process of writing).

In an attempt to shake off my mood at the end of this afternoon's work, I ordered that Champêtre be saddled, and we cantered off on a tour of the grounds. I should be uplifted by realizing that all the glory of this place is mine now, but I am not consoled.

Funeral services loom. Will mother attend?

❦

6 FEBRUARY, 1806 PEMBERLEY

It was raining, of course – the Gods must watch our affairs more closely than we realize. Apparently they will not send a member of the upper class into the grave without the proper weather as a background to sorrow.

My mother did bestir herself, and looked most gloriously beautiful in her 'widows weeds', most inappropriately named in her case. My mother's gown clung in graceful folds to her slender body, and the black veil made her appear especially delicate and exquisite. I took her arm, and as we walked to our pew I revelled in the sensation that she needed me and appreciated my support. Georgiana followed us, such a sad wisp of a girl! When we were seated I bethought myself that it would content my mother if I took her hand. Surely, it would have been a contentment for me! My gesture was rejected.

The church was full, and full of the folk that my mother seems to prefer. These all returned to Pemberley for a formal reception. Soon our house was resonating with the charming and shallow chatter of many well dressed women and well attired men.

As the great silver trays of filled wine glasses were passed one could see the fluttering of many gloved hands all lifting at once, for all the world like the scene in a ballet. I wanted most awfully to quit the scene and be alone, but it was apparent that as the master of the manor there would be no such dispensation. At times I felt as if in a dream, so wrong did it seem to hear such jollity. Even my mother seemed to share in this upward mood.

Georgiana? Georgiana had disappeared, and no one appeared to miss her, as no one asked for her. I bethought myself that I should search for her upstairs, but each time I tried to quit the scene, there was a new order of participation required of me.

At last the long day ended, and the last guest departed. My mother's smiles faded. The study door remained closed, there was no grand presence behind it, nor ever again shall there be. Mother bade me good night and went to her room – now a tragic queen ascending the grand staircase alone. How delicate she looked. How defeated.

❦

27 JUNE, 1806 PEMBERLEY

The summer wears on. Tedious indeed! Sameness? No! A different problem every minute, it seems. Various tenants come to me with their various problems. Theirs are so much more difficult than my own that I am ashamed to complain, even to you. I try to be of help to them in so far as I am able, but it does seem that most men are asked to prevail against unprevailable forces. They shake off one ill only to be beset by several others.

Into the middle of all this flutter scores of little white invitations which await me each day on the credenza in the grand hall. They come from scores of mothers who have trembling young daughters who must be wed, and who have noticed me all at the very same moment, it seems. (Could it be the moment I became master of Pemberley?) Fie! I, who need to be consoled in my grief, am to be hunted down quickly and swept off to the altar before another can corner me?

Folly and foolishness. And me thinks Georgiana needs a friend. I wish to be here if she needs me.

3 JULY, 1806 PEMBERLEY

I have added to the establishment a new servant whose name is Edward. It troubled me to learn that my Mrs. Reynolds was frequently disturbed at night to attend to mother. I did not fancy Reynolds carrying the heavy trays up and down stairs at all hours. I protested to her. I asked her to appeal to the head butler. She protested that she would not.

Once, in fact, I tried to take a tray from her to carry it myself, but her reaction was so extreme that I eschewed the gesture.

I set about finding a young and strong man to manage her chores, and in order to assure her that she was in no way being lowered in status, I elevated her to the position of Housekeeper, which pleases her mightily. She is much grateful, and I am certain will be excellent in fulfilling the requirements of her position. I feel somehow reassured when Reynolds is in evidence.

I do not see Georgiana often. She keeps to her room, or spends long hours with her music. We dine together most evenings. On occasion I accept an invitation. Not she. She cares not to cover the social circuit.

We miss Mother at the table. And Father too, of course. But I do not miss the lessons and lectures about how to manage my heritage with success. I feel I am doing this quite well. And I must confess that I am not averse to a good part of the responsibility. I like to leap in when there are emergencies. I have helped with floods, fire, with various accidents. I have gone on raiding expeditions against various villains who have attempted various nefarious misdeeds. I have even helped in the breech births of not a few colts.

This makes for full days and not much time for reflective sorrow. The work is firming my body with new strengths. Strengths that come from heavy labor, not from sports. Thomson once wrote, "Health is the vital principle of bliss, and exercise, of health."

Health, I know full well. Of bliss I know naught, and doubt that ever shall I know.

❦

6 JULY, 1806 PEMBERLEY

Edward came to my chambers this morning, saying that my mother wished to see me. She is in bed most of the time now. Several doctors have been sent for but not one has found anything to point to by way of illness.

She bade me enter when I knocked. I stood stiffly by her bed, quite mute save for the usual amenities. Then as if from nowhere she commenced to upbraid me for my aloofness and coldness. I could say nothing by way of response.

"And Georgiana! Where did the two of you learn to be such unfeeling *sticks*?"

What did I mumble? An inconsequential "I am most sorry, Mother."

"SORRY? Never a kiss or a sweet word of comfort from you since ~ since. . ." She could not say it.

Again I said that I was aggrieved to be such a disappointment.

"Fitzwilliam, why can you not put your arms around me? It would be so such a comfort to be able to put my head on your shoulder. It would be such a comfort."

D., I tell you squarely, I could not move. In truth, I realized that it would be an impossibility *to touch her*. So I continued to stand there – dumb! DUMB! – and numb!

She became agitated and ordered me from the room.
Sick at heart, I left.

⚜

7 July, 1806 Pemberley

D.!

My mother died last night. I was awakened this morning by a frantic knocking on the door. Edward. He bore this most desolating news. As I leaped from my bed, not fully awake and in shock, I experienced a loss of balance and would have fallen if Edward had not been there to steady me.

Pemberley has been *awash* all day with agitated and frantic visitors, commencing with Dr. McPherson, who sent for other physicians (one had need to be in attendance on Georgiana the entire day) apothecaries, tenants, friends, tradesmen, besides all of the various family members who could be reached. All the day one could hear the mournful knelling of the 'passing bell" from the parish church.

The physicians are at a loss to tell us the cause. I? Somehow I attach myself to this strange death. Why could I not perform even that small tender gesture which she had craved from me? The gentleman-like gesture for which a lady had cried. WHY?

⚜

10 July, 1806 Pemberley

D., Is there no bottom to grief? I sink down, down, endlessly. I pace the floor, hour after hour. I go for long rides. (Poor Champêtre. When I finally bring him in he is completely lathered. The groom looks at me strangely, but does not comment.) I swim constantly – at all hours. The lake is bitter cold at night. I care not.

I do not understand what killed my mother. Nor do the physicians. Was it grief for father? She acted no different when he was alive. Passing strange.

Let us suppose I had the power to summon her back to this world. Would matters be different? Could I set things to rights?

Yes! I could! I imagine a reunion, a glorious reconciliation, an openness between us, allowing us to talk and talk. I would pour my heart out to her and tell her how I adore her, how I idolize her. She would – what would she do? D., I realize that I am doing all the talking in this fantasy, nor can I imagine any words which would be appropriate to her. However I *can* visualize her smiling sweetly at me, the way she smiled at so many of her friends.

Georgiana is now my responsibility, yet I feel too numb to help her in *her* grief. She is quieter than ever. I fear she will faint again, yet I am unable to say any of the right words to help her. Yes, I am in charge of it all, and I feel totally unequal to the task.

I am ranting – it is late. I bid you a doleful good night.

⁂

10 January, 1807 Pemberley

Reynolds asked permission to address me at breakfast this morning. I stood and motioned to her to sit down, but she would not. She said she could not speak if *I* were to stand thus, so we rearranged ourselves.

"Mr. Darcy, would you not like us to change the upstairs so that the Master can take the master bedroom suite?"

I was overcome with confusion for a moment. But not for long. As my thoughts cleared I realized that I could never live comfortably in those rooms. It would be like claiming the throne room of our King.

I thanked her and told her that I cared not to make such a move. She looked so disappointed that I relented and told her that it would be most acceptable if she cared to make a few changes in my own suite, such as lighter colors on the walls and in the fabrics. I would be also happy, I told her, to take possession of the grand bathing tub that my parents had sent from France. Otherwise I would like the servants to clean out the rooms, dispose of the clothing somehow, and shut down the suite for the time being. Later it might well suffice for guests.

⁂

1 May, 1807 Pemberley

Awoke this morning, fervently wishing that I could turn over, shut out the day, and avoid the bitter pursuits to which I must tend – Overcame, arose, bathed, dressed.

When I descended to breakfast I was surprised to find Georgiana seated there. In the mornings one can almost forget that she resides at Pemberley, except for the lovely sounds of music which float through the house, gladdening one. She looked frail and pale, and her eyes betray that she has been weeping overmuch. She came to the table, she informed me, because she had a request. This turned out to be a desire to reopen the house in London, to go thither and study music. She requested this in a grave and serious manner. I was much moved. She said she would like me to arrange this for her, except for the lessons, of which she has taken charge.

"Excellent!, Georgiana! I am proud and pleased that you have such an ambition and have acted upon it. I shall arrange it forthwith, and find a proper gentlewoman to accompany you. And now I have a favor to ask of you. I have a task for the two of us. Please come into the study after our meal."

When we entered therein she walked around the room, studying the pictures on the walls, the books on the shelves, the bibelots on the desk. Finally she remarked, "How often you were summoned here. And how sad you did look when you left the room!"

I must say I was surprised. How knew she all of this? Did she too "spy" from the upper *parapet?* I demurred from pressing her and told her that the business at hand involved Mother's jewels. I told her that there were many pieces, that I and several solicitors had searched everywhere for some document which might relate to the disposition thereof. Nothing. It appeared that it was up to me to dispose of these articles. I needed assistance.

She accepted with alacrity. I pulled out a variety of velvet cases from my desk drawers and turned them onto the table for her. She handled each shimmering object most reverently. The cases gave off a fragrance which recalled Mother only too vividly. Had I not been a well braced male, I might have wept.

She said, "How beautiful Mother looked when she went to a party! Do you recall, Darcy? How she brightened and shone?"

I did recall. I cared not to discuss it. Instead I told her that the jewelry all belongs to me by rights, I was surprised that Mother had given no thought to her daughter nor to the ladies who had attended her these many years; that it was my thought to *forge* (may the good Lord forgive me!) a note from Mother making individual bequests. Georgiana leapt to the plan. She said she wanted none of the treasure, that her life is such that she has no need of ornamentation. We argued. I won. (I do not have many confrontations, but it does appear that when I do, I prevail.)

We settled to it immediately, deciding upon trinkets for each of the staff, including some who have departed and need to be located. Finally, I persuaded her to accept some of the finest objects. Finally, she persuaded me to put aside some of the most handsome pieces for the future Mrs. Darcy.

('Put aside,' yes. *However*, the thought of another woman wearing Mother's necklace? NEVER!)

I must confess I felt lighter of heart when we finished the job of sorting. It felt bright and nice to be practicing such a deception with my sister, and for such a pleasant benefaction. I sat down to compose the letter, while she waited. When I had put the pen down and had blotted the ink, I rose to my feet, cleared my throat, and read aloud to her. She remarked with delight that I had transformed myself and had sounded for all the world *like Mother*.

I must take care that when the staff is convened and I am reading the letter, that I remember my own voice and do not assume so vividly the voice of an other.

6 MAY, 1809 PEMBERLEY

Nothing much to report, D. Life goes on. (Is that a platitude, Father?) I have not much care for society, and avoid most opportunities to mingle with my peers. I ride to Rosings to see my Aunt Catherine de Bourgh. I have just returned from another such jaunt.

It has been a grievance to my aunt that she was abroad when Mother died. Why do I think that my sorrow can be eased in being in company with her? These two sisters were in no way alike. (In one way, yes, both took *most* seriously the pairing of couples so as to enhance the family tree. Their plans for me were – and are! – *gruesome*.)

Aunt C. does amuse me with her idiosyncratic behavior, and the trip thither makes for a good ride for trusty Champêtre and his Master. There are several fields with splendid hedges to jump, sparkling streams to ford, and where the vistas are most lovely to behold. I make plans to stay overnight at the Inn at C. – but usually I keep on riding.

Aunt sets a fine table, on occasion there are people of interest at her board, but generally one finds the usual unpalatable types – blunt men, and uninteresting women. My cousin Anne sits like a spectre, saying naught.

Inevitably, I am placed on her right. I try vainly to elicit some sense of life from her, give up the effort, turn to *my* right and test this lady for conversational possibilities. I have found silence profound, or, worse, a torrent of such inanities as to sink me. Where does it all lead? As I write, I see it now – pass the time! So be it. Let the others worry. I shall sit content with my own racing thoughts – unless, that is, I can find a one to share in a splendid exchange.

Resolve – I shall continue to go to Rosings on occasion. To be dutiful. It will not be for my own satisfaction.

Tonight, as I heard the melodies of Georgiana's music, it occurred to me that a happy project would be to find a second pianoforte for her to be situated in the London house. It will not be long afore her removal there.

Done! I shall send a messenger there to inform our London staff to open the house for me.

21 MAY, 1809 LONDON

Contacted today a gentleman named Burkhardt Tschudi, who is in partnership with one James Broadwood. They have an excellent firm. Spent the better part of the morning with the estimable gentlemen. Mr. B. has of late invented the soft pedal, enabling the player to make sounds both *forte e piano*. I listened and forthwith ordered a most handsome instrument.

Have feasted on theatre. Covent Garden and the Lyceum are both running splendid venues.

11 AUGUST, 1809 LONDON

A messenger arrived yesterday morning with a neatly folded, sealed missive which was brought to me as I was writing at my desk.

From Charles. "Capital!" thought I. NOT SO. Alas! It bore news of the death of his mother. I was on my feet and calling for my carriage on the instant.

Arrived after a great deal of anxiety. The weather has lifted, and it seemed that everyone in London was abroad, crowding either the sidewalk or the street. We were at a deadly crawl for most of the transit. The only possible reason for not being in a wretchedness was that I was so concerned with untangling mentally each grievous clot of personages in our way, that I had little time to dwell on the loss of Mrs. Bingley. But it came over me with full force as I entered the house and realized I would see her nevermore. As I recall, I gasped and leaned against the door post for a moment.

Charles greeted me wordlessly. Then finally found his voice. He explained that his mother had been returning home in her carriage when a runaway team came hurling down a cross street. The huge horses veered as they espied the obstacle in their path, and turned aside. But the heavy dray they were pulling slid sideways and into the Bingley carriage, overturning it, with the lady pinned inside. When the carriage was righted by a host of citizens and the melée had been settled, and the "charlie" had the door pried open, he found her with a broken neck. The coachmen told Charles that he knew the worst when the charlie looked inside and removed his cap.

I must have looked like a wild man. Charles asked if I were all right. I blurted I know not what response, and ran off down the street, nor did I stop running until my breath would carry me no more.

Returned to the house, did what I could to be of help, sat again with Miss Caroline. I can write no more, D. I mourn for this lovely creature. For her family. And for *myself.*

🕸

· 20 NOVEMBER, 1809 LONDON

Pemberley affairs seem to be running smoothly *at last.* Made a quick decision to join Georgiana, so here we are in London again.

In addition to theatre and the many good lectures, I have ventured into the social life here, and whereas I find most events to be pallid, and the majority of whom I meet to be deficient, I find that I have a great passion for the dance and am happy to attend the many balls which take place in town. Here I seem to cut such a fine figure that each appearance leads to more invitations, which come within days (oftimes within hours).

There are vast battalions of young women who lack either beauty, or charm, or wit, or esprit, or poise – often all of these qualities taken together. I could forgive them these insufficiencies if they were passable dancers, but even this merit is wanting in most. When I return a partner to her guardian, I sometimes find persons of the older generation who are capable of an interesting exchange, and I might stay and chat for a time. I most particularly seem to get along famously with the various mothers.

Last night I met such an one, the mother of an awkward little goose whom I had escorted back to her nesting place. The lady asked me a few polite questions, we commenced to talk, she soon made it most clear that she was without escort. I found her agreeable in every way. Decent figure, pretty face, tawny hair (although frizzly and pomaded like all London ladies – their hair is too contrived for my taste.) I grant that her dress did seem extraordinarily décolleté for a *grass widow*. What there was of it above the waist was a light green, sparingly draped over the bosom. The color *below the waist*? I seem not to have noticed.

I dared venture to her an invitation to dance. It was only too apparent how much she would have liked to accept, but she demurred, saying it would not be good form to take the floor in place of her daughter. I admired her integrity in the matter, and told her so. She suggested we walk to the terrace. So we did, leaving the daughter alone. It did occur to me that this was paradoxical behavior, but I did not pursue the thought.

I had been addressing her as Lady T., but within moments she had urged me to use her first name, and within moments after that she had thrown herself into my arms and kissed me passionately. I was stunned at first. She was, however, most helpful.

When the ball had ended she slipped into my hand a folded paper with her address and a key. (!!) And so I have been plunged into manhood sooner than ever I dared dream. I confess I was shocked when first she threw herself upon me, but I have been brought to the realization that I am an impressive figure now, and indeed find her a lady of infinite good taste and discernment.

Her morals? Not my business. She invited me for tomorrow – no, (since it is dawn, it will be *this night*). I confess that I shall live in terror that Lord T. will return from the West Indies and discover us. I can imagine a duel at dawn and if it be with pistols, I can foresee an early death. I am not enthusiastic about this.

26 November, 1809 London

The "Old Price" ticket riots are going on night after night at the Covent Garden Theatre, and my blood was racing at the thought of witnessing this. Persuaded my languorous lady to accompany me thither. We arranged for my carriage to fetch her up at the corner of her street, and then to come for me. I had suggested that she attire herself discreetly for the occasion, knowing full well her overblown style – even this lady's undergarments have an air of the ridiculous – but she had ignored this, and was done up in her usual frills and adornments, with too much jewelry by far. I suggested she place the valuables in her reticule, but she would have none of it.

We arrived to a riotous scene, which caused her to shrink and cling. As we entered, the mob was so dense that one was buffeted about. She took grave exception to the commotion, and to the fact that the cheval glasses, into which she is forever (and wherever) staring and primping, were totally obstructed by masses of people. Took her to our private box, the entrance of which is spacious and secure, this solaced her somewhat, but it was all too clear that she was not responding favorably to any of this.

Kemble's company was performing. Pantomime? One could not tell! From the moment the play commenced, it was the audience that provided the drama, and what a performance that was! This has been going on since the opening on September 25th, when Kemble had announced that there must be new prices because of the great cost of rebuilding. The only audible words to have reached the audience since that day were Lord Byron's prologue, which Kemble had read *before* the historic announcement.

I was thoroughly enjoying the antics. Not she. I said, "Just think, this is the kind of spectacle one reads about in the wildest days of the Roman Empire!

"Roman Empire?"

"Yes, milady. We may well be walking over buried ruins from their vast Empire, which reached throughout Britain, as well as Europe, and even across the Mediterranean."

"You say there were riots here?"

"Who knows. There were certainly great commotions in *their* Coliseum."

"Coliseum?"

"Never mind. Look below!" I pointed to where a crowd of rowdies had hoisted a huge man aloft, everyone shouting and laughing. He was waving an O.P. banner. Now a rival faction bore down upon them, with a similar arrangement, and there was a skirmish between the two groups – skyward types plummeting into the crowd with a great clamor. No one hurt. "I say!" I said, "how fortunate that they fell upon their friends!" She gave me a blank look. I turned and shouted, "Bravo!" to the more lively fellows in the pit, and they acknowledged me, although it is said that there is some resentment against this new tier of boxes "for the privileged."

My companion rose to her feet and ordered me to take her home. We exited in a sullen silence, which I broke when we had located and entered my carriage. "I am coming here tomorrow night. I shall call for you at the same corner. Dress yourself appropriately. This is what I care to do." She demurred, so I settled it by conquering her with a kiss. She agreed.

⚘

27 NOVEMBER, 1809 LONDON

Returned from a day in The City, ran up the steep stairs to see if my cravat were still white. A sullen gray, soiled by the heavy and unceasing soot of dear London. London! Even in the summer when the coal fires are abated, it is the very devil of a place. Changed the offending stock, took a fresh white kerchief, and ran to my waiting carriage.

"The same corner, please." As planned, there she stood. But *done up*, as the night before. I expressed my dismay, she told me she would not accept another such insult to her dignity, (and safety) and that we were to go to Lady Westland's for gambling games. I reached for the vent and whispered to my coachman, who maneuvered around the small park and headed in the direction of the address she gave us. When we arrived I did not wait for the attendants, but opened the door, leaped for the curb, handed her down, escorted her to the door. There, I kissed her hand, ushered her in, bade her good night and good-bye.

I was not disappointed in the hullabaloo at the theatre, but in retrospect I realize that I would truly have preferred to be able to hear the actors.

⚘

28 NOVEMBER, 1809 LONDON

As for the lady, there have been notes, and more notes, and flowers sent by messenger, and this evening she dared to come to my home and beseech for a "reconciliation." I am afraid I was most cold with her, but I was tactful. I did not tell her that the *bloom* of my attraction to her had worn off. What I did suggest was that this would be far better for her daughter, that I knew how carefully she saw to her well-being, that we were playing a dangerous game and had best desist, and that I prayed that her husband would soon return. I kissed her hand and I wished her well. When she lingered, I put my arm around her shoulder and firmly escorted her to her carriage.

❧

30 July, 1810 Pemberley

Dear D.,

Did I once write that I was ashamed to confess moodiness when so many of our tenants have such grievous problems, and mine were so simple and easily solved? Well, allow me to join the ranks of the benighted! Grant me high marks for irresolution, ill luck, bad management – any one of a long list of demerits in overseeing the affairs of family and Pemberley.

I will make short shrift of this confession. It is too painful to linger on't.

Wickham Junior has not been seen in these parts often (*Grace à Dieu.*) When he does return it is inevitably to importune for funds. A most distasteful session, throughout which I try to keep well in mind my father's fond sponsorship of him. I will say that the distastefulness of the session has always been mitigated by my awe for his versatility in the fine art of *cadging.*

I have tried manfully to give him *congé* before he could find Georgiana, but on several occasions he was able to meet with her. Seeing her animated and happy gave me pause. It was pleasant to hear her laugh, as she did with him, so although I had the impulse to order him off the premises, I withheld, for her sake. But I did plot to remove her from Pemberley as soon as I could arrange it.

Some time before Wickham senior died, he had recommended to me a certain Mrs. Younge as *duenna* for my sister. Located the proper file (what a grand confusion of hirings and firings since the year of my birth!), located the lady's address, located the lady, received Georgiana's approval, and sent the two off to Ramsgate for a proper summer holiday. Georgiana's age? Fifteen.

The second post I received from her bore startling revelations concerning visits from young Wickham. Realizing instantly that this could bode naught but ill for Darcy family matters, I went immediately by coach and four to Ramsgate. I arrived there within a day or two of the planned elopement. It is not possible to describe accurately my disgust and despair when I saw the three together – crafty Wickham, conniving Mrs. Younge, and my foolish and innocent sister. Does the word "despise" describe sufficiently my feelings toward the loathsome schemers? No word does. Toward Georgiana? Only a frantic sadness and pain.

Had Georgiana *not* been there, I swear, D., that I cannot vouch for the safety of either one of the nefarious pair. (A splendid philosophic concept of *antithesis!* Cambridge's Professor Proctor would be exultant!)

Georgiana, more downcast than ever (if possible) has returned to Pemberley with me. Would that father were alive and such a burden could have fallen upon one who could manage it well! I am striving, but certainly am not the one to cheer her. We are, the two of us, *a sorry lot!*

30 October, 1811 Pemberley

Another note from Charles has come this morning. I turned it around in my hands, almost in fear of opening it. What bad news *this time?* It turns out, happily, that there is only pleasant news – he has rented an estate in Hertfordshire known as Netherfield, and is planning a house party. I have known of the place; I believe my parents were friendly with the owners, who have removed to their large hunting estate in Scotland.

I am urged to join him. Should I accept? If I do not, what is there for me at Pemberley? Georgiana is in Austria, studying with the youthful Karl Czerny. I confess I have some uneasiness their ages being so compatible. A musician? Not an appropriate match for my sister.

London? The rebuilding of the new Drury Lane theatre commenced yesterday. Nothing for me in such. Not yet. No, not London until my sister returns there. Besides, I might cross paths with Lady T., and I have no desire to resume that folly.

All in all, I find that I prefer the country to the squalor of the city, especially in the warm months. The country has the fragrance of grasses and flowers and the good sturdy smell of the animals, and the God-given quiet which is so welcome. The city is even more noxious (if possible) now that it is colder.

Temptations of the city – concerts, theatre, good lectures – conversations in the coffee houses, (assuming that one is with interesting companions) The Edinburgh Review – tempting. Certainly not available in the country. (Not until days later, that is.)

Temptations regarding Charles' party – does the list of guests fill me with happy anticipation? No. All Bingley sisters, Mr. Hurst, now married to Louisa. Some others.

Charles? *Yes!* He has described wonderful fields for riding, great moors, good streams. Apparently a fine stable. And in spite of my criticism, with these people I have a comfortable sense of belonging. I like that well.

Not a bad choice! My sophisticated world in a fine country setting. I reach for my writing paper this moment and I shall accept.

⁂

10 November, 1811 Netherfield

Are you comfortable here at Netherfield, D.? It is passing fair, although nothing to compare to Pemberley. Certainly the facilities, although pleasant enough, do not compare to my own. The hip tub is sufficient for my needs, but not a commodious ocean of a tub such as mine at P. The staff is shaping up, but have much to learn and I am not certain how well the Mlles. Bingley do as managers. Getting hot water brought to the bathing-room is a chancy affair. It does arrive – eventually.

There are fewer of us than planned. Very few, in fact. Charles, Miss Caroline, her sister Louisa and her Mr. Hurst, and *moi même.*

My room is large (though not as large as mine at P.). I overlook a garden which catches the morning sun. There is a desk, sufficient to my needs. And there are great stretches of time for writing, so I can be good to you and atone for past neglect.

I am not certain how lively this will be. Consider Mr. Hurst. Mr. Hurst is a crashing bore – spends his few waking moments over food, liquor, and cards. The rest of the time one will find him capsized on a couch, chaise or whatever, *whenever*, noisily snoring. His position is such that I am frequently tempted to pull him by the boots off onto the rug. I have seen beached whales. He is not beyond being compared to same.

Mrs. H. appears to ignore him, and spends her time in close exchanges with Miss Caroline (when the latter is not attempting to draw close to me) engaged in foolish and inane twaddle.

Charles is another matter. We have fine times together – riding, examining the woodlands, fishing, going over the merits of the house. One day he is set to buy it, the next he is dubious, and worried about this or that, so we set out to investigate this or that. Today was a ripping good day. We decided to check the roof, went out an upper mansard window and climbed over a great stretch of it, a vantage that affords vast views of the rolling property. Charles returned to safety as soon as we had ascertained that the structure was well guarded against any weather problems. Not I. I felt exalted and cheerful in such an open yet inaccessible place, and stayed there until I was summoned to noon dinner.

Often I walk alone, accompanied by Beau, a handsome brute of a dog, almost as big as a pony.

There are neighbors. Undoubtedly we shall be meeting them.

🙊

11 NOVEMBER, 1811 NETHERFIELD

A Mr. Bennet came to call. He is a neighbor, apparently lives near, apparently has five daughters, all marriageable. A pleasant enough gentleman, but in no way distinguished. It does seem that we shall not find many of our equals here. So be it.

Charles is determined to return the call and urged me to attend with him, but I have declined. I see no possible interest for me in again seeing Mr. Bennet or his eager (I presume) daughters.

Idiot chatter tonight after supper, a game of whist. I left early to return to my book. There is not much point in reading in the drawing room when the group is gathered, unless they *are* at games. Miss Bingley seems to have a rare connection to anyone who is reading, and darts in like a homing pigeon to interrupt. It so happens I am reading Sydney Smith's *Sketches of Moral Philosophy*. It is an excellent work, (as he was an excellent speaker!) but takes concentration, and the relentless gander has a grand capacity to destroy that very attribute.

Good night, D. Sorry to sound tedious, but tedium seems to be a cloud which finds me wherever I am to be found.

🙊

13 November, 1811 Netherfield

Dear D., I am in mind of Egyptian paintings of the earliest period. Perspective not yet devised – figures of no dimension, sideways and flat, Depict me as I am today you would need to draw me as FLAT.

Few visitors. Potential for any person of interest? Doubtful. However, there is a good stable and excellent fields for riding and passable games for our pleasure, and – of course – reading, although the library here is woefully undersupplied. It is fortunate indeed that I brought books with me.

⌘

14 November, 1811 Netherfield

It seems we are destined to attend the Assembly Ball this evening. I would prefer to stay here and read, but Charles will not have it, and I wish not to inaugurate my visit here with being even more difficult than usual. I have agreed to attend.

Later

Arrival at the site of the Assembly dance was even more discouraging than I had anticipated. Dilapidated structure, muddied approach, planked over so haphazardly that it was the cause of screams and shrieks from the ladies trying to traverse the walkway, and slipping into the soupy ground.

When we entered into the hall we were greeted by a blast of humid air, musty, dusty, and – I shudder to say – reeking strongly of perspiration.

The ball was as I expected – a typical case of overreaching for a gaiety which is never truly attained – loud voices, scratchy and ear-splitting music. The men? Of no distinction. The ladies, likewise. I espied an animated group of young ladies. This proved to be the family of the Mr. Bennet who came to call. Five sisters, all five are "out" in society. Judging from the deportment of two of these girls, it would be better for society if they had been sent off to France to be entered into a convent. These two (I presume the youngest) soon were galloping about the room in totally unbridled jocularity. Where was their mother? *The mother was there!* And looked *dotingly* upon their antics. (!!)

There was a solemn one who sat apart, with a dour face. Then, there were two dignified young ladies. Strange that they were of the same family. Different from one another, and certainly different in deportment from the three mentioned. One could not take one's eyes from the oldest. She has fair hair which fairly shimmers about a face of classic mold. She is serene as a goddess, and all eyes turned toward her as she glided about the room. Charles did not exaggerate in extolling her beauty. Her sister is another type entirely. Raven dark hair, and whereas she has good comportment, one could not call her "serene." She fairly crackles with energy, and appears to laugh a great deal. As I write this, am I reminded of my Mrs. Bingley? Certainly I am not.

Charles confirmed to me that the fair young lady was indeed the eldest Miss Bennet, then advanced hurriedly in her direction as a man who had surrendered all his power of will. Thereafter, he danced with her as often as he could manage.

He tried to induce me to join in the dance. He suggested the brunette sister, who was sitting unattended. I reminded him that I require that I must be well acquainted with whomsoever I am to approach.

My aversion to the whole situation was rising. Charles, oblivious to my mood and to the general sense of derangement in the hall, did not abate his urging. The more he pressed, the more I resisted. The more gregarious he, the less amiable I. He was arousing in me a discomfort which I liked not. I reached the end to my patience, and told him in no uncertain terms that I had no humor to give consequence to young ladies who are slighted by other men. He referred to her as pretty. I countered by declaring that she was tolerable but not handsome enough to tempt me.

It seems the lady overheard my remark, for she colored and bit her lip. I was sorry for this, and if I had felt more lively I dare say I would have tried to amend such a *faux pas,* but as it was I turned and walked away, wishing I could be anywhere but in that hall.

Soon there started a low buzz in the room, which I sensed immediately. One could see that it generated from a circle surrounding the mother Bennet. It was not difficult to ascertain that the subject of the *contretemps* attached itself to my unsavory remark. Many glances in my direction, and words which winged themselves my way as surely as arrows, words which clearly referred to the young lady's mortification and my role in it.

I stole a glance at the maiden, expecting to find her undone and sobbing. To my surprise she was talking with animation to a friend and laughing merrily. There were intermittent glances in my direction as she spoke. The object of her jesting was only too apparent. I!? She was laughing at *me*!!

I wanted to leave, but Charles was clearly not so inclined. His manifest joy in his new acquaintance only made me the more disconsolate. There was nothing for it but to stare out of the window, wishing I were in another place. At this moment Miss Caroline materialized to appropriate me, and made remarks about the boorishness of the scene and of the people. Now my displeasure rose against *her* as well as against myself. How sounded we two? Why should one take against a scene of such liveliness?

I wanted not to be like Miss Caroline in her vain absurdities. I wanted not to be like Fitzwilliam Darcy in his towering discomforts! When would this evening end???

It did, after an eternity of discomfort and regret. I regretted being where I was, saying what I had said, being laughed at, being too tall, being so frequently remarked – I took Miss Caroline's arm. Did this bring pleasure to me? Indeed she looked superior in every way, and would have *been* superior in every way if she were not so intent on proving it.

⁂

19 NOVEMBER, 1811

I have been awakened, D., by a strange dream which shook me from a deep sleep against every desire to be awake and aware. So strange! Its meaning? I will never know, but I must set it down in order to clear my head and return to a hoped-for and more tranquil rest.

Vague memories of a brutal battle, with my self in the very center. A huge shape grabbed the lance I was bearing and pulled me toward its great dark looming presence. I could not let go of the lance; I could not resist the powerful grip and its pulling. I tried to call but had no voice, nor was there anyone to see my plight. Then was I seized with a great force from behind. And now started a pushing and pulling forward and back, back and forward. And I with no voice. Suddenly I was in another place and bound tight in some kind of an infernal machine, calling, calling for succor. A figure appeared; now were there shouts from all directions to "start the machine." Now I could see a huge wooden wheel, somehow part of the device which was caging me. The figure started to spin this wheel. Terror overcame me! I would be tore into twain! I tried to shout, but no words would come. Then, just as suddenly, I was in a shadowy room and a woman was sliding toward me. She was far away but she reached out her arms, which were somehow elongated, and did seize me. I was pulled toward her and fell upon her. Then the horror came, and I awoke to the usual calamity.

Blessings on you, D. It is a rare anodyne to be able to pour out my tortured thoughts to you.

Now I shall stretch out on the chaise and try to find some comfort in a dreamless sleep.

⅗

22 November, 1811 Netherfield

This night there is to be a party at Lucas Lodge. In view of my behavior at the Assembly Ball, Charles consulted with me as to whether I might prefer to remain at Netherfield and not annoy myself (and others) with my distaste for the "inane and unfastidious country life."

My reply stunned him. I told him that I should like to attend. I did *not* tell him that I had been thinking about Miss Elizabeth Bennet, with regret for my rudeness to her, and with anticipation of seeing her again, not only to make it right, but in order to further our acquaintance. I could not forget the expression in her eyes, nor the sound of her laughter, and the charm of her playfulness. I have noted that she appears to be a champion of the art of conversation, seeming to engage her companions by her concentration and liveliness.

Above all I am drawn by the fact that she laughed at me. A new experience!

I shall wear my new dresscoat tonight, and I shall approach Miss Bennet as if she were of the highest rank.

Later

The lady is too alert by far. At the Lucas' I stood near whilst she was speaking with Colonel Forster, when she turned to her friend Charlotte Lucas and asked, "What does Mr. Darcy mean by listening to my conversation?" Miss Charlotte suggested that she ask me direct, which she did, and was then so mocking of me that Miss Charlotte hastily suggested that she sing for the assembled. So she did that also, not capital, but by no means unpleasing. An encore was demanded by many, but her eager sister, Mary, took her place at the instrument and so deadened the air that it was demanded that she cease, and play something danceable (and bearable).

I? I desired to engage this zesty Miss Bennet in conversation, but was *shunted* by the arrival of a cake to mark a belated celebration of her birthday. Then Sir William cornered me and I could not get free. How he did go on.

Indeed, although he was my host, and a titled gentleman, such attributes do not a hero make. One cannot help but note that his attire shrieks aloud that he is new-minted to the coin of *the good life*. His tights only too well outline his dumpling of a figure, the bows below the knee are a trifle too blowsy; the shoe buckles, too large, too bright – by a hairsbreadth only, to be sure, but just enough to destroy the illusion of gentility; the stockings, a shade too white, too swelled and curved to his overblown calf; his swallow tails just enough too long in the back to cause one to wonder if he would not be trapped if he chose to seat himself. As for his conversation – ludicrous, ludicrous in every respect. As I was summing him thusly, he prattling on and on about the good life, Miss Elizabeth happened to pass near us, and he decided immediately that we must dance together. He took her hand and pulled her toward *me*. I was surprised at his boldness, but happy enough to accept the opportunity, when she declared sharply that she had not the least intention of dancing.

Sir William persisted. I asked her for the honor of the dance. The words came easily, to my surprise, and I was happy for that. Again she refused me. This was even more of a surprise – she had truly *meant* what she had said. She left us.

As I was recovering from the unexpectedness of this, Miss Bingley was suddenly near (only too near!) and whispered that she could guess the subject of my reverie. I told her that I should imagine not.

Her guess? That I was fuming over the insipidity and grossness of the society we had entered. A few nights ago, perhaps. But this night? Off the mark!

I silenced her when I told her that I had been meditating on the pleasure which a fine pair of eyes in the face of a pretty woman can give one.

When she demanded, and received, the name of such a one, she gave me the answer which I had known to expect – she asked, when was she to wish me joy? There was nothing for it but to tell her that her rapid imagination was only too characteristic of her, that I knew she would go on to fabricate from my "admiration" *an immediate trip into matrimony*.

My words only stimulated her devilish spite. She proceeded to outline my future relationships with the Bennet family, the most ridiculous being that 'my mother-in-law' would frequently be our guest at Pemberley. In her nastiness she was even more diverting than her usual, so I let her rant on. Which she did, until the evening did end.

It is late, D., and I should retire, but it is a tonic to think on the events of this evening. In spite of my stiffness and basic shyness in society, I have never until this night suffered a rebuff. Not ever! Not until this night. Who is this lady! Is she an enemy so soon? If so, is it because of my unfortunate remark?

Shall I see her again? Will she be more friendly?

❧

23 NOVEMBER, 1811 NETHERFIELD

The inertia has been lifted at Netherfield despite the inclement weather. This morning, the eldest Bennet sister rode over on her dripping horse, a sodden bundle of a girl who, having accepted an invitation to lunch, was determined to fulfill her promise to attend, despite any inconvenience such as a drenching storm.

When we returned from our outing, Charles brightened the moment he laid eyes on her. Did I say "brightened"? He was positively effulgent! He put Apollo to shame! In fact, if it were not so immediate a transformation as to be implausible, I would be tempted to suspect that he has fallen in love with the lady. She is indeed most beautiful, even when shivering with an ague. The exposure to the elements wreaked such havoc on her that she needed to be packed off to an empty bedroom, and there ordered into bed.

Charles was the perfect illustration of a paradoxical situation – *Distressed* by her illness; *delighted* that she was to stay the night. Word was delivered to her family that she would not be able to return as promised.

Some time later her sister, Elizabeth, walked into our *encampment*. Walked! A good three miles, through the mud and slush, most of which appeared to have settled on her skirts.

She was a delightful sight to behold – rosy from the exertion, eyes sparkling, her face alive, but with a sweet and anxious look. Is this the lady whom I declared "tolerable to look at" at the Assembly dance? While I was examining my disdainful and impetuous conclusion of that evening, she excused herself and went hurriedly to her sister. Immediately the spiteful ladies started to cackle about her disgraceful appearance. The remarks did not sit well with me. When the object of their scorn returned to the room briefly, I made certain to overhear her, and found her remarks to be bright, amusing, crackling with deft wit, pronounced in such a melodious voice!

She spends most of her time with the invalid. All too little time with us. I find myself awaiting her return.

LATER

The weather has lifted, and I happened to glimpse her going from the house. I watched her from the window. She was playing with Beau. Apparently they were engaged in deep conversation. (I can sympathize. The dog surely has better observations on life than most of the group here.) Beau was sitting regally, ears forward, from time to time cocking his head, apparently recognizing some word he knows. At such moments I could see her laughing with obvious delight. At one point she reached for him and pulled him to her. I will not say that this move left me unaffected. The dog responded by bathing her face with his enormous tongue. Still laughing, she pushed him away, took the hem of her dress, found a clean spot (not easily, and exposing a most well-turned ankle) and wiped her face with her hem.

A sharp question from Miss Caroline interrupted my revery. I led her hastily from the window before she could espy what I had been viewing. I desired to hear none of her sneering remarks.

I returned to my book. She brought hers over next to me, but read not a word, babbling continually. For once the interruption mattered not a whit – I was dwelling on memories of the lady and the dog.

And so to bed. Let us hope, D., that she will not intrude into my dreams. Elizabeth Bennet is not a lady whom I may take into consideration. Her position is not distinguished, and her family (with the exception of herself and Miss Jane) is *disgraceful*.

❧

24 NOVEMBER, 1811 NETHERFIELD

Today while riding Charles' horse (at his request) in order to sharpen her on her leads, I espied Miss Bennet, who was out for a walk. After inquiring for her sister I asked if she were not concerned for the weather. She looked up to the lowering clouds and replied that if they worried not about her, she would not worry about *them*. (As she tilted back her head there was opened to my gaze the full curve of her white throat. I wanted to dismount and to put my hand there, wanted it so badly that I had to bite my lip to control the surge of such an impulse, then cursed myself, "What is it with you, Darcy?")

At that instant came a loud clap of thunder. (A rebuke from on high?)

The lady laughed, looked again at the roiling clouds, "I dare say they have other undertaking!"

Now came a brilliant display of lightning flashes against the hills to the north, with violent claps of thunder and a grand race of black clouds scudding directly towards us. I shouted to her to gather up her skirts and climb on, leapt to the ground, held out my hand for her foot, and hoisted her athwart the mare's rump, behind the saddle. Swung aboard and galloped in a southerly direction, racing the storm. Her arms were clasped about my waist and I had not much need to worry for her safety, as she sat the gallop uncommonly well. (As I write this now I do wonder at my forwardness. Had she fallen from the horse we would have had a fine confusion. But she did not.)

A house came into view, and I headed the mare in that direction. Slid from the saddle, threw the reins over the animal's head, ran and pounded on the door to see if the family was at home. The wind was up, and the first spattering of cold rain was felt. The door opened, I turned to dash to the lady and help her alight, but was amazed to find her running up the path. How got she down without me to help her? As I pushed her in front of me and into the house, the heavens opened.

Slammed the door, apologized to the owner, thanked him for the asylum. He bade us welcome, and commented on our luck in the timing of our visit. Before I could introduce myself, he excused himself and disappeared into the adjoining room.

Miss Bennet's comment was a surprise. She did not discuss the weather (the usual subject even when *unextraordinary)*; she merely said, "Your poor horse. Will it be safe from the lightning?"

"She will survive. Animals seem to know how to do these things."

"*Noah* would have let her into the house."

"But this is not my house. And I venture 'twas not built for animals."

She said then that we were having a conversation without the benefit of having been properly introduced.

88

"And have we not met?!"

"Yes, but on uneven ground. Yesterday I was so covered with mud that I am not certain that you can recognize me today."

"Surely you jest!"

"Surely, I do."

I looked at her, knowing not how to reply. The room filled with a brilliant flash of light, followed by the thunder immediately upon it. We both jumped. I shouted, "the horse!" and ran to the door, had started to open it, when I felt her tugging at me, and turned, surprised.

"You just told me that animals know how best to handle these situations. Either she is safe or she is dead. You are alive and I suggest you *remain* so."

The rain stopped as suddenly as it had started; the thunder grew more faint and one could hear it moving to the south, and the skies began to brighten.

She said, "Perhaps now it would be safe to open the door."

I halloed a 'thank you' to our host, opened the door, espied the horse leaning against the side of the house and offered the lady a ride to Netherfield, which she refused. She thanked me for my gallantry, bade me au revoir, said she would prefer to walk.

"But the ground is now wet."

"Twill suffice."

We parted.

LATER

Late this evening Miss E. returned from the sick room and joined us in the drawing room. She had changed into a graceful gown, freshened herself, done something pleasant to her hair, and looked lovely. We were playing at loo, she was invited to join, she declined saying she would prefer to read. *Mirabile dictu!*

The ladies moved to make sport of her remark, teasing her that she took no pleasure in anything else. Miss Bennet valiantly defended herself against the accusation. I took displeasure that she should be driven to defend a desire for *reading*.

Charles (who cannot brook any form of unpleasantness) quickly turned the conversation to the subject of the welfare of Miss Jane. A brief and negative report, a quick turn, and Miss Elizabeth went to the table where lay the few books we had at our disposal. Miss Caroline used this moment to discuss my library at Pemberley, the inimitable beauty of Pemberley, my sister – all with a calculation to establish her prerogative with me and to distance Miss Elizabeth from any intimacy. How malicious a woman can become!

When we turned to the general topic of women in our era, there came the golden moment I look for when I choose to enter into conversation. From Miss Caroline's praise of the talents of my sister, we moved to discuss the subject of women of excellence. I disagreed with Charles' fulsome estimate of the accomplishments of so many, saying that I could not boast of knowing more than half a dozen, in the whole range of my acquaintance, that were really accomplished. Now entered Miss Elizabeth, "You must comprehend a great deal in your idea of an accomplished woman."

Miss Caroline came quickly between us with standards of her own – music, singing, drawing, dancing, languages, and a certain something in her air and manner of walking, tone of voice – etcetera, etcetera. The manner in which she was posturing suggested that she might have imagined herself as standing in front of a pier glass and enumerating what she saw reflected as she detailed it.

I felt it encumbered me to add to her list something more substantial, in the improvement of her mind by extensive reading.

Miss Elizabeth deftly dismissed the whole farrago with, "I am no longer surprised at your knowing *only* six accomplished women, Mr. Darcy. I rather wonder now at your knowing *any*."

I responded to this, hoping that she would turn her serious attention to me and we could discuss the issue at a level at which I now knew her to be capable, but they were into it now, and very soon Miss Elizabeth left the room. When she returned it was to inform us that Miss Jane was worse, and after a discussion about sending for the doctor in the morning, she retired. As soon as she was gone, again I had that sense of flatness which I have detailed to you, D.

※

25 NOVEMBER, 1811 NETHERFIELD

As I gazed out of my window this morning I spied Miss Bennet skipping merrily towards the meadow, with Beau bounding at her heels. Did I say "skipping"? I did. She was. What a pleasant sight. The women I have observed walk, sway, mince, glide, shuffle perhaps. Skip? Never.

The very look of the dog was also gladdening. He was bounding with joy, tail straight behind, taking great leaps around her. Then he sailed over the fence some distance from the stile. To my astonishment the lady hiked up her skirt, scaled up and over, jumped down and ran after the dog into the meadow, where they disappeared in the tall grasses.

I waited their return. This they did, she with a bundle of flowers. These she placed in the shade of a tree, and proceeded to romp with Beau for a few minutes. Then she headed for the house, and I reasoned that they would be going into the conservatory.

I dressed hurriedly and descended to that place, inquiring after her sister. I was informed that Miss Jane still has a fever and is most uncomfortable. "The flowers are for her?" I asked, but Miss Elizabeth answered not, as an alarmed look crossed her face.

She said in a low voice that something "crawly" was on her shoulder, and would I please help her. She turned her back to me. In obliging, I found that it would be necessary to push down her bodice slightly. She did not object to this move, and shall we say that I did not mind the inconvenience. I must confess that her skin was most wonderful to the touch, and I was disappointed to find the creature (a spider) so quickly. I threw it to the floor and moved to step on it when she pulled on my arm, begging me to spare it. Then she stooped and enfolded the invader in her kerchief and took it outside where she released it. As I say, I was astonished. There is no other woman I know who would not have leaped to a chair and stood there shrieking to the heavens.

We parted pleasantly, an agreeable surprise after her sharpness the other evening.

❦

26 NOVEMBER, 1811 NETHERFIELD

Well, D., we had a grand performance at Netherfield this day. I especially enjoyed the antics because Miss Elizabeth came to my defense when I fell under an attack from her mother.

This day Mrs. Bennet arrived with the other three of her brood in order to look to her ill daughter. Miss Elizabeth had sent for her, but soon after the young lady had taken a turn for the better. By the time the mother had arrived, Miss E. felt that Miss Jane now could well be moved. Mrs. B., however, pronounced her to be gravely ill, and *not to be moved.*

Miss Elizabeth must stay on as nurse, so I am content. Charles is in every way consoled. The ladies are irate, and one hears an orchestration of complaints and expostulation.

The conversation went approximately as I detail it now – First, a group discussion led by Mrs. B. concerning Charles' temperament, followed by a soliloquy about country living, which somehow led direct to *me*, and my contrariness. Thereupon I received a direct hit from this shrill lady! She accused me of having *the wrong disposition* by comparing me invidiously to Charles, whom she allowed to have the right disposition.

I have been well trained to be courteous at all times to my elders, and I would not protest this charge on my own behalf.

However, Miss Elizabeth interrupted, saying to her mother that she had quite mistook me, and attempting to clarify my meaning. I cannot tell you how pleasant this sounded to my ears! I tried to catch her eye, in order to recognize this boon with a smile, but she would not turn toward me.

Now Mrs. Bennet went on to such assertions about the glamour of country living, that the sophisticated Netherfield group could hardly contain itself. Smug smiles, knowing and satiric winks. I felt sorry for Miss Elizabeth whom I could see was wilting with humiliation.

But she is gallant, D., and she is quick! She stopped and deftly changed the course of her mother's remarks by diverting her attention with questions about the Lucas family, at which point the mother was given an opportunity to glorify her own daughter Jane, whilst demeaning Miss Charlotte Lucas.

The lady was only too obvious in this *maneuver* (clearly calculated for Charles' benefit), again obliging Miss E. to diffuse the woman's foolishness.

This time she chose poetry as her subject. Capital! Here is a subject ripe for the picking! We two should have begun a lively discussion, but Miss E. finessed the opportunity with a wicked quip about the efficacy of poetry in driving away love. I shall not forget her remark, "If it be only a slight, thin sort of inclination, I am convinced that one good sonnet will starve it entirely away." This was so on the mark that I had to smile.

It caused me to recall a short-lived attraction on my part to an exquisite but simple young thing, whom I had invited to dance, and into whose delicate ear I had then proceeded to quote a sonnet. She had declared that I was "too clever by far for her," and requested that I escort her back to her seat.

While I was remembering this long-forgotten incident, good-byes and thanks were started. Miss Lydia, who had been prowling the outer edges of the room, now approached Charles and reminded him of his pledge to give a ball at Netherfield. He assured her that he had it in mind.

Exeunt omnes Bennets, save for Miss Elizabeth who returned immediately to her patient. I was sorry for this, as I would have liked to pursue her thoughts about poetry.

The others proceeded to demolish the Bennets with a savage barrage of ill natured jesting, which I found unpleasant. I then retired to you, D., 'ere I would lose the words I wished to keep in my mind. Now you have them.

LATER

Frustration this evening. Desired to write a letter to Georgiana, sat me down, followed by Miss Caroline who would not cease her prattle. Then a conversation with Charles concerning his character, I being more stern than ever I meant to be, and Miss Elizabeth entering in to defend Charles, thus encouraging him in a mockery of me. To end the dispute the young lady actually urged me to sit down and finish my letter, and I did so although it was not easy to concentrate. I was startled that she had been cavalier with me, but also I was amused and stimulated. To the end that I soon asked for music, which Miss Caroline *hastened* to provide, almost trampling over Miss Elizabeth to be sure to get to the pianoforte first, little anticipating that I desired the music in order to invite Miss Elizabeth to dance with me.

Did so. Silence. I had need to ask her twice. In responding finally, she accused me of premeditated contempt, the very last thing on my mind; told me to despise her if I so dared; again, the last thing on my mind. I was, in fact, bewitched by now, and aware that if it were not for the inferiority of her connections that I would be in some danger.

She went to her sister, I said good night and came upstairs to write again to you.

27 November, 1811 Netherfield

As I was tumbling deep into sleep last night, I heard, loud and distinct, Mrs. Reynolds' voice chiding me. Her words came so clear that I can set them down to you, D., in perfect order, exactly as they hammered into me as I was letting go the imprint of the day.

"Fie, Mr. Darcy! You must learn to adapt to new places and new experiences, and be determined not to be ill at ease. Learn to accept that which is different. Often you will find a pleasant and refreshing surprise. A gentleman of your rank needs must learn to adapt, to travel widely, socialize broadly, and be at ease at all times, whether in familiar circumstances or not. Life is not everywhere the same, nor should you desire that it should be."

As I pen these words to you, D., I remember well the circumstance when I heard them – Reynolds was helping me pack my belongings prior to my departure for Harrow. She was trying to help me in my bitter mood, but I was not consoled. I did, however, appreciate that she was trying to cheer me. On the morrow, as the carriage awaited, I tried to give her a farewell hug. My father rebuked her, and, of course, *moi même.* "For shame, Mrs. Reynolds. You will make a mollycoddle of the boy."

Here I am, father. You should be well pleased. Tempered and strong, as you desired me. Only too well aware of my exalted position. Inclined to quick and fierce plunges of mood, and to barbed retorts. And a champion of the insult. Shall we salute one another?

And so it is back to sleep, D. Perchance to dream again? Let us hope not!

Later

I slept later than usual this morning. When I awoke I went to the window and was not disappointed. Although it was cold, the sun was bright, and Miss Bennet was seated upon the grass, toweling her wet hair. I was struck by the mass of it, the ease with which she tossed it about, and how, when dried, it caught and threw back the sunlight.

Then I saw Beau bound out and dash straight at the lady. In his exuberance he came close to knocking her backward onto the ground and she struggled to regain her balance. To my astonishment she was laughing.

To my further astonishment she threw her arms around him and gave him a most undeserved hug. The dog next took up her brush in his teeth. At that she provided the ultimate astonishment – she took it from him and proceeded to groom him! It was a lovely sight, and I felt gladdened to the core just to watch them.

I could not persuade the sequence of these images to be gone. When, sometime later, I was riding with Charles, he asked to know why I was so quiet. I told him I knew not. I could not confide in him the subject of my musing. We all agree in this house that the Bennet ladies are fine company (when healthy), but much beneath us. True enough. Yet I did not want to converse with Charles. I wanted to dwell with my morning images.

I pray to God they will not haunt me this night.

❦

LATER

This evening Miss Jane was deemed sufficiently recovered to be brought into the drawing room after we had supped. Miss Caroline had apparently been all solicitation for the invalid until we gentlemen joined their group. When we entered she looked up, actually dropped the shawl which she had been handing to Miss Jane, hastened to my side, and began a campaign which suited me ill. Should she ever take pen to paper (a doubtful possibility) she could write a compendium on how NOT to minister to a gentleman of letters.

I took up a book; she did the same. I tried to read; she tried not, and kept whispering to me, which I, striving to be the polite gentleman, tried to ignore.

She took up conversation with Charles, hard to shut out, because she was very close to my ear. Next she arose, approached Elizabeth, and persuaded her to take 'a turn about the room.'

When they came toward me I closed my book, but refused her invitation to join them, saying that joining them would *interfere with their motives*. Miss Caroline caught not my meaning and turned to Miss Elizabeth for clarification. Miss Elizabeth read my remark only too well, saying 'he means to be severe on us, and our surest way of disappointing him will be to ask nothing about it.'

Miss C. persisted in asking for an explanation, which, charitably, I provided, "You either have secret affairs to discuss, or because you are conscious that your figures appear to the greatest advantage in walking. If the first, I should be completely in your way; and if the second, I can admire you much better as I sit by the fire."

I saw Miss Elizabeth smile, taking me only too well. If only she would look at me! I have not met her eyes in all these days.

Miss C. comprehended me not at all, although my riposte had been clearly dead to the center of the target. She relied upon Miss Elizabeth once more, who counseled her to tease me and laugh at me, adding, "intimate as you are, you must know how it is to be done."

"Intimate as we are!" What a mockery! How can there be intimacy when there is a fathomless gulf between our understandings?!

But what a fertile field there is to be explored with this Miss Bennet! I engaged her in a discussion on the subject of humor and ridicule. D., I could have gone on for infinite periods with this lady on that subject, or any other.

Miss Caroline had long since been out of her depth, and her retirement would have been welcomed. All I cared for was to continue talking with Miss E. I not only relished the sparring and her wit, but the fact that she was now, forsooth, looking at me direct, and I was all but lost in the deep azure of her lively eyes. Is there danger in paying her too much attention. I fear there is!

And now to bed. I must stop my thoughts about this lady. Does writing to you avail? Or does it deepen the conflict I am enduring?

She is *not* the proper person for Fitzwilliam Darcy, heir to Pemberley. No! However –

꧁꧂

28 November, 1811 Netherfield

Awoke this morning, went to the window in hopes that I would have a refreshing view, only to see a carriage disappearing into the distance, with Charles waving a wistful farewell. It seems that our unexpected guests have decamped.

I could see Beau lying dejected, his great head on his enormous paws. Such a sad look!

Joined the group at breakfast with the full determination to be lively and entertaining, but my words fall into such hollow space, and are returned with such insensibility that I closed down abruptly. The twaddle resumed, followed by a languid discussion of how to spend the day. Archery and croquet were decided upon, to be followed with whist and commerce, and topped off with charades.

I determined that I should spend the day pacing. What traveling points should I pick for myself and my tattered thoughts? I felt strangely hollow inside, and had an unfamiliar sense of abandonment. I needed to think on this, and the company was not what one could term conducive to sessions of sweet silent thought.

⁂

1 December, 1811 Netherfield

It is all flat again. The very air seems stilled. What peril am I in that I can so attach my vitality to the presence of one person? There can be no possible grounds for us to be compatible. What could I be thinking?!

Of the lady, constantly.

What is our relation to one another? She listens carefully to the few words I utter in her presence and responds on the instant and to the point. She is not unaware of how I stare at her. She is not at all discomposed as most women are when I survey them. Whereas I, I am totally so when we meet face to face.

A pox on all this! It is a glorious day and I shall suggest to Charles that we ride into Meryton. Perhaps we shall find the Longbourn ladies there.

Later

Wickham, ah Wickham! How dare he presume to return after our agreement that he would never do so. I shall never forgive him for the Georgiana matter. The rest of his sins are paltry in the light of that offense.

I grant that he did not expect to find me in Hertfordshire. How ironic that he should! He was deep in conversation with Miss Elizabeth Bennet. *Deep*! I was aghast.

He was discomfited to see me. I? I was in *a fury*! I rode past, but in my heart I would have loved to single him out from the group and ride him down.

I could see that he has already fastened on the lady. And it was obvious that he was pouring some kind of poison into her ear. I doubt that he is attempting another seduction, since she is without prospects, but I am deeply suspicious that he was formulating some kind of mendacity about me, for she turned from him with a look of distress and shock on her face, followed by a cold and furious look *at me* which I liked not.

Charles would have liked to stop but I rode on and he was forced to follow. I could not explain my actions to him, as this would have entailed betrayal of the whole nasty business with my sister. I knew that he would seek to learn why I had changed my course so abruptly. To be sure, he asked "Earlier you were keen to ride into Meryton, Darcy. You *found the reason* for your haste; that is, I presume it was the Bennet ladies whom we were seeking. Then you rode straight on. What could this signify?"

I kept a stern silence and after a few questions he had the wit to stop questioning. Then I kicked my horse and shouted "Last one into the stables is a second son!"

We raced across the moor and jumped a few hedges and fences. I led, even though I ride one of his horses.

The chase did not, however, quiet my unease. If Wickham is spinning Elizabeth Bennet into a web of lies about me, and I dare say that such is the case, I should care not. Elizabeth Bennet is much beneath me and I should care not.

I am in great perturbation. I should return to Pemberley.

☙

8 December, 1811 Netherfield

No, have not departed Netherfield. Charles would not have it that I should leave immediately prior to the Dance. Perhaps I might have done so, in spite of his remonstrances, but I had learned that Wickham has been (the quotes represent irony, D.) "called away on official business." A more salubrious atmosphere for me! I stayed.

I could not rid my mind of Miss Bennet's angry face when she glimpsed me at Meryton, and I had hopes to change that look by persuading her to dance with me. My reason to remain? *Certainly not.* There is my host to consider, always so sporting and helpful to me. And other good reasons. *Not for the sake of the lady.* Yes, I stayed.

There was some concern that there would be a storm just as the party was to begin, but the weather held, and the guests began to arrive. The house looked festive, the tables were piled high with succulences, flowers placed everywhere.

I watched for the Bennet party. Soon they entered and scattered. Miss Elizabeth looked beautiful, as did Miss Jane. Charles, of course, moved to the latter. I tried to catch Miss E.'s eye, but she would not look toward me. I dared to approach and direct polite inquiries. After all, had we not recently spent four days under the same roof. Surely, we are acquainted. One would not think so, judging from her response. Curt, chilled, almost unpleasant. I bowed, and left the field.

As the music started I was wondering, did I dare ask her to dance after such a coldness, but was preempted by the odious little man in a clerical collar whom I had seen with her party that fateful day in Meryton. He took her arm with great familiarity, and proceeded to make a fool of himself on the dance floor. Awkward, solemn, not acquainted with the moves, pompous, and gloriously clumsy.

It was clear that Miss Bennet was mortified (as well she should have been). The music stopped, I was about to ask her for the next dance when the toady took possession again, and put her through the same vexation. Dance over, I watched her shake him off and go to her friend, Miss Lucas, where she certainly had a great deal to report, doing so with high animation. I saw the musicians leave, waited a few moments, gritted my teeth, approached, asked her to do me the honor of the next dance, and beat a quick retreat before she could recover from her surprise.

How would she dance? A countrified clumsiness? If so, I would regret my rashness. I watched for the musicians' return, and when they did I went over and claimed her with nary a word.

At the very first movement I realized that if I had mistrusted her skill, I was in error. The lady moves unlike any other with whom I have previously danced (and there have been many.) She glides, turns as smooth as air, knows the dances well – it all seemed so effortless and delightful that I gave myself over to the dance and to the music and *to her.*

She seemed not to feel the same, and when we were in line await-ing our turn to move, she seemed dispirited. Then, to my surprise, she started a conversation which she would not drop, even when it was our turn to lead the figure. It is not easy to dance the complicated and elegant moves of the quadrille (as complex in the country as in the city) when one is talking. Steadfastly I kept my silence until she said it is was my turn to say some-thing now. Thus challenged I said, "Do you talk by rule, then, when you are dancing?"

What a hum of verbal activity she did produce! And all the while moving like a zephyr, with exquisite command of the steps. At one point I had the insane idea of stopping her verbal sallies with a kiss. Can you imag-ine what effect this might have had! (Now, the mere thought of it is so delightful that I run it over and over in my mind.)

At one point, as we were poised for the next set, we were inter-rupted by Sir William, who *effused* compliments on our dancing. He then made a reference to Jane and Charles as if their engagement were a matter of record. This indeed gave me pause. Whatever was the man claiming?

As I was trying to make sense of Sir William's prattle, I nevertheless found myself looking forward eagerly to his exit, and soon it was our move again and off we went.

I was hoping against hope that Miss Elizabeth would feel what I was feeling and leave off the bickering. I tried again to divert her from the very personal line she was now embarked upon. Not successful. She insisted on bringing up our meeting in Meryton, and challenging me about Wickham. She insisted on prodding me about my character. I resisted. When she said "If I do not take your likeness now, I may never have another opportunity." I told her coldly, that I would by no means suspend any pleasure of hers. We parted in silence.

My annoyance and frustration cooled soon, and I tried to reapproach, only to find her seated near her mother who was ranting away in a dis-agreeable fashion, much of it concerning Wickham, and thus *moi même*. I could see that Miss E. was most dreadfully shamed, trying to quiet the lady, who was not to be silenced. Shades of the conversation at Netherfield!

I could not help but admire the daughter's forbearance and tact, and the gentleness with which she treated this most unbearable woman. Each remark was uttered in such a high piercing voice, that one could not help but hear *each*. If she were a man I would have had need to whack her with my glove, and duel at dawn. Luckily she is but a shrewish lady and should affect me not.

How came she to have such a daughter?

Supper was served. I was seated with my friends, when the grotesque little clergyman minced his way over to me and introduced himself. Name of Collins? Something about my Aunt and Rosings and his Parsonage. Insufferable. I listened a moment in silence and then rose and moved away. I was aware that Miss Elizabeth had been watching this folderol with dismay. She had blushed to her hairline.

I tried to catch her eye, but she would not look in my direction. Is she shy? Certainly not! Can she be warmed to me? Certainly. Should I try? *Certainly not!*

The evening ended on a note of ennui. I do suspect that Mrs. Bennet wished to be the last to depart, which indeed she was, keeping with her all her group suspended in delayed motion of flight. She is more than obvious in pursuit of a husband for her eldest. I have been watching Charles and Miss Jane since Sir William's gauche remark. I fear Charles is at risk in this situation, and I must guard him well.

To be sure the lady is charming and most agreeable with him. However she is so imperturbably cool and complacent that I fear he will wreck his ardor on indifferent shoals. I must see to it that Charles is not hurt!

And so ends another country evening, D. Part of it was most disagreeable, and part of it was most wonderful. I will dwell on that part – how she moves so easily and with such control.

Why does her gracefulness surprise me? I saw how she played with Beau, with such a fluidity of movement and purity of line and the breathtaking line of her breast as she threw the ball.

How came she from such a family?

⁂

9 DECEMBER, 1811 NETHERFIELD

It is early, the sun is still low in the sky. I have been out to ride the wild brute which is mine whenever I am at Netherfield. We are getting along better since our last contest – he had decided it was time to throw me, I had decided I did not approve his idea. I was more brutal with his mouth than I like to be, but decided that if it was to be his mouth against my life, that he would be the sufferer. We went around in some wild circles before he bolted and headed directly for a grove of trees. I anticipated the low branches in time, laid my head on the side of his neck, catching a blow on the shoulder, but still all in one piece. This somehow impressed him and he quieted. We had quite a long chat when we returned to the stables, I gave him lots of nice strokes and a carrot or two. I believe we are good friends now, but I watch him warily (as he does me.)

This morning he was only too delighted to leave the stables, early as it was. Glorious sky, full of billowing white clouds and the most tender sliver of a moon, still visible, barely a small tremble in the azure sky. I amuse myself when there are such clouds; they can be translated into extraordinary shapes. Usually I find animal forms but today there was a near-perfect tableau of a young woman, with long hair, seated before an easel, drawing – no, painting. One could even see her white arm, and the hand holding a paint brush. The brush was a thin scraggly vertical cloud of dark grey. Whoever designed that one I wondered? Her hair was silver and white, so she was not Elizabeth. (If I would put *her* from my thoughts wherefore have I written the name? Shall I blot it out? Do it in your head, Darcy. Do not smudge the page.)

My eye was caught by the movements of a hawk wheeling high aloft and I stopped to watch. The upward streak! The glorious planing! The downward plummet! The poor creature targeted below would not sense the glory of it, but to me it was exactly that, *glorious*. The experience of being in Church could not give one a more soulful feeling. Here one could see the splendid handiwork of the Almighty.

By now the cloud figure had metamorphosed into a scattering of small forms without much resemblance to any known object. I commenced to muse on how the shapes of clouds could be translated into one's head as an objective reality. I thought about the philosophers who have worked on the problems of reality and the human mind.

Would that I could return to Cambridge and listen to their words! Would that Elizabeth Bennet would drift out of my head and disappear as the sky lady has vanished!

Gave my good friend a nudge in the ribs with an encouraging "giddap!," headed for a few high hedges which he took in his stride as if they were insubstantial as clouds.

LATER

I am worried about Charles, D. Last night when I bade you good night, I thought I would sleep peacefully. The music was still in my head, and the feel of the dance and of my partner were still very strong. 'Twas not to be so, and I tossed and turned with an assault of thoughts and feelings. There were images of Miss Elizabeth floating and whirling. Joined by others of Charles and Miss Jane as we passed one another in the dance.

I have seen Charles in and out of many an infatuation. This time methinks there is a difference. Sir William's smugness regarding a union between him and Miss Jane now sounds an alarm. Is Charles at risk of marrying most unwisely? The lady looks at him with apparent affection, but I have seen the same look awarded to others. She is quiet (most unlike her sharp and saucy sister!) I have heard her speak but rarely, although I do see her in tête-à-têtes with my friend, and it does appear that she has a voice. Does she return the depth of his attachment? Unlikely. Nor can I forget the vulgarity of the rest of her family, (save for the one sister) (whose name I will NOT write.)

D., I have never had a friend like Charles. I treasure him beyond power of expression. We are especially close since our respective losses – this does indeed create a closer bonding.

Since I have promised to ensure that Charles makes wise choices, and since marriage to a cool and possibly calculating lady, of inferior birth, does not promise well, I spoke to him of my concern. He listened with shock, but carefully (he ever hearkens to my advice and counsel.)

He has need to go to London on business. I suggested that we all vacate Netherfield and follow him there, where the season is in full activity, certainly a benefit to Miss Caroline, and (to be sure) to ourselves.

It did not take overlong to persuade him. We shall be leaving here shortly.

11 DECEMBER, 1811 LONDON

Dear D. We left Netherfield early this morning. The hour had the ladies grumbling and out of sorts.

Miss Caroline especially is not charming at such an hour. As we finished our breakfast and were filing from the room, I pulled her aside. "A word with you."

"Perhaps you would like me to tell you what I think of your plan of leaving at this ungodly hour?"

"No, that is not what I wish to discuss. I need you to be all cooperation. We both want the best for your brother. This odyssey at Netherfield is not in his best interest, as we have discussed. London will bring him to rights quickly. I vowed to your mother that I would see to Charles' best welfare, and I feel that I am doing so. Now I ask you to behave in a proper fashion and not bring discord into this trip."

I did not wait for her answer but went out to check on last details with the head coachman. Beau was well aware that the outing was to include him, and was gamboling with delight. I patted him and told him that he was to follow me close.

As we pulled away, everything was sparkling with a handsomeness of early morning dew. There was a chorus of farewells from a large gathering of birds. The staff which had been left behind to close the house sent up a feeble cheer. They will return to their lives in the farm or village, or wherever, and can thrive on their reports of the fine life at Netherfield when they were in service there.

The ladies rode in the carriage, the gentlemen (Hurst and I) were astride, the household goods and luggage followed in a large wagon. I rode Brute (now officially 'Brutus') who put on a grand display for us before he settled down. Side slips, wild turns, half rears, full rears, loud whinnies. Name it!

As we went off down the road I did not look back. Had I solved a problem for *myself*? Indeed yes!

Miss Caroline, now all smiles, waved happily to me, and I saluted her.

The schedule was fine tuned – it included the best inn en route, with a well planned and festive dinner.

Shortly after we had left the inn I realized that Beau was not with us and signaled to the carriages to halt. I would need to go back, and if he were incapacitated I would need a carriage to follow me. Now started a mean debate about whether the ladies would admit him to their company. Miss Caroline was for *going on without him,* whatever had befallen. I told her to go ahead then, that I would manage it on my own. She looked sour indeed as I reversed my course.

I found him about two miles from where I had missed him. He was lying by the road with a bloodied paw. As I was bandaging the poor foot with my kerchief, he raised his huge head and licked my face. An instant flash of the dog and Miss Elizabeth. A sharp pang. What did I think I was doing!? I stilled such thoughts, "I am doing the *right* thing."

When I returned with Beau we had a *donnybrook* about the dog in the carriage. The ladies were adamant. Finally we lifted him into the wagon. (This took three of us, *excluding* Hurst, of course. Stout fellow!) Expedition resumed.

I did not have an easy time of it with Brute. He became restive late in the afternoon and we had a "duel" in the road. I told the others to keep moving, got him into a field, rode him hard through every discipline in the book. Then into the hardest gallop I could force on him to catch the caravan. He was too tired after that to give more trouble. (How glad I would be to see Champêtre!) How would this hulk fare at a London stables? I shan't worry it.

Good night, sir. It is very late. When first I arrived I asked the servants to open all the windows, cold as it is. The house stunk of must and dust, and needed to be aired. Then the night drafts blew in bringing all the pollution of this feverish city, with all its fetid odors, so I gave orders to close the windows.

Open, shut. Shut, open. Ah, the stinking city! As I write, I am trying to recall the sweet scents of a country night.

And *more* to recall, Mr. Darcy?

No more questions!

Ah yes, Georgiana, you ask? Georgiana will arrive tomorrow.

❦

28 December, 1811 London

Each day I have been at work in an office which my solicitors have set aside for me. I am hard at it to set up a new system of accounts for the management of Pemberley. Father worked from a series of notebooks, but there are now available ledger sheets which clarify the entries and which carry a great deal more information. I am making good headway, and am enjoying seeing it all develop into a cogent and practicable design. Every three days regularly I send work on to Pemberley, where our steward will put it to good use. All is well while the day lasts.

As evening descends I return to my home in order to prepare for the evening's round of festivities.

This is when you will find a strange and altered Darcy. I bathe and change into evening clothes, and join the Netherfield group in a mad dash from party to party, levée to soirée, to cotillion to ball. Pardon me while I yawn. Charles is possibly, (if possible) closer to gloom than I. He goes wherever he is bid, dances with whomsoever he is pointed toward, attends Georgiana with punctilious propriety, (she, as glum as he.) I had entertained dreams that the proper person for Charles might well be Georgiana, and Miss Caroline had been all enthusiasm for the idea. A sound exchange – his sunny disposition and enthusiasm (which will soon return, I am certain,) *vis-à-vis* her superior position, wealth and talent. It interests us, but not them, it appears.

The parties who *are* enjoying this marathon are the Bingley sisters. Mr. Hurst? A cipher no matter where or what, unless it be at the tavern, at cards, or regarding matters to do with the racing of horses.

Since I am the agent of our return to London, I feel responsible to keep the entertainment going at a lively pace. I have tried to arrange theatre parties on several occasions. Of late it evolves down to Georgiana and myself. The other ladies care naught for serious drama, and I cannot abide their shrill and idiotic laughter when we attend comedy. Hurst can no longer be suffered. He falls asleep when the curtain rises, and so rattles the theatre with his snoring that we have had to remove him on several occasions.

Georgiana and I attend concerts together, a rare pleasure! She is quite in earnest about her music, and studies and practices all the day in our London home.

The problem with our pursuits is that the others, on many an occasion, seem scarce to know how to entertain themselves without me, so I am a man divided. Most compelling of all is my urge to attend every possible Shakespeare performance, usually alone. Then I must atone to the others for "abandoning" them.

The whole *farandole* has me tired beyond sense. Sometimes I drift during the various rounds of conversations, and recall with regret the loveliness of the country and its quiet ways. Frankly, I am plotting to remove myself as soon as possible and return to Pemberley. I shall do so as soon as I can escape gracefully.

I must confess that I did not figure it thusly. I was depending on it that Charles would gravitate towards Georgiana, but one cannot control the heart of an other. She is fond of him, but as a sister. He, of her, as a brother. When I realized how useless was my plan, I dared to dream that he would be drawn to any one of a number of belles of the season, but so far that has not materialized. I am certain that it will.

As for me, I think not along these lines. I am heavy of heart. I cannot remove from my dreams a certain tantalizing, fascinating, and devilish lady who tortures me at night, and who will not go away.

I saw her sister, Jane, today. We were startled to pass one another on Bond Street, stopped briefly for the most formal of amenities, and went our separate ways. When the evening commenced I did not see fit to mention this to Charles.

⁂

13 March, 1812 London

This day, D. this day! Let me describe to you the most extraordinary development.

In the late morning Aunt Catherine's carriage clattered to the door with such a clamor of voices and slamming of doors that many of our neighbors came into the street to ascertain the source of such a hubbub. Such an audience not only does not perturb my aunt but seems to increase the hauteur and grandness with which she issues orders, commands and reprimands, as if to prove to the lowly (who dare to be present) that she wishes them to know of her contempt.

It seems she needs certain items for Rosings which can be obtained only in London. Her brief shopping whirl should well benefit those London tradesmen who will be blessed by her attentions.

She will tarry at my home but three nights. Over dinner I was treated to rapid-fire bulletins of this and that, these and those, some of interest, most *not* of interest. Then she fired off a bulletin of *real* interest – Miss Elizabeth Bennet is visiting the Parsonage at Hunsford because her best friend, Charlotte Lucas, had married Aunt Catherine's clergyman, William Collins (a cousin of Miss Bennet's). The Hunsford party comes frequently to Rosings, and will continue so doing. I found amusement in conjecturing the conjunction of Miss Bennet and my aunt. What a clashing and crashing of verbal sword thrusts and parries! Two sharp minds, thrusting and parrying, with wit to burn! It might prove indeed to be a dazzling exhibition!

Aware that my Cousin Fitzwilliam will be my visitor soon, I decided on the moment that we two should go for an extended stay at Rosings, and announced this to our aunt. She was delighted by the prospect. It occurs to me now that her delight was seasoned by the anticipation that cousin Anne and I can thus become more fully acquainted, and realize for aunt a dream of our becoming united. This does present complications, but I am confident that I shall handle them deftly without causing too much affront to the ladies De Bourgh.

I think a great deal, with pleasure, on the prospect of seeing again Miss Bennet, with or without the delightful prospect of the skirmishes which I anticipate between the two ladies. I have tried to rid my thoughts of this lady. I find I have not been able to do so. The more I see of other women, the more I am entangled.

I hear my father's voice, I hear my own – the solemn strictures, the solemn concurrences – Pemberley must have the proper mistress. I have run away from the lady, run like a madman. I have tried to fasten upon another, so many available, all so paltry and bloodless, or conniving and cunning. All of them, save her.

And now I am determined to indulge my own fancy, to be several weeks in her vicinity, to enjoy the proximity – to make a decision once and for all. To be!? Not to be?!

En garde, D. Prepare thyself.

⚜

20 March, 1812 London

Cousin Fitzwilliam arrived, eager for London's pleasures. He was taken aback when I told him we were to depart immediately for Rosings. He handled it sportingly, however, when I appealed to his sense of family.

He sued for the indulgence of one evening in London, which, munificently, I granted him. We supped at my Club, then I left him to his own devices in order to ready my valise. Took more than the usual care in selecting my wardrobe for the stay – Buckskin breeches, the tightest I have ever owned, (must I then remain *standing?*) New Hessian boots, a new short waisted coat with long tails (but not so long as Mr. Lucas.') A collar in the latest mode, so high I swear it covers the mouth (however do I manage to eat??) A new hat, not a tall hat, but a round hat with a tapered crown. (What is it with you, Darcy? You never take such care! Enamored is it?)

Fiddle de dee! Cannot a man replenish his wardrobe without having to account for it?

⚜

21 March, 1812 Inn at C. En Route To Rosings

I do not know at what hour returned the prodigal cousin. I know it was difficult to arouse him at early morning, and that the minute my coach lurched forward, his head rolled back and remained thusly, he in deep sleep.

Capital! It gave me a chance to study my thoughts about this frantic impulse of mine. To see Aunt Catherine? ('Be honest, Mr. Darcy. Me- thinks there must be a lady.' 'Yes, there is a lady!' 'A lady, is it?' 'Yes And such a lady! I have not before met a woman who can match this one.' 'And is she the proper lady as spouse and as the mother of your children?' 'A problem indeed. However, can I not train her to fit into my world and make my world learn to accept her? Indeed I can. We can and will remove ourselves from her unacceptable family. This will not be easy, but she will soon learn the advantages I offer and will succumb.' 'Take care, Mr. Darcy!' – Response to that, 'Faugh!')

I can be immodest with you, D. I am certain that I shall overcome any resistance with facility. Women come easily to my arms – most, too easily.

22 March, 1812 Rosings

It is the week before Easter. We arrived at Rosings in the morning. Aunt was all ecstasy to see us, and flew about the grand hall as if a great stormy petrel, ordering out the entire staff with shrieked commands to dispose of our luggage, thusly, accommodate us, thusly, make us comfortable, thusly. She is all energy, all fury, and all efficiency when in this state. The happier she was to have us, the unhappier were her servants, racing frantically in every direction. At one moment there was a collision between two – one entering a door, one exiting the very same door with the embellishment of a tray, which flew into the air and came down with a great shattering of glass and china. At this, my aunt pounded her cane, and I did think for a moment that she might use it on the lot of them.

She had made plans for us for the entire day, and we were travelled about her vast estates (in spite of our protests) and shown off everywhere in a high commotion. Many remarks from retainers who had not seen Fitz. in some time and who commented on how grand and tall he has grown. All seemed pleased to see me again.

As a manager my aunt is most impressive, and I cannot say I was not interested in the details she insisted to which we must attend. I was, however, yearning to visit the one property she eschewed, namely the Parsonage.

She did see to it that we should have a long tea hour with dear cousin Anne. A wounded partridge, she. One could enter a room and espy her not. She has a way of sinking into the most commodious piece of furniture and disappearing from view.

The next morning came Mr. Collins to call. The very Mr. Collins who had tried to thrust himself on me at Netherfield. Tried, I am told, to marry Miss Elizabeth Bennet, who had refused him. (I would like to have been present to witness that proposal scene. Such a glorious mismatch!)

I could see my opportunity, and bided the chance to visit his "humble home." 'When he takes his leave' thought I, 'I shall accompany him.' It amused me to think of his presence as *a gift*, but I had full intention of using it as a means to seeing Miss Elizabeth that very morning.

Such bowing and grimacing, and such an obsequious emphasis on the many comings and goings between the two residences. I dared to steal a glance at cousin Fitzwilliam. He dared to return the glance. I was able to keep a stern countenance, but not he. He could not restrain a loud guffaw, which he covered quickly with a coughing fit.

When the gentleman announced that he must return to the Parsonage, *I offered to accompany him.* He near collapsed with the joy of it, and then his bliss was trebled when cousin Fitz. declared he wished to join. Off marched we three.

My heart raced as we approached the residence. We were welcomed by Miss Charlotte, her sister Marie, and their father, Sir William, he of the blowsy rainment. Where was Elizabeth?

Enter Elizabeth. (For a moment I had entertained the hope that I would see her anew, find her plain, and would be able to laugh away the fancied enchantment.) When I saw her, D., I knew I was lost. She is, if possible, lovelier than ever I remember her.

I stammered a greeting, heard the sound of her musical voice. All I could manage was a commonplace query about her family, All I received was a commonplace response. Soon, cousin Fitz., a champion of the art of small talk, had things going at a lively pace, whilst I sat mute and strange.

Now, Miss Elizabeth looked at me and asked pointedly, "My eldest sister has been in town these three months. Have you never happened to see her there?"

I muttered that I had espied her once on Bond Street. Soon after this we left. During the entire return walk to Rosings but one question tore at my mind, When, sensibly, might I see Elizabeth Bennet again?

Not for a week it seemed. I went often to church, hoping to find her there, but 'twas not to be. I wanted to call, but could figure no logical justification for it.

At night, D., with the candle out, I imagine a tantalizing variety of encounters. In each I am easy, lighthearted, debonair in approach. And she, warm and responsive, full of charm and airiness. This inevitably leads to a melting together of our two selves, and all the rest of the drama –

⚜

29 MARCH, 1812 ROSINGS

At last the Collins party was invited by Aunt to dine at Rosings. The invitation was extended when we met in church this Easter morning. The invitation was extended *for this very night.*

I was dismayed by such a show of contempt, but Mr. Collins received the summons in an ecstasy that ill matched the fact that for this past week there has been a long succession of dazzling formal dinners hosted by my aunt, to include *every* person of quality in the entire shire. It stands to reason that invitations to these affairs had been sent *well* in advance.

Fitz., as always, has such an easy time of it. He carried the supper along, floating on a cloud of bonhomie. When we retired for coffee, he corralled Miss Elizabeth for himself, and embarked on such a conversation as I envied. Kent and Hertfordshire, traveling and stays at home, new books and music. Aunt was unable to contain her curiosity, demanded to be included, and finally took over the conversation. I, sitting next to my aunt, wished she would leave off that I could listen again to Miss Elizabeth.

It was suggested that she play for us. Graciously accepted. The instant she commenced, Aunt resumed her incessant dialogue. It was hard to ignore her, since she was talking into the immediate vicinity of my ear. I rose, strode to the pianoforte and stood there, gazing at my lady, able to feast my eyes on her radiant face.

"You mean to frighten me, Mr. Darcy, by coming in all this state to hear me." I assured her that she was mistaken.

Soon commenced a conversation, (between passages of music) in which I felt a part. It included Fitz., to be sure, but now I knew what to say and how to engage her. It mattered not that the subject was satiric of me – my coldness to strangers, my inability to master the art of approach. Cousin F. demanded of her to know how I behave among strangers. Her first indictment was not damning, although she had indicated playfully that 'twould be so. "He danced only four dances." I countered that at that time I knew not any lady beyond my own party.

"True; and nobody can ever be introduced in a ballroom." This ultimately led to some words of mine to the effect that I lacked the talent to converse easily with those whom I had not before met. Her retort –

"My fingers do not move over this instrument in the masterly manner which I see so many women's. They have not the same force or rapidity, and do not produce the same expression. But then I have always supposed it to be my own fault – because I would not take the trouble of practicing."

A direct hit! It made me smile. I said something to the effect that we neither of us perform to strangers. She had no chance to counter this remark (which I cherish because it united us, in a sense) because my aunt came our way and again seized all initiative.

I was aflame when I retired, D. The gulf between us has narrowed, she looks at me now. And we are again speaking to one another. She is – she is – she is a glorious woman, and I fear my heart is lost.

※

2 APRIL, 1812 ROSINGS

Today I dared to pay a call, and went to the Parsonage as soon as it was seemly. I was surprised to find Miss Elizabeth unattended, but she bade me to sit down, which I did, somewhat ill at ease, since indeed we were *entirely alone* in the house.

She was asking searching questions about our retirement from Netherfield and the while I was trying to parry same, my thoughts were on the upstairs of this house with her bedroom, and her bed; with the imprint of her lovely head on the pillow, – all this time breathing in the delicate fragrance which is hers alone.

She ran on, and so did my private thoughts. How could one say we were *alone* together. She was in one place; I? I was in the upstairs with her in my arms.

One part of me was discussing all manner of commonplace things with her – the Collins house, the distance of travel between various sites, the virtues of Kent. The other? –

We were thus engaged, when Miss Charlotte and Miss Marie returned.

After a seemly period of conversation with them, I took my leave.

❦

29 April, 1812 Rosings

These have been happy days for me. To be in Miss Elizabeth's presence seems to change my mood on the instant. And I have not been disappointed in the skirmishes between her and Aunt C. Dazzling! What I like most about Miss E. is that she plays fair – decently, with humor and proper respect for an elder. And I can see that my aunt relishes the challenge. Their subjects? The proper age for 'coming out,' proper chaperonage for young ladies, the proper education for young people, opera, and so on. Aunt is all hauteur and disapproval of the Bennet family's regulations. Miss Elizabeth eludes her disapprobation with deft skill.

Here at Rosings I have seen nary a blemish, not upon her behavior, nor her discourse, nor her manners. I observe that she has all the minor accomplishments upon which our elevated ladies pride themselves, and major accomplishments which few of them will ever attain. She plays well. (Aunt C. taunts her that she does not practice enough.) She has a lovely singing voice, pure, without artifice, and with accurate pitch. Her conversation is a delight. To cap it, D., the lady reads excellent books, with concentration, with relish, and, *mirabile dictu*, with retention. She is currently reading *Tristram Shandy* and from time to time one hears a delicious trill of laughter escape her. Yesterday I dared ask her, "Have you read Sterne's *Sentimental Journey?*" She answered in the negative. When I offered to lend it to her she thanked me, accepted the offer, and returned to her reading.

To boot, she is glorious to look at. A minor virtue, but of some importance. (Ho!)

And what of the standards which I was trained to apply to my choice of a mate? Position, social standing, significant relatives, governesses, schooling? Do I hurl these sacred banners to the ground and gallop off, unencumbered? "Yes!" a loud and affirmative "Yes!"

⁂

1 May, 1812 Rosings

I have taken to intercepting Miss Elizabeth in the park when she takes her walk. I join her, we talk a bit, but much of the walk is taken in silence. My thoughts are *not* silent. Once I offer her my hand there will be no turning back. I am in great conflict when thus with her, but in even worse trouble when away from her.

My appetite, usually so hearty, seems to have disappeared and I pick at my food. Luckily, my aunt has failed to notice this, or she would accost me.

⁂

4 May, 1812 Rosings

D., Say farewell to foolish Hamlet. "To be or not to be?" I, who make so many decisions so easily, I have been behaving as a blunderhead. I am ready to put an end to all that! "To Be!"

I have just run up the grand staircase to change my waistcoat. I have a call to make, D.!

The Collinses have come to tea but Miss Elizabeth is not of the party. She is at the Parsonage, quite alone. Is this not the perfect time to tell her of my love? Is this not the perfect time to open my heart to her and to propose to her. *I shall declare myself* . . . I have considered, and know that my problems can well be overcome. So why do I take the time D., to write you now? Because I am about to take the one step which will be the most important one of my life, and because it transgresses my vows.

I remember my father proudly showing me the family tree, and I remember his injunctions about the proper wife for me. He would disinherit me if he were alive. The loss of Pemberley I could withstand, but the withdrawal of his favor? Not that. I could not bear that. Nor of my mother's. And yet – and yet – it is my life, and my life is bleak and empty without Elizabeth Bennet. I go, D. I shall return a happier man.

LATER

A disaster! An unmitigated disaster. I am totally undone, my life lies in smoking ruins. Not only did Elizabeth Bennet refuse the offer of my hand, but she gave me reason to believe that I am the last man on earth who would be acceptable to her.

How could this have happened??

At first I was nervous and ill at ease. I paced silently. Finally I started, and with all the proper and acceptable words, but she looked pained and was most silent. I told her that I had struggled in vain, that my feelings could not be repressed no matter how hard I had tried to conquer them. I told her how ardently I admire and love her. *What did I do wrong?* I spoke at length of "family obstacles," of the difference in elevation between myself and herself, surely *she knows all this as well as I.* She remained quiet, and this encouraged me to continue. At length, I proposed.

And then of a sudden she told me that although she knows she should have expressed gratitude for my suit that *she could not.* This came as a dagger to my heart, at last exposed and totally unprotected, and just when I was feeling that blessed sense of relief that finally, FINALLY, I had faced up to it and avowed my love.

D., she was telling me that my suit was not to be accepted! A nightmare. I, Fitzwilliam Darcy, Master of Pemberley, was being refused.

I asked, "And this is all the reply which I am to have the honor of expecting?"

I should not have given her the opening! For I was then presented with an indictment of my faults and failings and sins which has left me reeling, all expressed in words I never thought could be addressed to *me.* They ring in my ears until I feel I shall go mad.

I defended myself. Especially as to my "meddling" in the affairs of Miss Jane. She denounced me as the man who has been the means of ruining, perhaps forever, the happiness of a most beloved sister.

She did not wait for my response to this, but went on to carry the indictment beyond all credulity – she denounced me for my mistreatment of Wickham! This was not to be borne! Luckily she is a woman, and luckily she is a woman with whom I had considered myself in love. If she had been male I cannot guarantee that she would have *survived* this remark. I, *I* was accused of reducing Wickham to poverty, of depriving him of his heritage, of depriving him 'of the best years of his life.' This was NOT to be endured. I lashed out at her – now I seemed to care not how I expressed my dilemma about her. I used such words as "the inferiority of your connections," spoke of her condition as being "beneath my own." When I was through she told me that my mode of declaration had spared her any concern for me that she might have had, had I behaved in a *"more gentleman-like manner."*

I felt as if the breath had been taken from me. I could say nothing. These words will haunt me for the rest of my days.

She continued, ". . . you could not have made me the offer of your hand in any possible way that would have tempted me to accept it." Still silent, I . . . She went on to speak of my arrogance, my conceit, and selfish disdain of the feelings of others, and concluded this death knell by saying that I am the last man in the world whom she could be prevailed upon to marry.

I could barely murmur my regrets, D. I told her she had said quite enough, extended my best wishes for her health and happiness, and quit the field, shocked, still furious, and – and heartbroken.

Goodbye Miss Elizabeth Bennet, I have grievously misjudged you, and you me. Let us say no more, ever, to one another.

🙢

5 MAY, 1812 ROSINGS

I slept not last night. Around four o'clock I must have drifted off, but awoke almost immediately with thoughts which plunged me into a terrifying abyss. How is one to survive such an unhorsing?

Perhaps 'twas the sound of my gnashing teeth which ended the brief anodyne of sleep. As I opened my eyes to the unbearable burden of consciousness, I was only too aware of the turmoil within my reeling head – Elizabeth Bennet's voice, her slashing words, my protests – a battle royal – and I, falling, falling from my steed, to be found lifeless on the ground and carried from the field. Mournful trumpets? Sound of weeping? Who will weep for Fitzwilliam Darcy? Only he!

I arose and paced. Whose voice was disturbing the early dawn? It was my voice, ranting to the unheeding air. I, Fitzwilliam Darcy, pleading with a woman, pleading that the record be set straight, pleading that my honor and my parole be cleansed of the devastating indictments which had been pronounced. I would need to tell her about Wickham, his distortions and lies, his extortion of monies, his refusal to take the Curacy which had been arranged for him; worst of all I would need to detail his dreadful and humiliating attempt to seduce Georgiana, a story I have long hoped to bury.

Sat down to write the letter. I referred first to the accusation against me in regard to Charles and her sister Jane. For this I made no apology. I have seen my duty to my friend, and have not shirked my responsibility. I would hope he would do the same for me.

Then I laid down my pen and rested my head on your pages, D. I was choking with a self pity I despise. What I could not deal with was her image of me. "Arrogance, deceit, selfish disdain of the feelings of others —"

Was this Fitzwilliam Darcy? I? The scrupulously trained gentleman whom my parents had designed to be the heir of Pemberley?

Each painful indictment pounded in my head with the dread clang of a funereal tocsin.

I – to plead like a ninny to Elizabeth Bennet? Never! *However* . . .

Again I took up my pen and commenced to write about the matter with Wickham – furiously. A letter? Nay, a *tome*. Page upon page. I poured out all the fetid details, my gut turning over as I detailed it all. Reread the lot when I had done. Does one hear the sound of whimpering? If so I needs must tear the offending document into a thousand and one pieces. No, I need not do this. Whatever the tone (and it did appear to have a dignity) I would deliver it. Who can bear to destroy the labor of several hours, a cry from the very soul!

Crammed the lugubrious lot into an envelope, dressed and walked to the park where she is wont to take her morning walk, found her not. I espied her somewhat farther down the road, just walking into the park – strode towards her, asked her to do me the honor of reading the letter, handed it to her. She took it from me. I bowed slightly, turned. I left.

Farewell, Elizabeth Bennet. You may destroy my heart, my hopes, my future, but not my honor . . .

7 MAY, 1812 LONDON

Returned from Hunsford this day, leaving a scene which I would quickly forget. Cousin Fitzwilliam came with me, full of questions. I would not speak a word to him, but sat silent, locked tight into my wretched thoughts. More woe, more confusion, more shock than ever I have experienced.

Returned from Hunsford hardly describes the reality. "Flight from Hunsford" would be more to the mark. There is news from the Continent of great wars and great retreats. I liken my action more to an event of this nature than to some commonplace event. I think of invading armies, excitement brimming, flags flying, bugles and drums churning the very air, hopes soaring. And then, the rout – everything in disarray, many wounded, many dead, flags torn to shreds, along with all hopes. Such high planning, such ruination!

How could I have been so blind? How could I have not noted Miss Elizabeth's displeasure towards me? How could I have so insulted her? How could I have overlooked the one salient glory of hers, her total integrity, which of course entails loyalty to her family, *howsoever* they conduct themselves. How could I think that blithely I could remove her from her family because they do not suit *me?*

How could I be so blind and so unfeeling towards the one person I have come to love above all others?

I must have started to talk to myself, because Fitz. asked, "What did you say?"

"I said naught."

"I distinctly heard 'Elizabeth.' Whatever *did* happen when you went to call on her?"

"Do not ask, and do forget whatever it is that you are thinking."

He studied me long and hard, and then told me that he was sorry for whatever it was that had taken place. He then started to reminisce about the visit, and of course, arrived at Miss Elizabeth, and went on detailing her merits and attributes until I was nigh undone. He intimated that were he the first son he would have proposed to her.

"No more, cousin. I have had enough of this lady, and would be alone with my thoughts."

"You are a strange one, Darcy. I am sorry if I have offended you."

We rode the rest of the way to London in silence. My thoughts could not be diverted from the collapse of my dreams – my intentions – my plans – and the loss. The loss! How am I to continue without her? And who is *she* to make me so lose possession of myself? This cannot be. No one person can defeat me.

Except, it seems, myself.

LATER

Hello D. I have not finished in regard to the "flight from Hunsford." Cousin Fitzwilliam's remark was stabbing at my entrails – a dagger in my very guts. No decent English gentleman would dare to venture the question I determined to ask. But then, it does seem – according to Miss Bennet – that I am *not* a gentleman, so what could be the harm? I ventured it:

"You say you would have courted Miss Elizabeth yourself were you not the second son?"

"You may stake your life on it, Darcy."

"And what would my uncle, your father, have to say about that?"

"Darcy! There could be no offer of my hand so long as my father exists. Your question is pure fallacy. Certainly I do not wish for his demise, but if he were gone you may be assured that were I the first son, I would indeed seek to be wed to Elizabeth Bennet."

"Assuming that she had not taken the matrimonial step to another."

"Of course! Assuming that – No! Hold! Assuming she had indeed been wed, I would ride up and abduct her. She would come willingly."

"And do you truly deem that such would be the case?"

"Who knows?"

"Elizabeth Bennet would not. She is ethical and principled above all else."

"You seem to forget, Darcy, that this is all in the realm of the subjunctive. My father is hale and hearty, I am the second son, my brother is hale and hearty. But you! Why did you dally so long? You have known her since November last."

"Excuse me. You are making an assumption without basis. You know nothing."

He apologized, again gave me such a searching look that I was forced to turn away. He took refuge in sleep. Not I. I was hearing her voice, clear and punishing – "You are the last man in the world whom I could be prevailed upon to marry."

How is it possible? How could I have been so blind?

※

14 JUNE, 1812 PEMBERLEY

I was awakened this morning by a great clap of thunder, followed by a blinding flash, and then another. Closed the window, and looked out upon a scene of storm-tossed trees, and an agitated sky, alternately dark and then blindingly bright. A scene as if tailored to match my mood. As I stood watching the display I thought that if a bolt of lightning were to come through the pane and strike me it would be the better for everyone. My thoughts strayed to Georgiana, who had come to visit me, and with that I threw aside my self-pitying and ran the long corridor to knock at her door. I called to her and asked if she were all right, and could I close her window for her. She was happy to hear me, and invited me to enter. She did not rise, she did confess that she felt ill at ease, and would I sit and talk with her until the crazed heavens quieted.

Conversation with her is difficult – I asked would she not let me read to her, and she complied. I searched her shelves until I found a copy of *King Lear*, and read to her from the last act. Eventually she murmured "How well you read!" and slipped off to sleep.

I regarded her for a moment. She is soon going to be a lovely young woman, already her features are beginning to emerge with clarity. I see traces of my mother's exquisite face in hers. I tucked the covers around her gently, and returned to my chambers.

Blew out the candle, but knowing that sleep would not find me again, I watched the storm, all the while thinking on Elizabeth Bennet's words, and cursing my foolish pride.

When 'twas light enough I prepared to go off to the fencing academy. The storm had passed over, and Pemberley was washed clean and pure. The trees soughed in the wind, the first birds were beginning to stir and call to one another. I saddled Champêtre (was he surprised to see me at this hour?) and we rode long and hard until the day was begun.

Luigi also was surprised to see me, but organized the weapons quickly, handed me the blade and the mask. I told him to leave off the mask, it is heavy and cumbersome. He assented most reluctantly, but insisted on replacing the weapons with a blunter version. "En Garde! In Line!" and we went to it. I know not how long we had been lunging and parrying before he shouted, "Disengage! Signor Darcy! You are dueling like a man possessed! One of us is going to be wounded! I have never seen you thus! You act like a man who has been scorned by the woman he loves!"

I wanted to go on, but he demurred and suggested that we "fight" again when I am in a quieter mood. He told me to surrender my epée, that he was afraid to walk away with his back to me. A sobering statement! I leaned my head against a column and tried to quiet my breathing. He put an arm around my shoulders. It was comforting. He said –

"Ah, women! So marvelous, so enchanting! They can take us to the heights! They can plunge us to the depths."

Ah indeed!

Champêtre was rested, so off we rode again to the fields, where I could forget everything but the speed and the wind on my face and the soaring sensation as we took the fences, and the essence of the glorious animal strength and grace of the steed beneath me.

31 July, 1812 London

I have neglected you again, D., but I am certain you care not to hear my "bootless cries." I have ridden a thousand miles, back and forth. Pemberley to London – London to Pemberley – Pemberley to London.

I have fenced a thousand rounds . . . My London fencing master will not even go to the floor with me unless we wear those hideous masks. I have kissed the hands of a thousand worthless women. I have troubled to find those whom I had romanced, and left them as abruptly as I found them. Now Charles has written and suggested that we plan a large house party, this time at Pemberley. He has all his sisters collected, and some "jolly men" (turn of phrase or a true picture?) I feel I owe him a good turn. He is not the same since we left Netherfield. He is no livelier than when we were in London last December. He smiles, to be sure, and is responsive to all suggestions, good or bad, but he seems *unsolid* to me. So I have made the plans as necessitated. Perhaps he will regain his geniality.

Georgiana is at Pemberley, and has attended to the many details which devolve unto the lady of the house, and it follows that Reynolds is a master at managing. Apparently she is happy to show off the new guest wing, so it appears that I have satisfied many people, (the one exception being myself – but who cares for that one – surely not I!)

I am leaving a day earlier than I had planned. I have some concern for the Hunt. I want it to come off well.

⁂

4 AUGUST, 1812 PEMBERLEY

I shall not sleep this night, D. I have sharpened several quills, and there is much to write. *Elizabeth Bennet came to Pemberley today.* No! I shall not sleep this night.

I had need to spend the day with attending to all the demands that would have come in my absence from far and wide.

First, from our tenants. Second, from the various stables which will be involved in the Hunt. Then to Champêtre. He seemed glad to see me, and I to see him. He was pawing the ground and nickering loudly as I returned *early* this morning. It did my heart good to have a friend welcome me with such joy. I put my arms around his arching neck and buried my head in his mane. The stable hand stood silently, not knowing what to make of the early hour nor such a show of emotion from the master. Nor did I.

We saddled up hurriedly. I told Harold that I would return as soon as possible, and please not to mention to the household that I was already in the neighborhood. I would explain when I returned.

We rode long and hard. We took every fence we could find. We galloped through the clear places, dodged through the forests, practiced a few difficult *maneuvers*, discharged a great deal of pent up energy – and I attended to each and every detail which needed attention.

Finally came near the house, threw the reins over his neck, tore off my boots and jacket, and dove into the lake. The water was cold – cold. Shockingly so. It almost took the breath from me. Deep deep under its weight, the sky somewhere above me, the depths beneath me. The thought entered my mind that it would be fine never again to emerge, but my chest began to hurt, and every instinct in my gliding body came to rescue me and pull me to the surface.

Harold was holding Champêtre by this time. We headed for the house, going our separate ways. As I came through the tall shrubbery *she* was standing there. Miss Elizabeth. At Pemberley. Was I deluded? No, it was she. She seemed as shocked as I.

I knew not what to do or to say. It was not only the surprise at seeing her. It was my drenched and dripping condition. I have been taught poise, D., since my earliest years. I lost it all. All! Eventually I regained control of myself to greet her, to request that she introduce me to her companions. Apparently she was as stunned as I, but did find her voice to introduce me to her aunt and uncle, with whom she is traveling, Mr. and Mrs. Gardiner.

We chatted. I came soon to like them both. He was interested in our stream, and I urged him to return and join me there for a morning of fishing.

I wanted Miss Elizabeth to know that I was happy to have her at Pemberley, that the words which had passed between us mattered naught. Feverish thoughts ran through my mind when they announced they must be leaving soon. Cast about for a delay, then suggested they take the southern walk before departing. "The rhododendrons are in full bloom and will be the subject of certain tours next week. Perhaps you might like to take a look." They agreed.

I excused myself, dashed into the house, up the stairs, changed into dry clothes and hastened back. When I came upon them on their walk, I escorted Miss Bennet, but we both acted as total strangers, spoke not a word, yet I wanted her never to leave. Soon Mrs. Gardiner called her, and the party bade me goodbye.

The equipage pulled away and I watched, feeling that my heart was being wrenched from my breast. Never have I felt so alone.

Then Miss Elizabeth turned her head, and I fancied that our eyes met. Was there an expression on her visage which I have hitherto not seen? By now she was too distant for me to be certain. When they were far down the drive I went back to the house.

Had I imagined it? Was she softer, more kindly disposed? Dared I to hope that she had seen me anew, that my letter had opened her eyes to a Darcy she had so misapprehended?

I knew at that moment, and know now with a deep certainty that the love and respect I feel for her is for her alone, never to be extended to another, that there is indeed no other to match her. Wherever she is there is a quickening, a charge of life, an energy, a fascination.

D., what am I to do? She is not wrong for me. She is right for me, and I dare to presume that I can learn to be right for her. There is something between us that can no longer be gainsaid. And yet – and yet she has rejected me most firmly. How to overcome?

When I reentered the house I willed most desperately to be alone in my room, but Mrs. Reynolds was hurrying towards me. I awaited her, but I most wanted to sort out my thoughts about my visitor, and all the other thoughts that were smashing and crashing about in my brain so that I was in the full bloom of a Brobdingnagian headache.

"Oh, Mr. Darcy! Welcome home! Such a surprise! We did not expect you until tomorrow. Such a lovely group we had here, and so appreciative of Pemberley and of everything I showed them. I do not often take such trouble with visitors. The young lady seemed so interested in your portraits that I took her upstairs to see the most recent one, of the matured Mr. Darcy."

"Methinks you inconvenienced the young lady."

"Not so, sir. Not at all. She studied the visage for a long while. There was such a play of expressions upon her face that I could not avert my gaze. She is indeed exceptional to look upon.

"Of a sudden there was a shout from below, and Galahad came bounding up the stairs, with Edward in full cry behind. The dog ran straight to the lady. She knelt to greet him and there appeared an instant accord. I fear he may well have removed his affections from you to her."

"Then that will make two I have lost."

"I do not follow."

"Reynolds, I must tell you that you have met the young woman who lately refused my hand."

"Not possible! Refused you? What young woman in all of England would refuse my master?"

"This one, Reynolds. Let the matter be a closed chapter."

"And to think I considered her of a superior intelligence . . . "

"She is such – she has intelligence of the highest rank."

I turned my back and left her abruptly. She was still muttering to herself as I closed my door and flung myself upon the bed.

Thank the stars above that I have you to tell this to, D. I am in a storm of conflict. What means this tale of Mrs. R.? Could it be that Elizabeth has new thoughts in regards to me? Could there be a turning?

Now arrived our house party, with a clamoring of slammed doors, loud chatter, hectic arrangements, luggage dispersing in all directions. Good god! Three more Bingley sisters than the usual quota. A raft of young men, whom I could not distinguish one from the other. Introductions, and not a name I could remember. I could scarce attend to all this, but it somehow was managed, and I got through the evening.

6 August, 1812 Pemberley

Awoke this morning, to the sun streaming through my windows, to the liquid sound of the meadowlarks trilling to one another. Men were already about, working in the fields. I could hear their muffled shouts as they called to one another. Somewhere a cow lowed. What a comforting sound!

I was determined to follow up on the events of yesterday. I want not to force the matter, but I will not let it drift into nothingness. I have seen a different Elizabeth Bennet and I wish to have her here again at Pemberley. (And on, from now until eternity.) What strategy could I devise to bring force to the issue, but yet not compromise our delicate "truce"?

The house was astir, with a babble of unfamiliar voices. A pox on all that, I must get to the inn!

Georgiana! I shot from the bed, dressed hurriedly and sent for her in the study. A milling crowd in the halls. Each eager to greet me. Did my best to wade through. Did.

I told my sister of Miss Elizabeth Bennet and of her sincere interest in music. Would she enjoy meeting the lady? Yes! Bless her! I suggested she get ready, ordered the curricle, and informed Charles that we were driving to the Inn at Lambton.

"But Darcy!! –"

I left him, gasping with surprise.

As we drove, the skies kept drenching themselves bluer and bluer and serving up marvelous clouds to enhance the glory of it all. Came to the inn, requested to visit with Miss Elizabeth Bennet, were ushered in, my heart hammering the while.

Miss Elizabeth! I dared not look overlong – just to note again how she seems to radiate light from her beautiful self. She flushed when she greeted us but seemed unable to meet my eyes. She made up for this with her graciousness to Georgiana, who indeed seemed to spring to life. Bingley now joined us, so happy to see her again. She appeared to be holding no resentment toward him and engaged him in conversation. I pulled my sister aside and suggested that Miss Elizabeth and the Gardiners be invited to Pemberley on the morrow. She did so. I enjoined Mr. Gardiner to bring his fishing gear. Accepted! Charles tugged at me, "Darcy? The Hunt!" We left hurriedly.

7 AUGUST, 1812 PEMBERLEY

Early this morning (but not early enough) the party arrived. Mr. Gardiner came to the stream where we awaited him. The ladies went to the house. Mr. G. was beaming with delight, and indeed the water was aswirl with fish. He knew exactly what to do, did so, and was a man content. Not I. Cared naught – caught *naught*. I was waiting, waiting to return to the house and see Miss Elizabeth once again.

At long last we put aside our rods, carried the catch to a side door of the house, proceeded in to join the ladies. Ah!

Reynolds looked out from the pantry, caught my eye, and took the sign for food to be carried in. Now came a great procession of platters of fruits and such, arranged in splendid cornucopias. A tongue, with red currant sauce. Great towers of pastries, creams and tarts.

Lady Caroline was at her worst. Whilst elegantly dishing out the viands for all guests, she gave said guests but brief notice, and continued her conversation with Mrs. Hurst in hushed tones, such as to exclude the others. Then she started calling across the table to Mr. Hurst to know which fruits he would like to be served, would he care for scones, if so, with which condiments? She kept forgetting the Gardiners' name, as if she *really* could not remember it. She did all she could to make it difficult for my visitors. I noticed a wicked little smile on Miss Elizabeth's lips. As she held out her plate, and Miss Caroline, head averted, moved to put upon it some slices of fruit, Miss Elizabeth herself turned her head to speak to her uncle, and in so doing moved her plate just enough that the serving ended on the table. Consternation. Apologies from both ladies.

I was privately relishing this small drama when the mood turned ugly. In the sweetest possible voice Miss Caroline turned to Elizabeth and asked, "And have you seen Mr. Wickham of late, Miss Elizabeth?" What a scurvy thing to do! Here, she caused perturbation in a quarter she did not intend. It was clear that she had wanted to cause discomfiture to Miss Elizabeth, but it was Georgiana who bore the shock. A tea cup crashed to the floor. Miss Elizabeth rose on the instant, and went to Georgiana's side. She suggested to Miss Caroline that since she was so intent on assisting Mr. Hurst that perhaps she should move to him, swiftly placed a chair between Georgiana's and Miss Caroline's places and sat herself down. Since my letter to her, she knows more of Georgiana and Wickham than anyone, save the principals in the event. We share a secret, and I relish that sensation, but did not relish the moment.

Miss Elizabeth moved deftly, attempted to involve Georgiana in the conversation, and when this did not avail, she suggested they two play duets on the new pianoforte. *Hare and hounds!* (How well I remembered her artful dodges at Netherfield when attempting to head off her mother!)

G. shook her head, and stayed quietly in her chair.

Miss Elizabeth was tactful about this refusal, went in to the salon and proceeded to test out the instrument, exploring its improvements with shining eyes. She commenced to play. Some of us moved.

Soon Georgiana followed, quietly sat down on the bench with Elizabeth, and, as if they had been friends for years, they commenced to play duets. I cannot remember a happier moment for me. I was gladdened to see my sister animated, and gladdened to see the two heads close together. Georgiana suggested that E. should sing, whilst she accompanied, and we had the pleasure of a sweet and pure voice with extraordinarily beautiful piano accompaniment. (At least I took pleasure. Caroline and Mrs. Hurst chattered meanly all through the performance.) All the while I could not take my eyes from the songstress – had she looked in my direction she would have had no doubt of my feelings! I kept thinking could there come a time that she will be at Pemberley with me – for all time?

As she concluded she looked at me – finally. Our eyes met and my heart turned over. Did hers? Is there therefore hope for this love-stricken man?

Just now, D. I have decided. I shall ride to the inn in the morning, and renew my offer. I can no longer ignore or evade my feelings for her. I love her. I wish to be wed to her. At this moment I dare to hope that she will not refuse me if I summon up the necessary courage and the right words. What should they be? What will she say? Will she forgive me for my folly in interfering in the Charles-Jane matter? Has she seen a new Darcy?

May God be good to me.

❦

8 AUGUST, 1812 PEMBERLEY

Saddled up Champêtre and we went sailing over fences and stiles, and across streams, my thoughts racing with the racing pace, and my spirits lifting, lifting.

Alas! When I arrived at the inn I found Miss Elizabeth in a most dreadful state. I made her sit down, took her hands in mine, tried to minister to her "illness" until I learned the cause of her distress.

An event of most deplorable circumstances has befallen the Bennett family; wretched Wickham has run off with none other than *Lydia Bennett*! A deplorable situation. The idiot girl is over five years away from one and twenty. And what could *he* be up to? Certainly to no good!

A wicked thought entered my mind – at least now he has met his match! Miss Lydia Bennet is undoubtedly the one person in the world who can and *will* drive him to despair! But immediately I began to realize the consequences, not only to Miss Elizabeth, but to the entire family. All prospects destroyed!

I wanted to take the sobbing Elizabeth into my arms to comfort her, but this was an impossibility in view of the circumstances. How could I press my suit at such a time? Moreover, my head was reeling from the urgency that something must be done to undo the undo-able, and what would that be? Whatever, it needed to be accomplished apace.

Miss Elizabeth was awash with tears and in need of drying, which is what most I would prefer to have done, but I rose and left. Something is needed! But what?

❦

14 AUGUST, 1812 LONDON

D., I have brought you to London.

When I returned to Pemberley I could not sleep, in fact, paced the floor for all but an hour of same. Back and forth, back and forth . . . what could one do to alter this dark sorrow? I could not help but think that I should have warned the family about Wickham. I have known where he is billeted. What manner of man am I that I kept my counsel? Have I had a role in this terrible turning?

No! No word would have prevented this headstrong foolish youngster from her folly. I should have warned, but I know full well that she would have 'fallen' in spite of it. I should have – she should have – her parents should have – *did not*. Enough, Darcy! There is work to be done. The couple must be found, wherever, however, and I shall set about the job.

So saying, I threw you into my case, D., awakened the staff, told Nielson to make excuses for my sudden departure to my guests, ordered the carriage, and set off for London.

A terrible twisted tale, which must somehow be solved, but how to do it, where to start, how to find sources who might be able to lead me?

The corrupt Mrs. Younge perhaps? Whatever the connection to Wickham, there is a connection. I will need to find her. I will! There are five marriageable sisters, and the thought of what will happen to them if this is not satisfactorily concluded is unthinkable. I must prevail! (But HOW?)

❦

17 AUGUST, 1812 LONDON

Have not written because of the bone aching fatigue in which I return from my daily searches. "Daily" does not refer only to the hours of light. Much can be accomplished in London by night, and frequently I have returned in the early morning hours. I explore every dark and unpleasant tavern and shop. Does anyone know a tall striking woman of approximately forty years of age, named "Mrs. Younge?

This night was a bottomless descent. I am lucky to be alive, but am beginning to sense that the quest may well be hopeless.

The desolate areas of London are not conducive to longevity, especially in the matter of a well-dressed gentleman prowling for an elusive quarry in a dense yellow fog. Last night it all might well have been terminated for this determined man.

As I was returning to where I would find my carriage, the fog being so dense I could scarce know in which direction I was moving, I felt a hand in my pocket, another at my throat, and that hand holding a cold metal which I first took to be a dagger.

I wheeled to encounter the rest of the person, could see naught, and was flailing in a nightmare of undetermined and elusive movement. All I knew in that sea of unsubstantiality, was that some force ordered me to feint to the side, and kick out with my left leg. I heard a gasp, an instrument clatter to the ground, and then a thud.

For some inexplicable reason the fog skirled away at that moment, enabling me to discover my assailant writhing on the ground (apparently I had well connected that foot to his groin). I could discern a figure fleeing the scene; mine eye caught the glint of an unpleasantly wicked knife. A poker lay on the ground, which I quickly retrieved and held to the fallen assailant's throat. In his hand he held my purse. He was babbling in terror, and pleading for his life.

I retrieved my purse, threw a coin behind him, ordered him to find it *if* he could, *when* he could, kept the poker and strode off into the fog. I did not further pursue my quest, but returned to Mayfair as soon as I was able to locate my carriage.

My London house does not have the amenities of Pemberley, but there is a tub of sorts and I roused Batson to fill it with hot, hot water. Soaked awhile, soaped off the feeling of filth and degradation that was upon me. How can it be that one finds in the same city such a foulness, alongside such sophisticated and attractive elegancies?

To bed, but not before placing the poker on the wall above the mantel in the salon, "The wealth of seas, the spoils of war . . . "

⁂

18 August, 1812 London

I value my life too much to embark on any more such futile combings of the dreadful places in London town. Put my head in my hands, said to my brain, "Go to work! Find a method!"

In a moment the name of Horace Walpole floated across my thoughts. Horace Walpole! He was a friend of my grandfather. He is dead.

Went to the window, stared out at the gray city. Horace Walpole? He was the author of *The Castle of Otranto*. Devilishly good book. Gothic novel. The first, I believe. Derring do events, schemes and villains, (Manfred, is it?) A prophecy, ghosts, heroine named Isabella, she escapes with the hero, name of Theodore – a peasant as I recall – Horace Walpole! How would Walpole have gone about such a mystery as the whereabouts of these feckless people?

"Tell me about Mr. Wickham, Mr. Darcy. What are his weaknesses?"

"The first is his need for the good life, the second is his relentless need for money, the third is his total unwillingness to work for it honorably."

"Well then, Mr. Darcy, would he not have need to go to a money-lender? –"

"Of course! Why I had I not bethought myself of this earlier? I thank you with all my heart, Mr. Walpole. And congratulations on your masterful book."

⁂

20 August, 1812 London

No more fumblings in the dark. I have started this day a methodical visit into the lairs of the benighted moneylenders of London. What a scurvy lot. Such dank holes of greed and desolation. I encountered a pathetic group of wretches in these places, but also (surprisingly) sons and heirs of the high born, some of whom I know. Usually we pretended we have not seen one another. (Let them think what they may of the reason for *my* being in such a place.) Some were classmates, some were members of the same set when we danced at the same balls. Some approached me to invite me to an evening festivity at the very time they were asking for a loan. The irony!

At each place I asked for and received a referral to the next. From the flotsam of this murderous town I received information, such as they have, and it was because of such questions and such information that I uncovered today . . . FINALLY! . . . the whereabouts of Mrs. Younge.

Went there, had the door part slammed in my face but got my foot in to prevent the closure, swept the cowering charlady aside, bearded the lioness in her den (cliché. Sorry, Father.) My gorge rose when I saw her. Such an engine of meanness and destruction! All the locked memories revived and swept over me so that I was deadened for a moment, but not for long. As the anger rose in me so did my strength of purpose. I denounced Mrs. Younge for her willingness to betray the innocent Georgiana who had never had an evil thought or desire, and to ruin such a promising young life. "I *shall* disclose this matter, a matter which I had cared *never* to disclose. Although I live not in London I have solicitors who *do*; once informed they will to *the watch* and all the way to King's Court if necessary."

I was ablaze with fury by the end of this tirade and I dare say that if she had continued to deny me I would have strangled her. She must have realized her peril and so gave me the information I needed.

She told me where Wickham and his lady had taken up residence. I took my leave. EXCELSIOR!

⁂

2 OCTOBER, 1812 LONDON

Well, D., I have done everything I can think to do. I have seen the miscreant couple wed (Wickham going through the motions like a somnambulist; Miss Lydia blithely ignoring all signs and portents, happy as a silly lark.) The church was empty save for the principals – the craven groom, the aloof minister, Mr. and Mrs. Gardiner, and the 'best man' (myself – *quel taradiddle!*) – the bride – a chattering majority of one – herself. She could not understand where were the honor guards, and where were all the friends?

I have arranged with the Gardiners to allow me the burden of the "ransom," have arranged that Mr. Bennet be apprised of what shall be his responsibility, without telling him of my role in the matter. The share allotted to him is small indeed, but I doubt that he will overmuch dwell on this.

I took me to Belgravia, told Charles of my intrusion into *his* affairs. It was not easy to confess to him my role in this matter, especially that I had known that Miss Jane had been for several weeks in London whilst we were there, and had not shared that knowledge with him. He was appalled. There was a verbal skirmish but I did feel cleansed that I had revealed my plotting to him, and we ended on good terms. I know he will forgive me – in fact, I feel he had done so when we parted.

However, I cannot be certain that Miss Elizabeth will absolve me of this transgression.

Lucky Charles! People of a sunny disposition find such a clear way. Mine is dark and thwarted at every turn. I could not bear a second refusal of my hand – but how else can I storm the gates of heaven if I do not risk?

3 OCTOBER, 1812 LONDON

These lines from *Macbeth*, made me throw the book to the floor, "When shall we meet again? In thunder, lightning, or in rain?" "When the hurlyburly's done. When the battle's lost and won."

It has all come sweeping over me – Elizabeth's entrance into Netherfield, caked with mud – her arms around my waist the day we outran the lightning storm, my dumbwitted "Surely you jest!" and her "Surely I do." – Her back to me, the feel of her flesh as I captured the errant spider – the sense of her as we danced at Netherfield – my body will remember always – always. So few moments! So overwhelmingly powerful!

And why do I sit here? Why indeed! I have grievously offended her, I cannot forget her drawing of my character. If she once saw me thus, how can I offer myself to her again?

It was so clear and so easy that final day when I rode to Lambton, suffused with courage and assuredness. But that moment has passed, and I am grievously *cumbered*. If only one could look into another's thoughts, *her thoughts*.

She is Titania and Miranda and Juliet and Mab, and ALL of the glorious heroines who have moved me, together with the airiness and impudence of Ariel and Puck.

Is the *hurlyburly* done? Is the battle *past and won? Where* is my daring? My assuredness? My courage? Darcy, Darcy! What manner of man art thou?

5 OCTOBER, 1812 LONDON

Today! Ah, this day . . . Today Aunt Catherine descended like a howling banshee. At first she was so angry that I could not understand her incoherent flood of words, but finally I calmed her sufficiently to be able to comprehend, and what she was saying has opened up the gates of a hopeful heaven.

It seems that word had reached her that I had become engaged to Elizabeth Bennet! A mystery, but I am not interested in fathoming how this came to be. Not at the moment. Aunt told me she took Anne and set out with her for Longbourn, where she confronted Elizabeth with (to my aunt) the dreadful charge. Eventually, E. apparently drove her "almost to madness," finally allowed that the rumor was *unfounded*. Then, dear Aunt Catherine, (how foolishly she does behave!) demanded that Elizabeth vow to her that she would *never* be wed to me. My seething aunt then informed me (as if this would be the nail in the coffin!) that the offending Elizabeth mercilessly *refused to pledge this!* To Aunt, the ultimate crime. To me, the lightning flash of hope!

D., know you how very foolish indeed was this last move? Thinking to triumph over me in this one infuriated moment, I dare believe *she lost the game*.

I am a man released from purgatory. God, I believe, has answered my prayer. We are off to Netherfield. Charles has adjourned there. I shall accompany him when he calls on Miss Jane. As for me, I shall risk it *all* on one question to Elizabeth. If she refuses me again, all is lost. Yet I dare believe that she will not refuse; *why else* did she refuse Aunt's ultimatum? I dare believe that she recognizes a different Darcy and knows, or at least senses, *as I know full well,* that we are destined in the stars for one another.

೮ಾಎ

7 OCTOBER, 1812 NETHERFIELD

Ofttimes it takes more courage to walk into a country parlor, I imagine, than into a field of battle. This was such a time. I found myself feeling grateful to Mrs. Bennet for her chatter. I dared not look at Miss Elizabeth. Miss Jane sat as a statue, a slight blush on her cheeks the only proof she was not of marble. Charles was as a sailing ship marooned in the doldrums. The deadly stiffness did not improve with time.

Not until we took our leave. At that moment Charles began to address himself to Miss Jane, and a slight breath of liveliness stirred. *He* was urged to return (Mrs. Bennet can scarce bring herself to greet me, let alone extend an invitation to return!) We left, much subdued.

೮ಾಎ

8 OCTOBER, 1812 NETHERFIELD

We dined at Longbourn this day. The mood of yesterday's visit did not lift. I exchanged but a very few words with Miss Elizabeth, she with me. I tried to be near her as she was pouring coffee but the sisters formed a phalanx around her and I was blocked from her. I had hoped there would be a chance when the tea things were cleared. Not so. I was corralled into a game of whist, and thus passed the time (a call for dirge-like music, here, please). Frustration and ennui!

I have had another discussion with Charles about Miss Jane, and my role in their relationship. He is still shocked at my interference, but has, I believe, found it in his heart to forgive me. He will not hold a grudge, I know him too well, so I have no real concern for our friendship, although he is still furious at my hiding from him the fact of the lady's presence in London for so many weeks. He looked sternly at me, said severely –

"You are in my debt, Darcy. But for you my marriage would be an accomplished thing, and I would have been spared these months of misery. How could you have so misprised Miss Jane's devotion to me?"

"I was wrong, Charles. I cannot say more. Shall I make it good with the first colt that is born at Pemberley next Spring?"

"A whole pasture full would be more to the point." Then he gave me a clap on the shoulder, pushed at me, and said, "Bygones are bygones. I only wish you the same happiness I am experiencing now."

THEN he informed me that he had proposed to Miss Jane and had been accepted! Congratulations! Lucky man!

As for myself?

"I am hoping past hope, good friend."

We shook hands on that.

⊗

22 OCTOBER, 1812 NETHERFIELD

And so it is, D. I have proposed to Elizabeth Bennet. This time not only did she not send me away in grief, but she has accepted me and I dare believe that she loves me! She has agreed to be my wife!

There is much to be done, plans to make, affairs to be settled . . . I needs must return to Pemberley, journey to London, with a sea of matters to be put into order. Georgiana must be informed, Reynolds alerted, I needs must contact all my solicitors, the list goes on and on. How soon can all these matters be settled by one who wants only to "walk out" with his beloved? (And much more than that, but we are a most proper society and I needs must behave most scrupulously.) I am so dreadfully, desperately in love that I desire only to mutter "I do," and race off with her, to carry her over the threshold and into the bedchamber.

And how came this about? Let me set it down. It is very late, but certainly I cannot sleep!

This morning I returned from London, and Charles and I rode to Longbourn. With Miss Kitty accompanying us, we five set out for a walk. Lost Kitty quite early, and soon thereafter we lost Charles and Miss Jane. We two walked on – silence.

Was this to be another frozen, Arctic waste?

Not so. Miss Elizabeth finally broke the silence, shocked me by expressing thanks for my kindness towards her sister Lydia. Thunderation! *How knew she this??* The Gardiners had given me their pledge of silence!

I learned then that it had been *Lydia's* thoughtlessness and not the Gardiners' treason. Lydia had let a remark drop about the attendees at her wedding, mentioning my name. It does appear that Miss Lydia can always be counted upon for rare surprises.

I told Miss Elizabeth, then, that if she would thank me it had to be for herself alone, that I had thought only of her.

She was too embarrassed to speak. As she blushed, I said to myself, 'Do it Darcy. Now or never again. *Now!*' The words came, "You are too generous to trifle with me. If your feelings are still as they were last April tell me so at once. My affections and wishes are unchanged; but one word from you will silence me forever."

She said very little, D., but it was sufficient. "Indeed, Mr. Darcy, my feelings are quite different from a certain event which I now wish I had the power to erase from every record. My sentiments have undergone so material a change that I receive with gratitude and pleasure your present assurances."

In all the books I have read or dramas I have seen, this should have been the dramatic climax, followed by a heavily charged emotional scene between the lovers.

And we? We went on walking, heedless of the direction or of the hour. And yet, I have never been so happy. Never! She was to be mine. The drama would come soon.

We realized the time. Where had it flown? We hurried back to Longbourn. We supped. The ladies rose. The men rose. Mr. Bennet excused himself and retired to his study. The ladies began to file out from the room. As Miss Elizabeth started through the door she turned her head and gave me a questioning look. I gave her a nod, but moved not. D., I had had no trepidation when I prowled the nasty London streets, I knew naught of fear. This moment, my heart was hammering so loud that it could be heard, I swear, from across the room. The servants came to clear. If the hammering of my heart could be heard they gave no sign.

I took a deep breath, and followed Mr. Bennet from out the room. I was reminded of the Bridge of Sighs in Venice as I traversed the vestibule to his study. Reminded myself of my breathing, and inhaled deeply. Expand the ribs, let the air fill your chest. Breathe out –

He was reading when I entered, seemed surprised to see me, but put his book across his knee and invited me to be seated.

As luck would have it, Mr. Bennet was reading Molière. *Tartuffe!*

"In French, sir?"

"Eh? Oh, the book. Yes, of course, in French. You know it?"

"I played the title role when I was at Cambridge."

"Did you?! That rascal! Tell me about it."

"I shall be happy to, sir, in the future. But I wish to make a request, if you will attend me, sir."

"Indeed. What can I do for you?"

"You can grant me the hand of your daughter, sir. I would marry her."

The look on his face quite banished all my nervousness. First he took his glasses off and wiped his eyes, then dropped the glasses. In retrieving them he dropped the book. I bent to pick it up, but so did he, and we almost knocked heads. He kept saying "Dear me!" Then he asked, "Does Elizabeth know of this?"

"Yes indeed, sir. This is not the first time I have so addressed her, Mr. Bennet. But this is the first time she has accepted me. I hope you will give us your blessing."

"Indeed, Mr. Darcy, if Lizzie will have you, then I wish you every happiness, and be assured my blessing goes with the wish."

And so it goes, D. I am to be wed!

ɛ̃ɜ

25 OCTOBER, 1812 LONGBOURN

D., I write you from Longbourn. Good desk, good pen, GOOD NEWS.

This afternoon we again walked through the groves of Longbourn. (How many miles think you that betrothed couples tread before they can get off their feet and engage in that in which they most care to be engaged?)

(Young men of Great Britain, if you would be apprenticed into a trade may I suggest that you present yourselves to a cobbler!)

Once more I begged Elizabeth's forgiveness for my inexcusable interference in the matter between Jane and Charles. I said to her that, "I swear that I shall go to my death without absolving myself of the guilt for my malicious and dreadful meddling."

She said, "Be not so stone hard against yourself. I do wonder, will it make it easier for yourself if I inform you that in every conversation I held with Jane about your *treachery*, Jane took your side and had no care but for to give you credit for your good intentions in your actions."

At this, I emitted a terrible groan and sank to the ground with my head in my hands. She knelt beside me and pulled my hands away, "I meant not to slay you my dear Mr. Darcy. I prefer not to be widowed ere I am wed. And in one way you were quite correct; Jane is indeed very cool, and I am certain that it was only too easy to mistake her feelings."

I thanked her for her charity. We made a vow that we should not again bring up the subject of my "perfidy." *She* said the word, not I. The minute she uttered it she put her hand to her mouth and begged my forgiveness. Then she smiled with one of those smiles of hers which lights her whole face. I still do not know how to sport with such changes of spirit. How do I cross from my tidal (nigh unbearable) waves of desire, when I cannot talk at all, to a mood which she inspires with her witty and remarkable conversation, where I can sport and jest with her as she does with me? I said naught for a space, just kissed both her hands. Again, her response to such a gesture amazed me. She looked distressed for a moment, flushed, drew in her breath, and looked at me with such a look that I almost lost all control.

(How long must we wait to be lovers? The days are too many!)

Finally it was I who spoke; "And is her sister as cool as Jane, think you?"

"Indeed she is, as cold as –?"

I finished the line for her; "Cucumbers."

She thanked me for the assistance and asked did I know the derivation of the adage. I was able to tell her *Cupid's Revenge*, by Beaumont and Fletcher. Next I knew I was telling her about my English literature courses at Cambridge, and she listened raptly, with such shining eyes, and my heart was singing for here is a friend with whom I can share my love of books and poetry and of ideas – and (remembering poor Professor G.) a person *of the proper gender!*

Then I stared at her long and hard, apparently with such ardor that she became shy again. I told her "I think you are not so cold as a cucumber, and I think we had better both rise and resume our walk."

And so we did, but I would have had it otherwise, and judging from her demeanor, I think she would also.

28 October, 1812 Longbourn

This day we four set out, two by two. Passing strange, how soon we became separated and wandered far from each other.

E. and I found ourselves deep into the woods. I stopped to turn to her, and she returned my gaze with such lovingness that I, giving way to a longing that could no longer be stayed, pulled her to me. I placed my hand where I had longed to do so – on her throat. I tilted her head back and began ardently to kiss her lovely face, from time to time murmuring such nothings that I cannot even repeat them to you, D., to whom I tell everything. Nor can I repeat the thoughts that were racing through my mind; such disrespectful and dangerous thoughts that I recall them with the same self despair I felt then.

Of a sudden her legs appeared to give way, and if I had not held her she would undoubtedly have fallen to the ground.

Blackguard that I am, I berated myself for saving her from falling. The natural conclusion of a fall would be her lying on the ground, which is where I most earnestly desire her. With myself lying next to her, or preferably –

D., I am a wicked, wicked man! I tell you earnestly that the nearly six weeks until our marriage are too much to bear, so in love am I.

❦

30 October, 1812 Netherfield

I return to my room at Netherfield, knowing full well that it will be another dreadful and lonely night. The days, ah! The days! I rise at dawn, post orders attending to the necessary affairs at Pemberley, especially with our tenants whose needs I follow closely. Then in a happy mood I turn to the arrangements necessary for the acquisition of a lifelong tenant, namely, a certain Mrs. Fitzwilliam Darcy. (How I like saying that aloud!)

Breakfast with Charles. This morning he looked haggard and miserable. I inquired; "Are you not well?"

"This d _ _ _ _ _ courtship period is hell's fire to a man. How is it that you appear in such excellent health?"

"If I do appear so, it is only because my nights have been a torment since *'a time which passeth all understanding.'*"

"Shakespeare?"

"No, the Bible. Where *are* your thoughts when you are in church?"

"I fear they are with Miss Jane."

We both smiled. I then remarked that I wondered if the Bennet sisters held such conversations.

" Mine did not. When Louisa was to be wed I overheard only such matters as fabrics and jewels and furnishings – and the names of who was to be invited."

I waited silently in the hope that he might desire to explore the theme of female confidences, but he changed the subject and we discussed fowling pieces and the need to stock the larder with pheasant. Soon he went about his business, I went to the stable, helped saddle the stallion I have been riding (big brute, rough ride) and rode off to be with my beloved.

All very fine.

As to my own health, the outer man may look hale, but the inner man is having trouble. I find myself as if divided at the shoulders. The head is in a state of enchantment and delight; below the shoulders there is a great deal of travail. It is but two days, yet I have permitted myself to kiss her only once. The moment I touched her lips I found that I was not to be trusted. Sweet, dear lady! Has she any idea of what a tempest her presence (and equally her non-presence) has caused? Methinks she does know. Methinks she experienced the same as I when we kissed. I dwell constantly on the recollection of the way she melted into me. Methinks she knows what may lie beyond such a moment. There is every promise that this will be a marriage paradisiacal.

Yet there is something so pure about her every move that I dare not taint her. She is so unlike the women I have hitherto known, even those met at St. James Palace and other such splendid venues. Each one so tarnished! And my "grande amour" of those days, even she.

From their insufficiencies I came to know what it is that I desire in a woman. And I have found it all, and beyond in Miss Elizabeth Bennet. I count the days, nay to be precise, the hours. (A staggering number.)

❧

1 November, 1812 Netherfield

I am making arrangements for Miss Elizabeth to move to Pemberley directly following the nuptials. I had considered the Grand Tour for our honeymoon and had proposed it to her. Of a sudden she asked me straight out, "Mr. Darcy, I would love to see the great sights of the Continent. But I detect that truly you do not have high enthusiasm for such a trip. And is there not a great deal of unrest and warfare at this time?"

For a moment I could scarce reply. Is this lady a mind reader? At length I took her hand, kissed it, and told her that my dream was to have our honeymoon at Pemberley, and did she consider that a disappointment.

"Mr. Darcy. How could time together with *you* be a disappointment under any circumstance? Please raise your head. I am not certain you heard my answer."

Then I looked at her. "Elizabeth. I scarce know how to thank you."

"You need not trouble yourself. Your eyes say it."

Need I tell you, D., that I ride to Longbourn almost daily, and stay as long as I can? It is a rumpled, hectic scene there, with many activities taking place simultaneously – fittings, preparations for the sisters' departures, and Mrs. Bennet flying everywhere at once, shouting orders and frequently collapsing, necessitating mad dashes for the smelling salts. The two elder girls, busy as they are, attend to her with comfort and soothing words. I am impressed with their sweetness, tact, and yes, I must say it, with their deep affection for their mother.

I find myself surprisingly content in Bedlam. I never knew family life could be so intense and close, and I am a keen (and dare I say?) fond observer.

I am becoming acquainted with Mr. B., and find that we are fast becoming good friends. His relationship with his second daughter is a joy to behold. It is clear from whence she has received her wit. His is wry, wicked, and ironic, and he proves to be exceedingly well read. I react in the same way I did in the early days with Professor G. I am stimulated, amused, and in high spirits when we converse.

Some days I muse on what would have been the substance of a meeting between our two sets of parents. I invent the dialogue, (or try to . . . whatever my story, I have to change because, like Georgiana, I cannot seem to pinpoint the quality of Mother.)

Miss Elizabeth came upon me this morning, as I was sitting quite alone and happily constructing one of the possible scenes. She inquired as to why I was looking amused, but I would not tell her the reason, and she was most curious all the day. The advantage of this was that she kept coming round to be near me. She would not pry, but would look at me hopefully. I would not divulge my musings, but merely stared her down intently. At one point Mrs. Bennet descended and found us thus. I rose.

"Fie, Mr. Darcy. You two must not be overlong together alone."

Elizabeth began to reproach her but I told her that this colloquy was between her mother and me and to back away. Mrs. Bennet looked at me with her mouth agape. I assured the lady that I would treat her daughter in a most honorable fashion, and that I am to be trusted. I kissed her hand and awaited her departure, which she took in some confusion.

One must acknowledge that certainly Mrs. B. has done one thing quite admirably – she has five healthy, individualized daughters. The two oldest are superb females. Mary is a "find" for me – we discuss philosophy and I am amused by her solemn pronouncements and her pontifical manner. Miss Kitty is improved (since naughty Lydia has taken her bad influence off to the north) – being most considerate of me, and very kind. – Lydia's miserable escapade (and my role therein) has served as a *Deus ex Machina* to unite both sets of lovers, so one may forgive her her trespasses.

I shudder when I think what my future might have been without Elizabeth Bennet in my life. I would need soon to be wed in order to produce an heir. Caroline Bingley? Cousin Anne? Any of the availables in London? And if I were not to wed? Farewell to the future of my Pemberley!

Tea has been announced. Wait for further bulletins, D. It is to be a double wedding. Mrs. Bennet keeps moaning, "So soon!" Hearken to me – not soon enough!

Writing calms me a bit, but I find myself pacing like a caged tiger. I am counting the days.

＊

13 November, 1812 Longbourn

Today was a glorious Autumn day, almost as warm as summer. I had carried with me a large portfolio of documents which needed attention, and was offered the use of Mr. Bennet's library, a splendid room with a spacious desk, good firm chair, excellent pens, and excellent light. I persuaded Mr. B. that he need not vacate, so he remained in an easy chair with his book. He is reading Madame de Sevigné's letters in the original French. One hears more than a few chuckles from time to time, but otherwise there is always a comfortable silence in the room, conducive to concentration.

When I had finished my work and pushed back my chair, he turned the book on his knee for a moment and asked me if I knew it. I told him of my French classes at Harrow and Cambridge, as well as the Pemberley tutoring sessions when I was young.

"That, Mr. Darcy, explains your excellent accent. The youngest years are the best time to get it established. Here, take the lady and read her to me, if you will." I took the book from him, and proceeded. From time to time he commented on how well I sounded. We were thus engaged when Elizabeth entered and found us. She smiled with delight at the companionable scene, came behind her father, put her arms around him (lucky man!) and listened intently.

The day was proving even more beautiful, and even warmer. I (in my best French) solicited her to walk out with me. She went to fetch her bonnet.

She directed me to one of her favorite groves telling me of the wealth of birds which were wont to congregate therein, and indeed she was accurate in every respect. It proved to be a sylvan delight, to be sure, with a rapturous "concert" in progress. My lady looked up with joy, searching for the musicians. Not I. I concentrated on the exquisite line of her throat when her head is raised thusly. However, she was standing directly under one of the trees which seemed to be the stage for our entertainers. It behooved me to suggest that she move out from under the branch, as even Paradise can present us with a contrary side.

She smiled reflectively; "Do you deem, Mr. Darcy, that there is no pure Good, no pure Paradise, no escape from Evil?"

"The accident to which I alluded would not, in the opinion of the creature, be an 'evil' but a good thing. And whereas you would not take it so, the earth would be grateful for the addition. At least, so it appears to me."

"And, by extension to a wider subject, what think you?"

"If you wish to be serious, I shall tell you what I *think* I think. Mind you, I may alter my opinion tomorrow. Today I think that our Maker has created Change as a constant factor. Where there is Change there will be gain for some and loss for others."

"Do you, then, not believe in pure Good?"

"How can I listen to Mozart, how can I look upon you, dear lady, and not believe in pure Good?"

She smiled. The very light transforms when she smiles. I was emboldened to make of her a request I have been wanting to propose for some time. Would she remove her bonnet? Preferably, would she vouchsafe to me this privilege? She moved toward me, lowered her eyes, lifted her chin, and waited demurely.

Her tresses! So alive, and deliciously fragrant with herbal fragrances to make one's heart sing. All restraint gave way, and I pressed my lips into that richness. I heard Joe Chifney's voice from long ago, "Never the body!" He should have warned against the locks!

It would all have started anew despite my resolution and promises to her mother, if I had not moved away in desperation and turned against the tree. She came behind and leaned her head against me, saying –

"Now we are *both* in danger from above. Perhaps you should return my bonnet."

I muttered into the tree, "I fear we are in danger from other directions. I had thought your tresses would be a safe retreat, but I know now that nothing is *outside the pale* where you are the subject. I would not and will not traduce my promise to your mother. You go home like a good girl. Here is your bonnet."

She hesitated.

"Go, Miss Elizabeth. I shall follow along."

"I shall do as you bid. If I am the cause of your travail I ask your pardon."

"Not you, my love. It is this damnably long courtship. Who do think you *sets* this period at such interminable lengths?"

"I dare say it must be the seamstresses."

And so saying, she left.

***

18 November, 1812 Longbourn

How fortunate it is that Charles and I must ride back from Longbourn, whatever the hour. It gets more and more difficult to tear ourselves away, and we are in rum shape when we do. The ride is a tonic, and does help one to fall asleep. At least our horses can be content in their warm stalls with their good blankets. I rise when I awaken, light my candle, and I pace. How many miles I wonder?

This evening with Elizabeth was glorious, a clear sky and a moon of blazing silver. The air was strangely warm. (Who looks after the clime? God? Angels? Unknown forces? Whosoever must love lovers.)

After dinner we four excused ourselves and went into the garden to "take a turn." Of course, we soon separated. Charles and Jane drifted off to a wooded copse. One could hear low voices and occasional laughter, with increasingly long silences. How could I have been so wrong? They are deeply in love and Charles is his old enthusiastic self. How I missed that brightness of his during our idiotic London "romp."

Elizabeth and I walked to the top of a hill. Was she warm enough? Yes. I commenced to trace the constellations for her, and drew her close, her head leaning back against my shoulder. As we were watching the sky we were treated to a shower of falling stars.

"A good omen, my dear." She replied that she had often come to this hill at night, but had never seen such a generous display.

"Did you ever want for a man's arms around you as you stood here?"

"I wanted for something more than that which I had, but I knew not what it could be."

"I hope this is the answer." I turned her around to me, studied her face, luminous in the moonlight, and had just moved to kiss her when we heard Mrs. Bennet calling her name. It floated through the air sounding *almost* sweet, since it *is* my beloved's name. Elizabeth was looking at me with such an expression as almost stole my heart from me, and I sensed that she would not answer.

"ELIZABETH!" (Not so dulcet this time.)

"Answer your mother, my sweet."

She sighed, returned the summons and was ordered to come in "on the instant." Elizabeth gave me a rueful smile;

"I wonder how many ladies accept marriage simply in order to lead their own lives."

"And is this *your* reason?"

"Indeed it is. There will be no more orders to obey, and if there are, I shall not do so."

"Surely you jest."

"Surely I do *not*."

You may be sure, D., that of a sudden I faced a pottle of questions. I cannot be certain, but it seems that she must have read my thoughts, for now she laughed merrily, and told me not to worry, that she would be a dutiful wife. As, apparently, I looked relieved, she laughed again, and added, "To a point."

I decided the only thing for it was to kiss her, started to do so, was stopped short by another "ELIZABETH! THIS INSTANT!" Lucky at that. Another second and I might very well have shocked my lady with my need for her. Strange; her very *contrariety* arouses me.

When we entered the house she was chided. She was furious. "Why do you call *me* and not Jane? Why do you single *us* out?"

"I *trust* your sister and Mr. Bingley."

Elizabeth gasped. I asked, "You trust Charles and not *me*, nor this obedient daughter of yours?"

The lady was unable to answer for a moment. It was as if, in her fury, she had forgot my presence. Then she said, "I was young myself, Mr. Darcy, and I know how these things might go."

"Perhaps, Mrs. Bennet, you did not trust *yourself.* There is no call to judge your daughter by the same model."

Elizabeth's eyes widened and she looked at her mother as if for the first time.

Mrs. Bennet blushed, became speechless, and fumbled for her fichu – I felt a sudden fondness for her, took both her hands, looked square at her and smiled. She returned same, tremulously, and fled the room.

From the daughter I received such a look and such a radiance as I shall remember all my life.

Now came Miss Jane and Charles. Miss Jane inquired for her mother. Elizabeth replied;

"She has gone to her room in order to reread her memoirs."

I laughed aloud at this statement. My lady looked at me with delight.

Time to say our good nights. Charles gave me a significant look. I knew full well what this communiqué intended. Now there could be *unchaperoned* good nights exchanged.

I pulled Elizabeth into the drawing room and suggested a good night kiss.

"Must you request permission?"

"I was afraid."

"Afraid?"

"Afraid lest I offend you."

"You would offend me if you did *not* ask."

"Well, then. We shall assay a gentle, friendly kiss. Close your eyes."

She did. I tried to behave as I had announced. Foolish notion! The minute our lips touched my hunger for her took hold. Was she shocked? I think not.

When I released her it was clear that she was shaken. I tried to bid her good night.

"No! Do not leave, Darcy! What shall we do?

"Do not tempt me too far, Elizabeth."

"Yes! No! Let us run away tonight. Tonight!"

I held her away from me; "Would you then emulate your sister Lydia?"

She gasped, sat down abruptly onto a side chair and then she laughed.

"Thank you, sir. And good night, my dearest. I dare say you are worth the wait."

I put my hand on the latch, feasting my eyes on one last look. She had risen and stood in the door to the salon, the candlelight behind her, silhouetting her body.

Charles joined me, we gave one another a knowing look, and ran for our steeds.

⚜

23 NOVEMBER, 1812 LONGBOURN

We have attended a hastily improvised celebration for Elizabeth's birthday. All guests quickly expelled, including the bridegrooms, despite our protests. I vowed to my lady that next year we shall arrange a true gala for her.

Yesterday we could not see our ladies at all.

This day we have had our last "family dinner." Now we cannot see our brides until we meet at the altar. A ridiculous convention. What is to be feared? That we might reconsider? *Not likely!*

The "temper" at dinner has quite changed as the days have drawn down. I remember the evening after I had requested Father Bennet's permission to marry his daughter. Constraint and rigidity. No longer. Now we two are as old friends. As for my future mother-in-law, enough surprises have been handed the lady as to have shocked her into a different quiddity. She no longer dominates the conversational drift. Mr. Bennet and the young people are in charge. Conversations with him are particularly lively. This, of course, galvanizes my Elizabeth, and she enters in with flashing eyes and high spirits. Mary, too, is a welcome part of the mixture, so fetching in her solemn high-mindedness. Tonight she was embarked on one of her grandiloquences when Elizabeth told her she was monopolizing the discourse and that she should be quiet and listen. I reprimanded Elizabeth that she herself had not been interrupted, and should allow Mary the same courtesy. Elizabeth apologized immediately, and then thanked me for the rebuke, which she acknowledged was well deserved. I looked at Mary; her small smile of gratitude warmed my heart.

Although the "waters" certainly were not disturbed by this unimportant tiff, Mrs. Bennet looked fearfully at both of us, actually blanched, and seemed certain that this interchange spelled the end of our engagement. Not even after Elizabeth turned to me and gave me a radiant smile, and I took her hand and kissed it. What thought Mrs. B.? That a spat with my lady would end my intentions?

As dinner concluded and it was announced that the evening must end, I requested leave for a few more moments, as Charles and I had a few "trinkets" to hand round. We excused ourselves, went to the entry whence we had removed our saddle bags. We each had a gift for our fiancée, and a special one for Mrs. Bennet, with thanks for her unstinting and unsurpassed hospitality. These were not trinkets. These were gifts of jewelry which had belonged to our mothers. Mrs. Bennet's gift proved to be an amethyst brooch from Charles, and an amethyst necklace from me. She was well nigh speechless (in regards to her, this was a record evening in all respects!)

When Elizabeth took her gift from its leather pouch, my mother's pearls, she seemed almost bewildered, put her hand to her mouth, looked at me, but spoke not a word. Mrs. Bennet could not be contained; "What have you, Elizabeth. Show us!" Still, she moved not. I went to her, removed the gift from the pouch, and placed the pearls upon her. The reaction in the room was potent, but nothing compared to mine. If there had not been others to witness, D., I would have knelt to her, in all her majesty.

Time froze for a moment. Elizabeth looked at me with such a look, still voiceless. Then, there in front of such an audience, she stood, reached up to me and kissed me on the brow.

The shocked silence which followed was quickly covered with a babble of voices and shrill comments on the gifts. The diamond bracelet given to Miss Jane was admired, Mrs. Bennet paraded to all her amethyst "wardrobe." We passed around trinkets for the servants, who have been so kind to us. And finally, good nights were exchanged. I had hoped beyond hope that Elizabeth and I might be left alone, but this was not granted.

A day and a half more! Shall we say that the bridegroom is ready.

❦

25 November, 1812 Pemberley

The last time I attended a wedding it was in London, and a most disagreeable event in every respect. Not this! This was *my* wedding, and to the woman I have craved for a desolation of months. The church was full to overflowing. The anticipatory mood could be felt. Rustling, whispering, exclamations as the various principals arrived. When first Charles and I entered there was a sudden silence. I took a deep breath, tried to still my pounding heart, looked around for a brief second and espied Signor Luigi with a handsome lady whom I assumed to be his wife. My instructor was all smiles. He knows me only too well.

I did not look to see if my Aunt Catherine were present. I knew she would not attend. Nor cousin Anne.

We took our positions. Charles and I kept our eyes fastened straight ahead, stood at the altar, stiff as dragoons, facing the Minister. When the organ music *seguéd* into the wedding music I was not sure that I would be able to turn. And when I did, I paid no heed to Charles' hand on my sleeve, but shook him off and strode to Miss Elizabeth. Gasps from the congregants. I did not know I would do this, but found myself at her side before I knew I had done it. Wry smile from Father Bennet. Jane, who was on his other arm, was obviously startled.

Sporting chap, Mr. B. He handed Miss Elizabeth over to me with bravura, first giving her a long and tender kiss on the brow. She was a vision. One could not escape knowing that she was amused at my breach of decorum. One could not escape knowing how ravishing she looked.

I led her to the altar. Charles did quite the right thing, remaining in position until Mr. Bennet and Miss Jane approached. He received her with the broadest happiest smile I have ever seen. Mr. Bennet stepped away and took his seat. The minister began.

I stole another look at my lady. She was wearing the pearls I had given her. A simple headdress, a graceful gown. Some words more (did I say *some*? The sermon went on and on and on) and she would be mine, to have and to hold . . .

The ceremony concluded (ask me not what the minister was saying) we stood for congratulations; hordes of well wishers from town and country, farm and village. I remember the Collinses, she with a set expression, he scraping and fidgeting and trying to make excuses for my missing aunt; various Bingleys, Miss Caroline sour indeed. A fond farewell to Mr. Bennet, a kiss to Mrs. Bennet which silenced her for a moment, but not for long. She was literally abuzz with joy. When would she see us? Soon, she hoped. (Not on your life, Mother B.!) FINALLY we entered a barouche and waved our farewells to our cheering guests.

At this point the proper thing for a well mannered groom is to kiss the bride properly, primly, formally. I knew indeed the right form, but the strictures were of no use, and the moment she responded to my lips I was a man possessed.

Luckily the chaise went over a bump at this moment and jolted us both, so a return to sanity was in order and I sat back, as did she. I took her hand, peeled off the glove, kissed the glove, and then kissed her hand. Just to touch her skin was sufficient for a time. When I looked at her, her expression stopped my heart for a moment. I let go of her hand, "Lady! What am I to do? Shall I follow the strategy you used when we danced at Netherfield? Should we not discuss the weather, the landscape, how beautiful you look. Perhaps even the fact that we are married?"

She smiled ruefully, asked for the return of her glove, then told me that she loves the sound of my voice and it would matter not what I said, I should just keep talking to her.

As I was absorbing the impact of this fine compliment she added, "There were so few words from you for so many months."

There was no answering this except with a look. She laughed, held my hand to her cheek, (so soft!).

By now we had come to the clearing where my large coach awaited us. Her luggage was already in place. I handed her in, and off we went.

Privacy at last! "Permission to kiss the bride?" I drew her to me . . . I cannot describe the rush of feeling that overtook me. Well nigh unbearable, and apparently for her too.

I said, "This will not do. Our lackeys can see in. I shall not reach for you again until we are truly safely alone. At such time I promise you naught."

She smiled demurely and suggested that polite conversation was indeed in order, and when did I discover that I loved her. Or was it presumptuous to assume that I did love her?

"My dear. I have deeply considered the matter, and deem that indeed I am in love with you. How long this will endure will depend entirely upon your good behavior. And what say you of yourself in regards to me?"

"As for myself, Mr. Darcy, I have prepared a syllabus of requirements which I expect to be fulfilled by my husband, and which I shall take very seriously."

This became a fruitful subject for exploration and we thus occupied ourselves until dusk. As the light waned I noted that she must be cold.

"Do you have a coat, Mrs. Darcy?" (How good that sounded!)

She told me that she did.

"Where is it?"

"In the bottom of my largest valise, I believe."

"At the very bottom of the stack on top of the carriage, yes?"

She agreed this must be so.

"How very sensible. Here, take mine."

And suiting the will to the deed, I placed it around her shoulders, against her strong remonstrances. Finally I said "Hush!" and buttoned the coat around her. Her eyes widened, she rubbed her cheek against the collar and thanked me sweetly.

"Mr. Darcy, the coat feels so warm. Will not you be cold now?"

"Not if you stay close to me."

"That, I believe, will not be a hardship, – I am sleepy. Would it be rude if I were to nap?"

"Not rude. Sensible." My thoughts were tumbling about rapidly. How best to accommodate her? What I would have liked in the most ardent way was that we should both stretch out on the carriage seat, head to head, but I quickly abandoned the idea. I then bethought that she could lie with her head in my lap, and immediately abandoned that plan as sheer unmitigated folly. I to lie down on the floor at her feet? Humbling yes, but not a problem that could not be overcome by a man so much in love. But the thought of the grinding bumps and the cold coming through the carpet ended the plan.

In the end I leaned against the side of the carriage, pulled her to me, (she moved to me so sweetly!) and told her to put her head on my shoulder.

"So much for this," said she, removing her headdress, then moved even closer, so that I could feel the slender strength of her, and laid her head on my shoulder. I may have murmured something like "Happy dreams." I remember not. I only remember the overwhelming thrill of it. I, drinking in deeply the scent of her, the lavender, the fragrance of her sun-blessed hair, the movement of her breathing . . . and then I drifted off too.

I had determined that it would be felicitous to break our trip by staying overnight at the Inn at K. Had arranged for dinner in the suite, for the requisite amount of flowers in the rooms, and – of course – roaring fires in all the grates. When we arrived there was a slight tussle over my coat. I would not take it from her. I told her that we would retrieve hers when the men and the horses had been attended to. She entered, still wearing it.

Somehow the inn did not look the same. To be sure, neither was I. My last visit had occurred not long in the past, but an eternity of change had occurred in every direction and one could not *expect* things to look the same. In view of my elevated mood – however – the environment should have looked *more* inviting, not less.

Learned that the Innkeeper's wife had died some few months past. Our host seemed harried and ill at ease. I expressed my condolence, then asked to inspect our quarters before I would take Elizabeth to them.

My intuition was correct. Nothing was right. Bath facilities? "We would be more comfortable down the hall . . . " An impossibility. What had happened to the bath? "Converted to an extra room." Impossible! Now I insisted that he uncover the bed. He hesitated, but when I moved to throw back the covers myself, he complied. It was all too clear that we could not stay here!

I ran down the narrow winding stairs to break the news to my bride. I was furious, but she, after listening carefully, managed to quiet me.

"Order some wine, Mr. Darcy, and let us toast our long ride on to Pemberley. How long will the horses require in order to be watered, fed, and rested?"

I let out a long sigh of relief, breathed a fervent "Bless you!" and hastened to arrange it. When I returned she was holding a goblet by the stem, handed me mine, and said, "I am happy for this, although I dare say that there will be consternation when we arrive so far in advance."

"Good lord, Elizabeth! I must see to our dinner."

"A toast, Mr. Darcy. I have been assured that dinner will be served shortly."

"The grooms. The coachmen?"

"Attended to."

I sank down onto a bench opposite her, relieved and grateful to have it settled. Toasted her, tossed it down in one long gulp, set the goblet down, and reached for her hand, looking long and hard at her. "Miss Bennet, will you marry me? I dare say you will be the perfect wife." She smiled that radiant smile of hers, "We have done that also."

Dinner arrived, throughout which we discussed the ceremony, the guests, the sermon (which neither could recollect), and other pleasantries.

When we left I quietly passed to the Innkeeper an extra "token" to ensure a proper headstone for his wife. How unlucky are some! How lucky are others!

Exited, a dramatic scene of torches and racing figures, the carriage awaiting. A loud "Giddap!", sounds of snorts and rolling wheels, on to Pemberley! I clapped my hand to my brow.

"What is it, dear sir?"

"Your coat! It is still at the bottom of the largest valise, at the bottom of the pile, on top of the carriage!"

26 NOVEMBER, 1812 PEMBERLEY

It was very late when finally we entered the Pemberley gates. The place was drenched in moonlight. I awakened Elizabeth gently. She roused, smiled at me, looked out and whispered, "How beautiful it is! How lucky I feel!"

How lucky she felt? How thinkest thou it went with me?

As the house emerged to view, one could see flickers of light appearing successively in the windows, and figures hurrying to them. I leapt from the carriage and swept up my lady before she could set foot on the ground. "I vowed to carry you over the threshold, and I insist on doing that." She struggled but briefly. The front door opened. Mrs. Reynolds stood there; "Bless me, Mr. Darcy! What a surprise you have handed us!" I set down Elizabeth, and introduced her.

"Lord, Mrs. Darcy, what a pleasure it is to see you again, and now as my mistress!" I began to introduce her to the others, of whom there were increasing numbers, all running in breathlessly, still adjusting various pieces of livery.

Elizabeth stood there, still wearing my coat. I, usually so precisely dressed, was without coat. I much doubt that any one of the staff has ever seen the master of Pemberley (father or son) in shirtsleeves when inside the house. Now there was a dead silence. Finally I recovered my voice and said, "Ladies and gentlemen. I bring you a new mistress to Pemberley. May I introduce Mrs. Henry Fitzwilliam Darcy."

A great cheer went up, and now there was nothing for it but to introduce my bride to each and every one. In the meantime the luggage was being brought in by the footmen, and being directed upstairs.

I had determined I would carry my lady up the stairs in my arms, and had so told her. This assemblage was not going to impede that promise. The introductions concluded, I gathered her up, against her protest, and started the ascent.

Another cheer went up from those crowded below. Elizabeth laughed low and told me not to turn my head but that we were being followed by three of the staff.

Next we met the footmen, *descending*. I murmured each name as we passed. Each bowed, trying to keep his glance averted.

My heart was hammering, but 'twas not because of the delightful weight I was bearing. How long would it be before I could end my bondage and be alone with her? I set her down at the door, and opened it. Our followers entered with us.

The chambers looked magnificent. Glowing fires had warmed the rooms (and looked most tempting!) There were flowers everywhere. "May I stay to assist the mistress?" inquired Mrs. Reynolds. My heart sank.

"I think not," said E. softly. "And I do believe that Mr. Darcy shall not have need of Edward."

Should Rose remain to help the madam? Should the valises be brought in? Would we like this? Would we care for this?

E., bless her, requested the smallest of her valises, professed most gracious thanks, and led the invaders to the door.

Thus, the reception was officially ended, with the master of Pemberley still standing silent. I was, in fact, backed up against the wall, a frozen witling.

Elizabeth closed the door and leaned against it. Still I could not move. If it were thus in fencing, D., I would be a dead man!

I managed to say, "I thank you. I fear I was not of much help just now."

She smiled and acknowledged my thanks, but seemed too shy to say more.

I came to my senses; "I shall take one step if you will do the same."

She did. She looked as if she were about to faint.

I said, "Do not be afraid."

"I am not afraid, sir. But do you suppose we shall still be standing here in a month's time, covered with cobwebs?"

"I very much doubt it." But still I moved not – I could not.

Then suddenly she called out my name, we both stepped forward, and as I felt the length of her against me, I let out a great groan of relief and bliss. The strange spell was ended.

I have never known such joy as I then experienced. I did not know it to be possible. During the night I must have called out her name a hundred times. It came with a torrent of words of love of which I cannot believe myself capable. Do I remember at which point Elizabeth became "Lizzy," when all the moments were so marvelous and overpowering?

In the middle of this night (morning?) I felt her stir, turned into her and gathered her into my arms. She comes so willingly! It is almost as if she melts into my craving self.

Her hair was marvelously disarranged and I took pleasure in pushing it away from her face. I paid especial attention to her ears, so dainty and exquisitely formed. I murmured something to that effect, and she replied, "I dare say they are tolerable."

Ensued a scuffle, and I need not detail where that was leading, until she called out my name, which halted me. She opened her eyes, and said, "I am hungry! Is there no food at Pemberley?"

Woman!! Has there ever been one like this one? I very much doubt it.

Told her that indeed it could be arranged from time to time. It just so happened that a repast may have been set for us in the sitting room. She slid out of the bed, reached for her dressing gown, which – of course – was not unpacked, spotted my coat, put it on and begged me to escort her to the place.

The scattering of clothes on the floor was notable. She stooped to gather them. I retrieved and held up the wedding dress and remarked that someday when I had the time to spare I intended to count the buttons at the back. How many did she reckon? I was recalling words between us when the buttons had become a *cause celèbre*. I had asked how had she got herself *into* the dress, and her answer had been that she did not recall, but that several had helped her. I had threatened to tear her free, but she had pleaded to save the dress for her sisters. It had been a crucial moment indeed, and when she started to laugh at the ridiculous situation we were both in, I had feared that she would be in no mood to match mine.

How wrong I was! Within minutes she had pulled her waist in, turned the dress around and had undulated out of it. As her body emerged from the folds of the dress and all the rest that went with it, I almost fell to my knees. It was then that she came into my arms and I could feel the *all* of her incredible loveliness. (As I write I am still wondering how these women manage to conceal from us the true lines of their bodies.)

"And then?" you ask. *Eventually* we came into my sitting room and indeed found a table set with an array of dishes to please a monarch. E. remarked that the scene made her feel that she was in *The Arabian Nights*. I pulled out her chair, seated her, sat down opposite and raised my goblet to toast the new mistress of Pemberley. It seemed wonderful and *right* to have her sitting there opposite me. I told her so. She liked that well.

We had much to talk about until she remarked on my laughter and said how good it sounded to hear. She wanted to know why had I always been so solemn.

"I am not now. Is that enough of an answer?" She gave me a searching look and then said, "I shall love you in all your moods."

My reaction to this remark took me by surprise. In one quick move I went to the floor and to her, and put my head in her lap, hugging her close, so moved I could say not a word.

She put her hand on my head, there was a long silence. Then she began to sing softly, low; airs I had never heard. I asked her what they were. She replied that they were airs her mother used to sing to her when she was little, probably Old English folk songs – did no one sing airs to me?

"Maybe Reynolds did. I recall not."

We were both silent. Then she began again. Such a suffusion of peace and blissfulness!

I know now, D., that there is indeed a heaven. I also know that there are angels here on earth.

It is dawn. My bride will be sleeping peacefully for quite some time, I dare say. I look over and I see her recumbent form under the froth of fresh embroidered linens and damask. Elizabeth Bennet! In my very own bed! Is it not strange, D., that I have never, until now, slept the night out with a lady. The bed – such a deep and private place, and your friend Darcy – such a private man. And there she lies, and it has felt to me, all the hours of the night (morning, to be exact) as if this is her destined place.

LATER

Elizabeth rose from the bed, which move awakened me on the instant. She asked me if I would direct her to the linen closet, a strange request and I asked her to explain. She was most unwilling to answer, but finally whispered to me that she was bleeding.

"I know where the closet is. What may I bring?"

"Sheets and towels. Here, here is the candle."

"No need."

"No need? It is ink dark."

"I know the way in the dark."

"How is that possible?"

"I used to hide there." And I dashed from the room.

As I was frantically pulling forth great piles of linens, I saw candlelight approaching. This proved to be Mrs. Reynolds who inquired about my dead-of-night mission. I told her as tactfully as I could manage that Mrs. Darcy (how well I like to say that!) was in trouble.

Relieving me of my burden, she suggested that I wait some moments before returning to the room. "Women know well how to handle these things, Mr. Darcy. Please do not worry yourself." She patted my hand. "She will be quite fine, Sir. We of the staff are most content with our new mistress, and may I say again, we wish you great happiness."

And off she went to my chambers, like a frigate in a fierce wind.

Elizabeth was resting comfortably when I returned to her. I could scarce speak, as I was overcome with a heavy sense of my own beastliness. I sat on the bed. "This is all my fault. I feel I have started off our marriage by treating you most unhandsomely."

"Darcy, enough! This is a most normal thing and I will hear no more about it. If you will just lift up your hanging head and tell me why you had to hide, and from whom, I will be most content."

"That was a very long time ago. I do not rightly recollect. Just tell me that you are all right."

She reassured me she was well, but murmured, "Nevertheless —"

I told her that I understood full well, gathered to myself the entire bundle of herself, until she fell asleep, and then I moved to write to you.

It is raining; a soft steady murmur; the roof gutters are commencing to warble with the waters' slow coursing down the sides of the house. Not so long ago such night sounds would have made me disconsolate through and through. Not tonight! This night I feel enfolded in something of tenderness and dearness which permeates not only me, but the entire world.

Bonne nuit!

⚜

27 NOVEMBER, 1812 PEMBERLEY

I fall to sleep with Elizabeth close to me, but it is not long before I awaken in torment for want of her, so I rise, and thus I commune with you at length, D. Your gain is because of my loss.

The rain has ceased and I am tempted to go to the lake, but am afraid she will awaken and be disturbed by my absence. I could not very well leave a note saying "Have gone to the lake for a swim."

And supposing she should come to the lake, the thought of her trying to find her way through the woods is dismaying indeed.

I care not for confidences, D. Such thoughts as I would be conveying are the very thoughts that would put me to worse *douleur*. Rest your pages. I shall read.

What goes through my mind? Thoughts about the delicacy of a woman's body, the strength of the male's. One must learn to balance this divergence. What says the Bible of this? Perhaps only the serpent understood?

⚜

28 NOVEMBER, 1812 PEMBERLEY

The sun was high when we awakened. The day felt fresh and new. E's hair was spread in marvelous dark waves over the pillow. I said, "Lie quietly, I would talk with thee."

"You will tell me why you hid in the linen closet!?"

"No. It is about our wedding night. When first we entered this room, so handsomely escorted, I went suddenly from fire to ice. I could not fathom such a lapse, but I know now I had realized of a sudden that I had been thinking only of myself and of my desire for you. I began to think of *you*, and later events only make this more urgent. You had said you were not afraid, but I was thinking then what would I be doing to you, you the innocent and uninformed and untutored, what would I be doing to you – and later I had to ask, "what *did* I do to you?"

"Mr. Darcy, you did nothing amiss. I am fine this morning. Should you be penitent because you are the first? And the only?"

I was moved, and bent to kiss her. She held me away.

"I needs must protest your assumption. I am not exactly 'untutored.'

"Your mother instr –?"

"Never mind my mother, I have lived near farms all my life. And of late I have had a most diligent teacher."

"A teacher?"

"You are forgetting that Lydia made her way home to be at our wedding. A seasoned, married lady, very eager to share her memoirs. I protested vigorously, but she insisted, insisted on telling all that transpires in the nuptial chamber. *ALL!* I covered my ears, but I heard. I tried, but I could not escape from her telling."

D., my reaction surprised us both. I laughed out loud. A rascal for a mate, and *I*. I, Fitzwilliam Darcy, now blessing Lydia Bennet, blessing the black sheep of the family!

When my laughter subsided I inquired if she were all right.

"I feel better than all right." She held out her arms to me.

"Elizabeth! Pray do not torment me with that which must be denied me."

"Nevertheless, dear Darcy, 'nevertheless' can safely be forgot."

It took me but a moment to realize the impact of this. I laced my fingers through hers, pulled her to me . . .

29 November, 1812 Pemberley

Last night I was on the very verge of slumber when Elizabeth said, "How could you have got like *that* when you are truly like *this?*

"Woman, I am asleep."

"It is so strange. You are still grave and mysterious and commanding and quintessentially noble, but I now know you to be sensitive, warm, most amiable, and with a delightful sense of humor."

I was by now fully awake.

"How could I have got like 'THAT'? What mean you by 'that'?"

"Oh, Darcy! You were perfectly miserable, and you made everyone around you miserable too."

"Everyone?"

"Well, almost everyone."

"I know not."

She now went to sleep, but by now I was hopelessly awake and rose to share this with you.

Sense of humor, eh? Nice to hear! Miserable to people? I know that often I discomfit some. My glance does seem to have a strong effect. Perhaps I am spared their foolish prying into matters which I care not to discuss.

Fiddle faddle! It is cold here, and warm and delicious next to my bride. I leave you.

30 November, 1812 Pemberley

I descended to the first floor today. Mrs. Reynolds greeted me. She inquired for Mrs. Darcy, and I informed her that my lady was taking her bath.

"And shall you be wanting to continue to take your meals upstairs, sir?"

I took her hand and looked at her straight, "I am being *rescued*, Mrs. Reynolds, right here at Pemberley."

She blushed scarlet. "I understand, Mr. Darcy. Just let us know when you wish to be served downstairs. But please, sir, take time to look into your study. There are some important missives, and reports for your consideration, piled almost to the ceiling."

She was quite correct, as usual. A blizzard of documents, neatly assorted. I rummaged through them, picked out a few which could not be ignored, took them with me and ran up the stairs. In the long hall I spied Elizabeth deep in conversation with Mr. Crowley, who stood hat in hand, with a long, long list. It seems they were discussing the spring vegetable garden.

I greeted him, he congratulated me. Elizabeth interjected, you must congratulate Mr. Crowley, Darcy. He is but ten days a grandfather to a fine little boy.

"Clive? A boy! Congratulations, Mr. Crowley."

"Indeed, Mr. Darcy. A fine little bairn. We have named him Norman for a relative who was mortally wounded during the Peninsular War."

"Was he with our fleet?"

"No sir. He went with the Spanish against Portugal."

Elizabeth rustled the pages he was holding, he apologized, and they resumed their planning. I listened to 'onions, sprouts, green beans, peas,' etcetera. I listened to 'parsley, rue, chervil, sage, bay leaf, mint, basil, hyssop.' Here, were she not so intense, I might have gone into Ophelia's chant as she floated to her death, but resisted. I had just moved to our door when she finished, thanked Mr. Crowley, and joined me.

"Planting in this weather?"

"No. Well, yes. We are discussing seeds, not plants."

"Have you had aught to eat, Elizabeth?" She reassured me that she had.

I closed our door. "Such a multitude of documents! I am in need of refreshment." Then I gathered her to me, lifted her, tossed her onto the foot of the bed. When she stopped laughing, she lay back. As I leaned down to her, my hair tumbled over my eyes. She brushed it back and for the first time saw the scar on my forehead.

She slid out from under me and sat up. "Darcy! What happened to you?"

I did not want to tell her the story of my mishap, but she persisted. This time she did not give way.

So I began to tell her of the melodrama of young Darcy and Bloody George. To my chagrin, the memory of that day returned with such an overpowering effect that I choked – such a dreadful sound. She pulled me to her and kissed my forehead most tenderly, so sweetly that something gave way, and I was of a sudden weeping in her arms. I was terrified that for this I would lose her respect.

I tore myself from her, ran to the window where I pressed my head to the pane, pounding my fists on the wall. I groaned that I was undone and knew that she could love me nevermore.

Suddenly I felt her hands on my shoulders, as she turned me around with surprising strength, and with eyes ablaze told me I was being foolish, that the contrary feeling was the case and that she was more in love, not less, for the event.

Such a redemption! I fell to my knees and buried my head against her. And lo! She sank down beside me and kissed me with an ardor I dare not describe.

I took her there on the floor. Neither of us could speak when we came to our senses. I carried her back to the bed, fell in beside her, and we slept close until I heard the supper being set for us in my sitting room.

This is for you, D. It is from *The Knight of Malta* by Beaumont and Fletcher –

"Of all the paths {that} lead to woman's love, Pity is the straightest . . . "

❦

1 December, 1812 Pemberley

Lizzie turned to me this night with a startling question, "Thinkest you that Jane feels what I feel when she is with (you know what I mean)," she lowered her eyes and blushed . . . "WITH Charles?"

What is a man to do? Again I laughed aloud. Then added that I of course could in no way give an answer, but that I doubted it, on the ground that Jane does not appear to be like her warm-blooded sister, and as for Charles – I told her I knew very little of Charles in such a role. Elizabeth commented, "I have always wondered what men talk about when they are in close converse. Apparently they will speak of indelicate subjects, but only on an impersonal level."

"And you, and your sister Jane?"

"Ask not, want not."

We lay back, her head on my shoulder. An owl hooted quite near, and was answered from the other side of the grove. There were some sleepy twitterings from the beech tree outside our window. Then silence. I began to think about the men in Elizabeth's life. My thoughts turned to the bowing and scraping and craven Collins. I remembered my introduction to him when he first sidled into my view and attempted to ingratiate himself with references to my aunt. I started to chuckle as I remembered his look as I rose to accept the introduction in my coldest possible manner, how I must have seemed to loom ever higher leaving him to stare up in surprise.

As I thought of his overtures to Elizabeth I had to laugh aloud. What a combination! Elizabeth queried as to the cause of my amusement.

"What I *want* to say is, what think you is the quality of the evening when Charlotte is 'with' cousin William Collins?"

Lizzie sat straight up and gasped. I liked my lead and went on, "I can fairly hear him." I imitated his voice, "My dear, would it offend you if I placed my hand on your inner thigh – here? – Perhaps here? – You are certain you are not alarmed? – A little higher – Tell me if I insult you. – You are quite certain?"

By now Lizzie was fairly rocking with delight. I pulled her to me, "My hand here, my dearest love? Perhaps here?"

⁂

2 December, 1812 Pemberley

When I awakened this morning Lizzie was on her elbow staring at me. What a lovely introduction to the day!

She greeted me, "Good morning, Mr. Collins."

I asked her might she not have preferred the good gentleman in my place. She replied that she had thought it over, and concluded that I would suffice. She then said, "Darcy, you are such a fine mimic. You were indeed, in every gesture and in every intonation, Mr. Collins himself. Yet, you did never participate in the charade games at Netherfield, you have not played the mime before – I do wonder why."

I brushed the question aside with murmurs of modest protest. Why did I choose not to tell her about my splendid short-lived career? Perhaps I shall someday.

⁂

3 December, 1812 Pemberley

This is the morning we descended for breakfast. At the head of the stairs Elizabeth remarked that her legs felt "funny."

"Must I then carry you *down*?"

"No. A jest." Then she added, "It will be nice to see Pemberley by daylight."

"Are you regretting –?"

"Indeed not, sir. Certainly *not*, sir!

Mrs. Reynolds was in the hall below. She espied us and ran quickly into the kitchens, where one could hear a great scurrying and commotion. When we entered the breakfast room she gave a deep curtsy and said, "We welcome you most heartily to the first floor, Mrs. Darcy."

Bless Elizabeth. Although she was blushing, she answered most promptly, "I thank you, Mrs. Reynolds. I am eager to have a second tour of the galleries with you as my guide."

Reynolds expressed her delight, then informed me that there were again matters for my most urgent attention towering high on my desk.

Thither I went after our meal, to find that Reynolds was not exaggerating. Went at it, eager to be done with it.

A brigade of servants was dispatched upstairs to attend to our rooms and to attend to E.'s valises.

Lizzie and Mrs. R. did the rounds, including, I presume, the galleries. Then apparently disappeared to the upper regions, for they were nowhere in the lower part of the house when I went to find her. Did so in our chambers. The two were in her boudoir, intent on the major chore of unpacking various objects of baggage.

"Ah, there you are. There is an invitation here from a Mr. Keith with whom I would have important dealings. It is for dinner this week. He says it is just a small gathering and he and Mrs. Keith would be honored to meet the new mistress of Pemberley. I would like to accept."

"Perhaps we should have gone to Italy after all!"

"Just a small dinner, my love, and we will certainly be home early."

❧

4 December, 1812 Pemberley

Last night I gazed at Elizabeth with unconcealed adoration and said, "I am besotted with you!"

"Bravura word! Where might we find Johnson's Dictionary?"

"Across the room." I fetched it for her and read – "Besotted" – silly, foolish, infatuated, stupefied as with liquor."

"I like 'infatuated.' As for the rest, they flatter neither one of us."

" 'Infatuated' is the word I intended. The others are off the mark."

"When first we met what were you feeling?"

"I cannot say. I have told you 'ere this that I was into it before I knew I had begun."

'If you were 'into it,' as you say, what were you feeling when you were so silent and remote?"

"Fascinated, and somewhat 'besotted.'"

"'Somewhat'! Why 'somewhat?'"

"Because I could not *truly* get to that feeling until I was able to do with you what so happily we do now."

I like to watch her blush. The color starts at the place between her breasts which so attracts me, spreads upwards through her throat and suffuses her dear face to the roots of her hair.

"Nevertheless, how was one to account for your *gloominess?*"

"That, Madam, calls for no response." I extinguished the candle.

I was just falling off when she inquired into the night, "I do not understand. If it is so very special and important to be of the gentry, why isn't one happy and cheerful when so endowed? I thank our good Lord that the Bennets were never so privileged!" And so saying she (at last) fell to sleep.

※

5 DECEMBER, 1812 PEMBERLEY

What a derangement this evening proved to be! The Keith party proved to be no "small affair" but a formal evening, with the ladies glitteringly bedecked, the dinner a banquet of two main courses, preceded by a salad course, with dessert as well, with an intermission after the first course whilst the servants removed the Worcester service and replaced it with Staffordshire. Discussion among the ladies regarding the relative merits of the porcelains. That is, except for my wife, who was sparking Captain Durward of the Household Cavalry to tell her of his exploits in protecting the Royal Family. I was afraid she would go too far, and indeed when she expressed dismay that Napoleon might invade all the way to London and make off with the Royals, I was sure the game was lost. Not so. The Captain swelled with pride and proceeded to invent all manner of derring do, while Elizabeth listened raptly. She was a success with this guest.

I am not so sure about the ladies. They commenced to scrutinize her, from the moment we entered, and when they were to be seen whispering behind their fans, one could be certain that the subject was not about recipes or children.

From one point of view my evening was a success. I was able to discuss a land trade with Mr. Keith which will be much to the advantage of Pemberley, and a happy conclusion for him.

The ladies were awaiting us in the drawing room when we had finished with the usual male ritual of port and cigars. Elizabeth was quiet, and I knew the ladies conversation must have seemed tedious to her.

Colonel Durward went full tilt toward her, and totally enveloped her in his enthusiasm. He drew her toward a place where there was a small Adams table with a burning taper upon it. With one wild gesticulation he knocked the candle from the holder and it fell upon Lizzy's shawl. He tried to brush the candle away, succeeded only in smearing her with the chocolate he was eating. The shawl caught, he fled, but his foot had caught in her dress and I heard a ripping sound as I was dashing to her side. I tore off my coat, smothered the flame in a trice, brushed her off, expected to find her discomposed. Instead, I could see that she was trying to stifle a burst of laughter. She motioned to me to bend down, and whispered in my ear, "God *indeed* save the Queen if Colonel Durward is to go to *her* rescue!"

By now the other guests had crowded around with a buzz of exclamations and praise for my quick thinking. Mrs. Keith offered to take Elizabeth upstairs to repair the damage, but the offer was rejected. The Captain was all apologies, and thereafter remarked in quintuplication that "Mrs. Darcy is such a grand sport. I almost set her afire, and she laughed in order to reassure me that no damage was done!"

We left as soon as we could manage it. On the ride home Elizabeth kept recalling the incident and breaking out afresh each time. Then she sobered and commented on my quick action in saving her from "suttee." "How is it that you know such deft tricks, my dearest?"

I told her of my training in the management of Pemberley affairs. "The laborers know how to manage these things, Elizabeth. One does well to learn from them."

"I am happy you learned so well, Mr. Darcy. I do believe you saved me from a possible disaster."

I stared at her a moment. Then I told her, "Elizabeth, I would go into the very jaws of hell for you."

No idle remark, D. I mean it.

⁂

6 December, 1812 Pemberley

Last night I wrote to you and was about to return to bed when E. awakened from her "soft" sleep. The moonlight was flooding into the room. I sat on the edge of the bed and quoted –

"'Soft stillness and the night/ become the touches of sweet harmony.' Guess who."

She ventured "Shakespeare?"

"Excellent. Now how about – 'The moon, Rising in clouded majesty, at length. Apparent queen, unveiled her peerless light. And o'er the dark her silver mantle threw –'"

"I know not. Who?"

"Milton. Perhaps that "peerless" could have been improved upon."

"You not only recite magnificently, but you are a critic too!"

"Thank you. Perhaps I could relieve the inane talk when I will be seated away from you at these endless dinners which we will have to attend. Perhaps I should just start declaiming –"

"I cannot think of many that would not deem you quite mad and would plan to have you put away!"

"This is about you, Lizzie – 'For of the soule, the bodie forme doth take. For soule is forme, and doth the bodie make.' I shall tell you who wrote it if you will do something for me."

"Thy slightest wish. Who wrote it?"

"Spenser. It is from *Epithalamion*. One wonders if he had not posed his mistress in just such a shaft of moonlight as is now in the middle of our chamber. And now for my slightest wish – I ask you to rise and go stand there in the moonlight."

Saying "gladly" she arose and went to the spot.

"And further, I ask you to remove your gown."

She gasped, then said, "Mr. Darcy! I cannot. All these years of training to be a most proper lady. I cannot do it. Besides, I shall be cold."

"I think not for very long. Did we not make a bargain?"

And as God may bless me, she *did.* Nor was she cold for long. What took possession of us both was what one might well term moon madness. In carrying her back to bed I murmured –

"Surely now you understand the meaning of 'besotted.'"

And now methinks she does indeed.

❦

7 DECEMBER, 1812 PEMBERLEY

A thunderbolt bulletin for you, D. I chuckle as I write the events of this day in the life of "infinite variety" of the Mistress of Pemberley, Mrs. Henry Fitzwilliam Darcy.

At breakfast I told my love that I was taking leave for a fencing lesson. She requested that she be allowed to accompany me to watch me in action. What could be more pleasant? Of course I invited her to join me, ordered the barouche for her, and soon we were off to the academy. It was a perfect day, brilliantly sunny but with a crispness in the air that made every breath a heady pleasure, leaving a taste akin to a vintage champagne.

The leaves, reds and ambers against the crackling blue sky, were a glorious sight. Champêtre felt my elation and did his dancing step as we rode beside the carriage.

It was apparent that E. felt the same exhilaration. She kept looking up to the *carnival* overhead and smiling with delight. When I handed her down from the carriage her face was aglow and I could not refrain from commenting on her rosy cheeks – and likewise her nose. Which (after this remark) I then felt obliged to kiss. When we looked up from one another, Luigi was standing at the door. He surveyed Elizabeth with a practiced eye, smiled and nodded to me, kissed her hand and told her how delighted he was to make her acquaintance.

I changed into my jacket and all, put on a mask (a lighter version these days, and I no longer resist.)

Did a few knee bends and other exercises, and we went to it. I was not in top form when we started. To say the least! The languid life of a full time honeymooner is not much conducive to athletic prowess in *the vertical* fields of endeavor.

However, I soon hit my stride and we went at the sport with relish and no end of bravura. It was clear that my spectator was fully enjoying herself. There were cries of approval, clapping, a series of gasps, and a final "Bravo!" all deeply satisfying.

I approached her, who greeted me with shining eyes. Would she could be there every time. What can be more of a spur to heroics than such an audience!

I put my arm around her shoulders, and turned to Luigi, who was studying the lovers with a broad smile.

"Surely, Mr. Darcy, this could not be the young lady who was causing you such *deep woe* the last time we fenced together?"

"Indeed it is she, Luigi."

Elizabeth was discomfited but reassured Luigi that our differences had been amicably settled. He assured her that this fact was more than clear.

She then proposed a most astonishing question – did he think that he could teach her to fence? We both gasped simultaneously, which caused a burst of merriment from her. Some bandying about the proper comportment for an English lady, some skirmishing between us, and then lo, she removed her cloak and bonnet, tied up her skirt, held out her hand for my foil. What could a gentleman do? I handed it to her (but not without hesitation.) What could the fencing master do? Shaking his head he went to fetch her a mask and whatever paddings he could find. He showed her how to hold the weapon. I placed the mask over her face. I shuddered. Where was Aunt Catherine?! Now I *really* needed her! She could have put my wife in her place.

Luigi held out his arm, true cavalier that he is, and escorted her to the floor, but not without a backward glance of sheer unbridled anxiety.

He showed my lady a few preliminary steps which soon she was exhibiting with facility.

She was splendid with the thrust, caused me panic with her parry. What could not be gainsaid was the grace of her movement and her deft footwork. Luigi now called a halt, wiped his brow and turned to me with an even more anguished look. Another dead silence, which Elizabeth broke with the expected but hoped against question – would he give her fencing lessons?

Into the silence which still pertained she sweetly said that they could confirm later, that she wished to discuss the matter with the lord of the manor. I gritted my teeth. *What a decision into which to be forced!*

When we returned to her carriage we stood in a long and earnest conference which (surprisingly) turned out to be not unpleasant. She was angelic about my problem with the decision, sensitive and considerate and preempted my confusion by saying we should sleep on the matter and she would accept whatever I ordained. I looked up and glimpsed Luigi peeping at us through the window. I had to laugh. I am certain that he, too, has never been placed into such a predicament.

Now, of course, E. wanted to know about Luigi's reference to the Darcy drama to which he had apparently been a party. I told her to hold off, I would tell her later.

You may be sure she did not forget to ask, and you may be sure, D., that since I had no desire to revive any memory of the dreadful days to which the incident appertains, I informed her that I had changed my mind. She gave me a beseeching look, but I held firm. Elizabeth does not coax (I love her for this.) (Should I say she does not coax *often.*)

Now I had achieved a position so that I could insist upon a compromise. She would take the lessons, but I would have modified for her and for Luigi, weapons which could not possibly inflict any harm upon her. I used the words upon "the form divine" which mollified her. And I made her laugh by adding "and for Luigi's safety also." We ended on the best of terms.

Do I dread the morrow? I think not. When I take her in my arms this lively woman melts like a dove. As for the fencing lessons? We shall see. We shall see.

❦

9 DECEMBER, 1812 PEMBERLEY

Last night Elizabeth told me that she had dreamed of me.

"Am I to be complimented or the reverse?"

" I cannot say. Dreams are so unreal. I dreamed you were as you were when first we met."

"Please spare me from going through that again!"

"It does seem that you are much improved."

"I cannot thank thee enough for such charity."

She studied me carefully. "Yes, you have the same thrust to your chin and your chin still has the same cleft – the same fine curl in your fine hair, the same blazing eyes, the same long, lean, graceful "figger" –

"You noticed *that*? *Then*? I am much complimented."

"In spite of myself – It was some weeks ago"

"When, to be exact?"

"I know to be exact. It was the day I was so humiliated to be discovered by you, when I was with my aunt and uncle who wanted to visit Pemberley. You came into view, soaking wet, carrying your boots. You were as startled as I. Your shirt was quite transparent, but before I averted my gaze I could not help but discern what a fine form was outlined against the linen. I believe it was at that very moment that my feelings for you took a very new turn. From that moment, good Mr. Darcy, I could think of naught but you, and I wept for fear that I had thrown away your feelings for me. But you had not —"

I was about to say that indeed I had not, but she ran her hands from under my arms to trace my ribs. The affect was electric indeed.

As you may imagine . . .

❦

11 December, 1812 Pemberley

Arose this a.m. to go fox-hunting with Meynell and a group which he had assembled. E. awoke, smiled adorably and suggested to me that I should take care of myself, that the sudden advent into the world might well be a shock to my system.

I could not get her out of my thoughts for much of the chase, and begged off early. Meynell suggested that he would come by with the *brush*, and I suggested that he not. He took me well, clapped me on the back and ordered me to give his regards to Mrs. Darcy.

When I entered our chambers I heard sounds from the inner room which indicated that E. had arranged for a bath.

I knocked.

Learning it was I, she asked me to wait. I heard a scrambling in the room, a hushed "where is my peignoir?" As I was about to offer to bring it to her, she exited, wearing my frock coat. One of the housemaids followed, bearing towels, and red as a beet.

I stammered a confused "good morning."

Elizabeth softly suggested to the girl that she should return later to remove the bath water. Poor girl. She knew not where to look!

E. ushered her to the door. The girl protested that she should leave through the back room. Elizabeth reassured her, handed her out and closed the door gently. My coat was trailing around her lovely ankles.

"Pray, return my coat!"

"It is mine. The penalty for leaving it last night. Moreover, it is the very coat which I wore almost the entire distance from Longbourn and I have grown most attached to it."

A struggle. I lifted her bodily like a sack of grain, headed for the bath whilst she pummeled my back with her fists. She vowed she would scream loud enough to bring up the entire staff, but of course did not.

I flung open the door, and slid her out of the coat into the bath. Trying uselessly to cover herself, she protested between gasps and efforts to dodge me, that she knew not of the manners of the upper classes, but that where she came from there was a code – I knelt and stopped her with a kiss. She threatened she would pull me in, I grabbed her wrists, assuring her of my undying respect and offered to soap her back.

Another tussle; by now I was half in the tub, half out, and she was rubbing soap in my hair. Since I was half in I used the opportunity to rinse my hair, managing to douse much of the soapy water over her luscious form. I then called for armistice, pulled her from the tub, tried to towel her dry – This was difficult, as she was convulsed with laughter, and by now so was I.

Finally I quieted down, and said, "What will the staff think when they see this flood on the floor?"

This started her all over again. Between gusts of mirth she added, "Do you think the water will seep to their ceiling? And imagine if the sounds of our great battle also floated through to them?"

Again peals of laughter. Again, too infectious to withstand.

It took battalions of servants a long time to clean the disorder we had created. In the meantime we sipped hot tea in front of our fire, drying our hair and waiting for them to be gone.

⸙

12 December, 1812 Pemberley

We have been much sought after since our nuptials. The affair at the Keiths' was noised about, and it seems everyone of consequence is eager to meet the new bride. Since that evening we have chosen to stay at home, but there was a dinner tonight at the Alexanders to which I had urged her, (and which we accepted.) Georgiana is with us, and I had learned that a young man would be present who might prove of interest to her, since he is a music student.

We gathered for the usual aperitifs in the salon. I introduced Elizabeth and Georgiana to various and sundry. Some we had met at the Keiths.' Mr. Clementi was introduced. Young chap, ill at ease, but with the proper manners.

Georgiana described to me what had transpired when the ladies had retired to the drawing room. Mrs. McIntyre, it seems, told Elizabeth that she had seen her in the village "gazing with rapt fascination into the window of the bookstore." Elizabeth had responded that indeed she had been there, and that she had seen Mrs. McIntyre gazing with equally rapt fascination into the window at the millinery shop. This inspired Mrs. McIntyre to many minutes of rhapsodic description of the several bonnets she had purchased.

Elizabeth interrupted this after some time by saying that she had bought a great many books, and asked whether the ladies would not want to hear the titles. Apparently not. They listened but a moment and returned to details of the trim on the bonnets, braid, lace, feathers, flowers –

Elizabeth had then remarked, "I fill my head with the magic and delight of books, Mrs. McIntyre, but I needs must do so one at a time. How fortunate that you, in one day, can don a succession of bonnets and at each change one can say 'What a magical and delightful bonnet, Mrs. McIntyre.' never noticing that there is nothing beneath it." Into the silence which followed this remark, (Georgiana insists they did not understand its meaning) Elizabeth had suggested that they speak of subjects even more interesting, and asked did they know that Georgiana had but recently returned from France where she had attended a reception *chez* Mme. Récamier, and had met a number of men and women famous in the arts and in politics.

Elizabeth interrupted. "This ended badly."

"How so?"

"I fear that in no time at all our dear ladies were clamoring for a description – here she broke into laughter and could say nothing for many moments – started again, again could not finish.

"Please, Elizabeth, finish the thought."

Finally she blurted out, "– a description of *the lady's attire!*," then buried her face in her hands and collapsed with it, joined by Georgiana, and shortly by myself.

Then she said, "Darcy, if you wish to be with others, do let us remain at home and invite them here. We could invite the young gentleman who took such an interest in talking with Georgiana. Jane and Charles are in the vicinity. Do let us have a small dinner at Pemberley!

"Indeed we shall."

And so to bed.

***

13 DECEMBER, 1812 PEMBERLEY

As Champêtre and I were wending homeward last evening, I was musing contentedly on the pleasures which awaited me at Pemberley – tea with Elizabeth in front of a cozy fire, reading the stack of correspondence, her droll comments on same, the amusing raillery on our way upstairs, the moment when we draw together – and then! I espied in the distance our large dray about to disappear over the brow of the hill.

This would be no cause for dismay except for the fact that I could discern that the dray was crowded with what appeared to be the entire staff of Pemberley. My first impulse was to go after them and learn what this could mean. I thought better of that, and instead galloped homeward in high passion. Stormed into the house, calling for Elizabeth, received no answer, shouted through all the living rooms and halls and galleries, then bethought me to search through the kitchens, calling, and by now thoroughly alarmed.

Then I heard her answering cry from somewhere deep in one of the pantries, traced this down, and discovered her with sleeves rolled up and her arms floured from elbow down. "What is going on? What nonsense have you contrived? How is it that the staff has deserted the manor?"

As my anger rose I began to hear Charles' voice saying (as he confessed to me), "I declare I do not know a more awful object than Darcy, on particular occasions."

I tried to bate my rage, could not, although I was realizing that as Mistress of Pemberley she is in full charge of the household.

Her reply? She said, "Do you remember our first dance at Netherfield?"

I roared at her, "And what has *that* to do with *this?*"

She put her hand on my arm, covering me with flour, tried to brush it off as she spoke, "You said to me something to the effect that 'you wished that I would not sketch your character at that moment, as there was reason to fear that the performance would reflect no credit on either of us.' I think this moment does *not* reflect credit on either of us, Sir. You have not asked me to explain why I gave the staff permission to leave today. You are angry. I am angry that you have not asked me to explain, and in one moment I shall either break into tears or I shall dump this bowl of batter over your head. I have not decided which course to take."

I looked at her with such incredulity - apparently - that of a sudden she burst into laughter. This did bring tears to her eyes, and in wiping them she smudged her face with flour. What could I do? I laughed.

"Here, Elizabeth, let me mop this adorable face." I tried, made matters worse. Finally she took the edge of her skirt and succeeded – more or less.

I told her I would listen, and I did. She explained to me that the Players were coming to the village, that she and Reynolds had determined that the staff had well earned a full day of pleasure and the release had been granted. Nielson would return at dusk to close the shutters and light the candles.

"And our dinner?"

"Would ambrosia and honey suit thee?"

"That is for the Gods."

"That is what you are to me."

How could I remain displeased? Besides, at every moment, as she was speaking, I was trying to quell the laughter which kept rising. She was, indeed, quite a sight.

She suggested that I tend to the post, saying that she had arranged for a dinner which we would partake in the clearing near the barn.

"And will it then be a *cold* dinner?"

"There is a bonfire ready to be lit. Never, as long as I live, would I *dare* serve the master a cold dinner."

"But it is cold outside. Do you forget that this is the month of December?"

"I have arranged for blankets. And it will be warm by the fire."

And that, indeed, is what we did, D. I was skeptical of the experience, but it turned out to be a rare delight. The bonfire looked more and more exciting as the night darkened. I actually enjoyed sitting on the ground.

To my surprise, (I had girded myself for a meager repast), we dined bountifully on breast of guinea hen, cooked to a delicious crisp; on fresh peas from our summer field, even potatoes baked directly in the fire. I had never tasted such and they were delicious. Equally good were the biscuits which she had prepared and toasted in a wire basket. Then bittersweet chocolate from Holland. She showed me how to break off a piece, place it inside a biscuit, and toast it in the fire. This was so hard to manage and yet so delicious that we ended by licking the melted chocolate from the basket.

She sang to me, we talked, we even fell asleep in the warmth of the blaze, contentedly together like children.

And so to bed. (How does one pen a contented *sigh?*)

17 DECEMBER, 1812 PEMBERLEY

This morning I suggested to Elizabeth at breakfast that I would like her to accompany me into the portrait gallery when we had finished. It was then that she told me of her gallery visit with Mrs. Reynolds back in August (how many years it now seems!) and of the many handsome things which Reynolds had said about 'the master.'

"To your great surprise, no doubt."

"I confess I was surprised, and I became much confused trying to rearrange my thoughts about you. Mrs. Reynolds was most insistent on ushering us upstairs to see the most recent portrait of you. As I studied it, my heart turned over. What had I been thinking, what had been told me that there could be two such discrepant views of the selfsame person!? Could I have been so entirely in error?"

"You in error? Is that possible?"

"Indeed I was, Sir. Even then I could not accept my feelings. I realize now that I was falling in love with you. What I *did* know *then* was that I had created a hopeless situation for myself."

"We shall have a portrait of you done soon, and it shall hang next to mine, and these two can settle their differences through the next many generations."

"I am most undeserving of such an honor, and I cannot let this offer stand."

"Perhaps I shall summon, then, a sculptor who can carve you in white marble. I can envisage a recumbent Elizabeth in long deep folded garments, her head thrown back, eyes closed, and such an expression on her face as I have seen on the few occasions when I have been able to open my own eyes."

"Fie!, Darcy. It sounds as if you would recreate me as St. Teresa!"

D.! I was thunderstruck. And in great confusion. Is it possible that she too had been on the Grand Tour? I much doubted that this could be so. Nevertheless *if* I asked her how she knew this, such a question might well lay myself open to the charge of being patronizing, a charge which had only too recently been leveled at me.

Elizabeth seemed to sense the source of my surprised silence. "Are you not going to ask how I have come to know of this statue?"

"Indeed, I did not *dare* ask it."

"Come, Darcy, you must show me where you would, in your imagination, put this imagined altar-piece. Meanwhile I shall tell you about the education I received from my father. He is an excellent critic, in addition to being well informed on many subjects."

As we moved towards the gallery I began to plan anew to have Mr. Bennet entirely to myself, and ascertain his various reactions to various works of art which have much preoccupied me these many years. Dare I ask him his reaction to the Bernini sculptures? Time will tell.

Several of the portraits in the gallery need to be cleaned. I pointed out to her the candidates for treatment, asked if she would work with Mrs. Reynolds on this problem.

"I shall look into it straightaway. Darcy? –"

"You have a question?"

"Please show me the portraits of your parents."

"Did not Reynolds show them to you recently?"

"I did not see them."

"They are down the line, in the proper order of succession." I took her arm.

"Should they not be upstairs with yours and Georgiana's?"

"No. They are down this corridor."

We walked, and there they were. Elizabeth stood quietly for a long time, then turned to me. I was studying my parents' faces. I know not what expression was on my own, but Elizabeth, who started to exclaim about mother's beauty, quieted suddenly, and said no more. I suggested to her that she enjoy the images and the skillful rendering of Mr. Joshua Reynolds, and please to excuse me, for I had work to finish. I left her there.

※

20 DECEMBER, 1812 PEMBERLEY

The holidays were happy, merry, bright – a great number of festive occasions (a good deal too many for my taste), a few days which enabled me to ride out. Time to work on the accounts, all entered carefully into the new ledgers.

Elizabeth has been toiling in the conservatory with Mr. Crowley, establishing all sorts of green exotica for the house, and culling seeds for spring planting. Our rooms upstairs are filled with bulletins detailing herbs, bulbs from Holland, roses, rhododendron, tree blight – name it! At night, when we are not being social, we often read upstairs, and she often sketches plans for 'the growing things.'

These are contenting nights – the crackling of the warm fire, the sound of my quill scratching away (not in regards to you, my sad friend. I have work of my own, involving the affairs of the estate and many of the shire proper. I seem to be needed as consultant on many matters.) And then there are the sounds of Elizabeth reading – the turning of pages, the low exclamations, the laughs.

Peace on earth!

※

5 MAY, 1813 PEMBERLEY

Charles has located an estate quite near ours, and thither we four traveled today. "Highlands," a handsome place, with splendid vistas, rambling hills, great vast meadows, stately woods, a find! The house is of red brick, early Georgian architecture, great rooms for entertaining and plenty of rooms upstairs for family. (We learned today that Miss Jane is expecting. Elizabeth's reaction was a wonderment. She fairly shone from head to foot.)

We drove up a long tree-lined drive, speculating as to just *how* long. The trees were just coming into that first fine film of new green. Once inside the empty mansion Charles and I dashed from end to end, from bottom to top, ending on the roof as we had long ago at Netherfield. The ladies were on the second floor and later told us that they could hear our feet on the roof, in spite of the intervening garret. I cannot say they were not discomposed; I cannot say they were not relieved to see us when we descended.

The garden is splendid; artificial ruins and various classical structures, including a temple which sits next to a lovely lake. "Lancelot Brown?" Charles studied his paper of specifications.

"Indeed! How knew you that?"

"Who knows? Possibly from a fop who escorted me through Europe and never stopped lecturing. Possibly from the many fine gardens of the many fine estates hereabouts."

Elizabeth suggested that Jane should be seated, and that we should take a rest in the temple. Miss Jane laughed, but was not too difficult to persuade, and we entered. As Elizabeth was about to seat herself on the circular bench, I pulled her back. "What?"

"Spiders."

"You and I have had dealings with spiders 'ere this." She smiled.

Jane asked, "Why is that amusing, Lizzie? I have a healthy respect for spiders. I know they are beneficial. You will never kill one, nor will I. But I do insist on maintaining a respectful distance. They do not seem to trouble you."

"Beg to differ. Your sister once implored me, a near total stranger, to remove one which was crawling downwards on her back. I believe it was that touch that caused me fall in love with her."

Jane demurely replied, "Mother was right. I am happy that I fell victim to the ague."

Now it was my turn to be perplexed. Elizabeth was laughing now and assured me that she would explain Jane's logic later.

Charles, by now, had concluded that this would be the place, and we heartily agreed.

As I am rereading the above, D., I realize that my wife indeed has not explained Miss Jane's remark. Nor will she. When I chided her for going back on a promise to tell, she reminded me of the many times when I have withheld, and claims to have learned the trick from me. 'Hoisted on my own petard,' I might add.

18 MAY, 1813 PEMBERLEY

Bathed and dressed this morning, and then awakened my sleeping beauty with a kiss. She opened her eyes and I said, "I have a mission and you must come with me."

She protested. I told her it was all settled and to get dressed. She sat up, stretched gloriously (tempting me to change all my plans at once,) but did not arise from bed. In one move I swept her out of it.

The carriage was waiting after our breakfast, and I hustled her into it. Our destination was a surprise, and I would not divulge. She rapped on the aperture in front and asked Gentry where we were going. He called back that he knew not.

Elizabeth laughed, "The man who is driving the horses knows not where to go!"

I told her that I had given the instruction to the horses. She was for once outwitted and settled back to enjoy the view. Trees a'bud with new lime green, so tender and bewitching. Sky, a clear Delft blue. Every bird in the shire singing full throated.

Soon we came to the village and went straight to my cobbler. As we approached, my tailor came from the other direction, his tape measure hanging from his bulky pockets. Elizabeth was (for once) totally without words or clues.

When she learned that she was to be fitted with boots and riding trousers, the trousers to go with her very own horse, she protested such a handsome gift. I silenced her saying, "You have heard me say, Elizabeth, that I like to please a woman worthy of being pleased."

All this while her measure was being taken, all this while her eyes were shining, all this while I was watching her with pride and joy. I was happy that she did not make a speech of thanks. She just said the word. The tone of her voice and the look on her face said volumes.

28 MAY, 1813 PEMBERLEY

Was working in my study this afternoon when Nielson knocked to inform me that the new horse had been brought to the stables. Hurried there to make sure that all was in order. It was. Gorgeous animal! A good height for my lady.

Found Elizabeth in the greenhouse with Crowley. Gave her the news. She quickly wiped her hands (on her skirt, of course) tried to smooth her hair away from her face, left wonderful smudges which I started to remove with my kerchief.

She put down her trowel, took my arm (smudging it, of course) and we hurried off. I could hear Crowley's chuckles as we walked away.

Several of the grooms were admiring the mare as we approached. Elizabeth caught her breath, finally got her voice, asked did the mare have a name. I told her that we once had a mare named *Dulcie*. She tried it out, liked it, asked when could she ride her? Consultation with the stable hands and Jarrow, who came limping up to join the "committee." Three days hence was agreed upon.

❧

4 JUNE, 1813 LONDON

I have business in London, D. When I told Elizabeth that I must travel here and invited her to accompany me, she responded in the affirmative without hesitation.

"You will be able to forego your communions with Dulcie?"

"I dare say I can manage without her."

"It will be very quiet socially. The Season does not begin until Autumn."

"I dare say I can manage. Oh, Darcy. To see London!"

I promised her that I would show to her the sights after finishing my affairs at the various ministries.

I have brought with us Rose and Edward in order to enhance the London staff. Elizabeth protested this "extravagance" at first, until I reminded her of how dirty London would be, and what oceans of laundry will need doing every day. I reminded her that we might be expected to do some entertaining, which would be pleasant for Georgiana. Elizabeth took fire at this suggestion.

This proved to be the slowest trip to London I have ever taken. Heavy summer storms preceded us, causing pretty tight work on the country roads. The Inn at C. was almost as disreputable as the Inn at K., and I was tempted as before to pass it by. But we were both hot and dusty, so stayed the night after the usual diligent inspection, this time undertaken by two Darcys. We exited at dawn.

Georgiana was at our door saying goodbye to her music teacher as we arrived. She was delighted to see us, introduced us to her teacher, a descendant of Dussek.

We took tea, heard about her work, relished her joy in what she is accomplishing. Elizabeth reported the news of Miss Jane's expectations, and of the Bingley's purchase, with *full* details about the house.

I finally had to break in, "Perhaps this would go more quickly if we gather up Georgiana and drive her back to *show* her the house?" Elizabeth rose. We three mounted the steep stairs. Rose was finishing the unpacking as we walked into the suite.

Georgiana opened the door to Elizabeth's boudoir and moved to acquaint her with the accommodations. I groaned, "Have pity!" Elizabeth kissed her, she bade us good evening. I added, "Good night." (It was still broad daylight.)

Elizabeth went to the window and sighed, "London! At last! What magic this city holds!" I came behind her, and pointed out some of the steeples which I could identify. She turned to me and murmured "And to think that I am here with Mr. Fitzwilliam Darcy!" Of a sudden, D., the city seemed magical and romantic and clean and dazzling to me also.

"You shall have all you want of the city tomorrow, Lizzy. It is late and it has been a grueling trip."

"But it is still broad daylight."

"Think how it must be for the Scandinavians in mid summer. How do *they* manage it?"

We bathed. She was still brushing out her hair when I fell into the bed. I called to her not to be long, and then I tumbled into a dreamless sleep. I must have awakened enough to take her into my arms when she came to bed, for she was there when I awakened, but I remember naught else.

The sounds from the city streets were rising – the clatter, the calls, the cries, the shouts, the odors, the clop of hooves, the jingling of bridles and sound of wheels, the tolling of church bells – kissed my sleeping beauty, slid from the bed, and was off to The City before the household had stirred.

7 JUNE, 1813 LONDON

Went to my club this afternoon and was informed that my sister and Mrs. Darcy were taking tea on the second floor. When I greeted them I leaned down to kiss my wife. Not many were present, nevertheless the muttering in the room was prodigious. Champagne was sent over to us, and as I raised my glass to the ladies I said, "There will be no need to announce our arrival in London. The news will be abroad within the hour."

I then saluted Lord N. and thanked him for the courtesy of the champagne. He looked expectant, and there was nothing for it but to invite him over to share a toast with us.

I was not happy for the intrusion, but I did relish his obvious admiration of my bride.

By the time we returned home the basket on the hall table already held several invitations. Thus began a round of social affairs (and for me, one must add the round of business obligations).

Elizabeth was full of reports. Everything was thrilling to her. She and Georgiana had "done" Kensington Gardens, circuiting Serpentine and Long Water, got caught in a thundershower, took refuge under the umbrella of a vendor. The skies cleared and they went to view Holland House. Seems Elizabeth was sketching the house, impressed by its fine Jacobean architecture, when the owner, the third Baron Holland, espied them and invited them inside. It seems Georgiana had met him at a concert where he had introduced himself as Henry Fox, (not mentioning his title) and they had found a mutual interest in discussing early church music. Seems in looking out the window today he recognized my sister. Seems he introduced them to the guests of the day, who numbered many statesmen and a few prominent writers. Seems they were taking a respite from their Conference, and were most hospitable to my ladies.

Seems that Elizabeth had learned that the house had once been leased to William Penn. She is an ardent admirer of the Constitution drafted in Pennsylvania for the United States, and an admirer of Mr. Penn. I asked, "Did you then challenge some of our British Tories on these upsetting ideas, Elizabeth?" Georgiana broke in to assure me that Lizzie might well have, save that the Conference resumed and the discussion died a'borning.

They then went to see St. Mary Abbots Church, and the Kensington Palace.

Tonight I took the ladies to Vauxhall, the London pleasure garden. A young gentleman came over to our table to greet us. Mr. Clementi, the young man whom we had met at the Alexanders.' I invited him to join us. He accepted with alacrity. When he left he suggested to Georgiana that there was to be an interesting concert at Vauxhall in several days and perhaps she would attend with him? She put him off, but one hopes she will give positive consideration. He comes from a good family. Prospects? (Foolish man! I sound like Elizabeth who is already planning the wedding.)

❦

9 JUNE, 1813 LONDON

Quelle femme! Tonight Elizabeth said, "Mr. Darcy, I have sinned."

I could not take this seriously. Never has there been a woman more ethical in all her dealings, nor more truthful. I asked her in what manner had she strayed.

"In St. Mary Le Bow Church," she told me.

This came as a surprise. She is dutiful, constant, reads her prayers faithfully, is without any major or even minor sins against others – How could this be?

"Darcy, you know how it is when we attend concerts together? How you are suddenly staring at me with your smoldering look. How you then take my hand, turn it palm up, and kiss it with great meaning. Between the lovely music and your look and the feel of your lips, I feel a strange epiphany, and at this moment I fear I might slip out of my seat and slide to the floor like a gooseberry coming out of its skin."

I laughed and then asked her how did this apply to Church.

"This is what you did yesterday. And that is how I felt yesterday – IN CHURCH! When my thoughts should have been turning towards God."

"And you have no doubt worried about this ever since?"

"Indeed I have."

"Lizzy, I am not ordained to the Church. Perhaps you should confess this to your cousin Mr. Collins."

Now it was her turn to laugh. I then reassured her that it is my conviction that "the gooseberry" feeling is much to God's liking and that she should worry her beautiful head no more.

15 June, 1813 Pemberley

Charles galloped over today, pulled up his horse, scattering gravel and setting our entire kennel aroar. I was in my study, heard the commotion. By the time I got to the entry hall he was striding towards me, eyes alight. "I say, Darcy! We are going to do a housewarming. I plan to invite the Bennet family, your Aunt Catherine, all the neighbors —" "Hold on, Charles. You have no furniture." He was not to be curbed. He would borrow. In fact, he was here in order to reconnoiter our supply as to what could be loaned. The party is to be twenty-one June. I reminded him how quickly that date would come, he reminded me that it was the summer equinox. "Solstice, Charles."

"Yes, of course, 'Solstice' — longest day of the year. Most of the festivities can take place outside. We can manage it. Matter of fact the invitations have already been sent."

June 21, 1813 Pemberley

The longest day in the year, to be sure. What a boon it is! All that daylight, and light late into the gloaming. The only problem — it rained most of the day. I hardly saw my wife, who was summoned early in the morning, and spent the rest of the day in mad dashes about the countryside, attending to this and that. Just before the party the skies cleared, thanks to all friendly forces.

Indeed, the entire family was assembled, with the exception of George Wickham. Lydia came alone, thanks to God on high, merrier than ever and (if possible) more showy.

My Aunt Catherine, accompanied by my cousin. A clutch of Bingley relatives, Charles' five sisters, Mr. Hurst and an uncle of his, a battalion of neighbors — a crowd! In addition to all the hurry-skurry, intimate relatives were staying at Highlands as guests! (Charles took me aside and whispered that he thanked God for the fact that the many guest rooms are far from the master suite. It was not going as badly as he had feared, for various reasons, the outstanding being that Mrs. Bennet is awed into silence by my aunt.)

Aunt Catherine watches Jane's and Elizabeth's every move and insists on having repeated to her every word uttered by my lady. (Waiting for her to breach some social convention? I dare say she will be disappointed. HOWEVER, knowing Elizabeth, I dare say she is capable of creating a 'breach' with due deliberation.)

Anne? Anne is her usual gray, silent self. She never takes her eyes from me. Has she nothing better to concentrate upon?

When we entered the party I went straightaway to Lydia, (with gratitude in my heart) took both her hands and kissed each, greeting her with enthusiasm. I left her gasping with surprise. She could scarcely collect herself sufficiently to greet Elizabeth whom last she had seen at our wedding.

There were tours of the downstairs, dancing, card-playing, and a concert on the pianoforte played for us by Mary (would that she were not so generous with her talent!) At least at such times I am seated next to Elizabeth. I can look at her from time to time. I can experience her delicious scent. I took her hand and kissed it. There was a stirring in the room, the humming of whispering females, grumblings from my aunt. I vow, D., no drama on the stage has ever caused such a rippling and susurration in any audience!

At length supper was announced, and we entered a sumptuous scene of gourmet splendor. (Lucky the new table had been delivered in time!) There were many to serve us (many of them from Pemberley) marvelous dishes at all corners. We went from one to the next, filling our plates to the full. As we stopped at a tray heaped with various breads, in company with a bowl of clotted cream and a stemmed crystal dish heaped high with some kind of confiture, Mrs. Bennet hurried to us and in her not so dulcet voice piped, "Do not fail to take the jam! It is Gooseberry! Such a treat and so very hard to find especially at this season!"

"In truth?" I replied. "Your daughter does not seem to find it so."

E. put her plate down hurriedly. I followed her onto the terrace and found her collapsed against the wall, in gales of laughter.

Put my hands on either side of her, pinning her there, and leaned into her.

"Go away, Darcy! You rogue!"

"I have you pinned, and shall not release you until you have recovered your dignity and are fit to reenter polite society. And as for my being a rogue, I find you a runagate. You left your dear mother in the middle of a dissertation on a certain jam. I am remiss in that I did not stay to explain to her the reason for your distress."

"You may lead me back, dear husband. I am quite recovered."

When we returned to the buffet we found Lady Catherine in the middle of a circle, demanding to know of "the business about the confiture" and "where had the Darcys disappeared," and no end of other furious questions.

I went straightaway to her, told her I had urgent matters to discuss with her, took her into the library, where I implored her counsel as to how we should handle the matter of poachers in the woods at Pemberley. All of which she was most delighted to impart. Kept her there as long as I could manage it.

Good night, D. It is late.

⚜

30 JUNE, 1813 PEMBERLEY

Surprises and more surprises. I returned this afternoon from my tour of duty and searched the house for Elizabeth. I was informed that she was to be found in the orchard. Thither went I and called. I heard her voice but saw her not. Then I espied her shoes at the foot of a peach tree and Mrs. Fitzwilliam Darcy on a branch of said tree. I was aghast.

"Shall I come down?"

"No, I shall ascend." And so I did. I flung off my coat and swung up (quite deftly, I confess) to where she was seated. I felt as if I were five or six years old.

Nevertheless I was concerned for her and told her it was not safe. She countered with the information that she had been climbing trees since early childhood. One does wonder whether anyone were watching out for her? I asked her what other unseemly sports she had been indulged to pursue.

"I used to ride."

"I know."

"Yes, but I did not ride like a proper Englishwoman on her side-saddle."

"An ordinary English saddle then?"

"No, bareback."

"In a long skirt?"

"Do you forget I was in a long skirt the day you rescued me from the electric storm?"

"How could I ever forget that day, Elizabeth!"

"You might be interested to hear that I persuaded my father to give over to me an old pair of trousers, which I tailored to my size. Then I outgrew them and had not ridden until our marriage. I know now that was hardly *comme il faut,* but I cared not. I admit that I had little knowledge then of just *how* critical the *haut monde* can be."

I reassured her that anyone who could use such a phrase was not exactly from the peasantry. I added, "and by now Elizabeth, the styles are catching up to you."

She smiled demurely.

"Darcy, is it not beautiful up here? Look how far we can see!"

Indeed, it was beautiful. We could see past the meadow, over the grove of trees, to the far horizon. It was a warm day and everything was bathed in a golden light, like the amber and gold one sees in a Renaissance painting. I could see Crowley's receding form, and he too looked as if on a canvas. The scene was indeed glorious, and so was she.

She was flushed from the sun, her damp hair curled in tendrils around her glowing face.

"Hold tight," I said as I leaned to kiss her. "Delicious! You taste of ripe peaches!"

She reached to pick one for me, but I informed her that I preferred to taste them from herself only, and kissed her again. "I can swing easily down from here, but how shall you do it? Shall I call for a ladder?"

"I am no fool, Darcy. Not in this hobble of a skirt. Crowley stays in the vicinity and he watches out for me, that is, when he is not driven off by the Master's presence. Also, he gathers the peaches which I throw down to him – I shall show you how I descend. You go first."

I scrambled down. I was perturbed about what view might be exposed to Mr. Crowley were he in my position, but she gathered her skirt from aft to fore, pulling it through her legs and tucking it into her waistband, scaled down to the lowest branch. I put up my arms and she slipped ever so sweetly into them. I held her fast. I confess my world was reeling.

Lady Catherine should see this! Inappropriate? To be sure! Yet the whole experience was enchanting, and I confess, it was productive too. On the ground I saw a giant bucket of peaches which I had not noticed before. I took a handful and said,

"Come live with me and be my love."

And she softly completed the couplet, "And we will all the pleasures prove."

And indeed we did.

1 July, 1813 Pemberley

D. I have this plan – I shall write Father Bennet and ask him to come for a fortnight, *alone*, using the excuse of some business upon which I need his advice. I shall express my regret that Mrs. Bennet cannot leave her daughters.

I want to learn from this estimable gentleman how he went about the education and physical training of his second daughter. There will be children here someday (not too soon, I trust) and I desire to gain from him his theories, his procedures, etcetera, etcetera.

3 July, 1813 Pemberley

Georgiana has been forwarding to us the invitations which arrived after our departure from London. One was tempting – a Grand Ball to be held by Lord and Lady Egremont who dwell in an impressive edifice with a gallant history which I knew would be of interest to E. I had heard news of the quality of the orchestra which would be playing, and I am most eager to dance to such music. Also, although abashed to confess it, I would like the *haut monde* to be able to view Mrs. Fitzwilliam Darcy in full regalia. (Thus speaks the very same gentleman who looks down on vanity and superficiality!)

We have had many an evening's debate. Finally the mistress of P. decided in the affirmative. Not to favor the master, mind you, but for Clive Crowley's young wife who is a creative talent, it appears, and whom Lizzie wants to encourage in her work as a seamstress. In short, Elizabeth and I will return to London to attend a ball, in order for Elizabeth to show a new gown, in order this to advance the career of a young, talented woman.

The level of excitement here has reached a crescendo. The Crowleys live nearby, luckily. Now we have many female conversations behind closed doors (many of which are unduly prolonged because of my wife's pleasure in the infant Crowley,) visits to the village, letters and packages sailing between here and Paris. Such flummery! Frequently I have cause to wonder as to whether we have made a sane choice.

Mrs. Bennet wrote and suggested she would like to come to advise on this project. Elizabeth refused her.

I cannot imagine myself wanting to take Mrs. Bennet's part, yet know that I look on her fondly at times; her character can provide a great deal of amusement (when taken in light doses) and she has certainly brought forth a Venus for me. In this case I felt sorry for her. Elizabeth did not relent.

Again we shall go to London, D. You may be sure that we shall have more trunks and valises than our mistress has hitherto encumbered upon us.

❧

17 July, 1813 London

Last week a special post arrived during the morning hours with a troubling word from my London solicitors who requested my immediate presence there. One of the properties in which we hold an interest belongs to a fine farming family in the north. A tragic accident has befallen the only son and heir leaving the widowed mother (a distant relative) and a family of six girls, with the dreadful issue of entailment.

Unfortunately the estate entails to me. Elizabeth found me in the study yesterday, and asked if I were feeling ill. I told her that I felt fine.

"You do not seem it."

"I have a problem that is vexing me."

"May I hear it?"

"Do not trouble your lovely head."

"'My lovely head' is troubled when you do not share with me."

I thought – What harm? Why not tell her of this matter? I am in no way forced to take her advice, and it may be that she will agree with me in any event. And so I did. I told her the whole sad story.

Her first concern was about the welfare of my cousins, not about the value of the estate. I must have given her a surprised look, because a smile came to her lips and then was suppressed.

"We are in agreement then. In no way can I dislodge this family."

She then asked, "Can not your solicitors find a way of transferring the property to the widow for many years?"

Strange, I had been thinking of the same thing. I told her so, she smiled demurely. Now we began to talk. Man to man? Hardly! Husband to clever wife. That was it!

Having decided that we both could well stand up to a few days' separation, I have come to London alone, as it will be business and business only.

She was alert and about her usual occupations as I kissed her goodbye in a lighthearted manner. The insouciance did not last; I felt sad and empty even before we had rolled through the gates of Pemberley.

24 JULY, 1813 PEMBERLEY

My febrile schedule in London could not allay the despondency, nor even the good solution which we agreed upon – the property rights to this unexpected boon will revert to my estate when the last of my cousin's next generation is deceased. Thus my own grandchildren will someday acquire the land.

I was ashamed that I missed my wife so desperately; her gaiety, her sharp remarks, her very presence. The very afternoon when we concluded the matter, I ordered my carriage for the trip home. My lackeys were perturbed at such a schedule but I impressed upon them the urgency of my return and they were most accommodating.

Reached Pemberley in the middle of the early morning hours. The house was dark and locked tight. Shook the front door, and sure enough, heard a snuffling at the base. Galahad! Good dog! Bark for me! Silence – except for the sounds of his delighted exploration at the base of the door. Went around to the french door. Open perchance? – shut tight. Dimly I could descry the dog plastered against the glass. I could imagine his tail a'wag, a silly grin on his silly face.

We had need to awaken Nielson. I crept around to his room only to discover that the window was above my reach. A few stones brought no results. Fetched our coachmen who, upon my instruction, formed a solid base for me. I climbed upon their broad backs and was thus able to knock at Nielson's window.

Nielson's astonished face appeared. The master! In the dead of night! Somehow floating at the window!

He descended to open the door for me. I thanked him and I thanked my "body guard" with warm compliments as to their valor.

Galahad was at my heels as I ran up the stairs, and I had to take care not to be upended. A contest at the door. Such a disruption to his regular schedule apparently decided him that he wished to be admitted to our chambers. How to shut him out, and myself in? Finally outwitted him and closed the door against him.

The most unwelcome thought beset me - that Elizabeth would not be there - that I might find a deserted room and an empty bed. 'Darcy, how could such an idea come into this foolish head!' But it did - and I was most grateful when I saw her sleeping form.

Shock and astonishment - was there another with her? My world reeled and then I ascertained as I neared her that she held in her arms only my coat, her beautiful head resting on the empty shoulder.

I sat on the edge of the bed and devoured the picture with my eyes.

She stirred, opened her eyes – when she saw me she floated (it seemed) into my arms.

As I kissed her and quieted her with the "hussshhh" which I know she relishes – (she was *not* unmoved) – an overpowering thought suffused me with the happiest sensation I have ever experienced – she loves me, she will never leave me. She loves me as I love her.

❦

21 AUGUST, 1813 PEMBERLEY

Georgiana has removed from London and is several weeks back with us at Pemberley.

She and Elizabeth are inseparable, even when E. is attending to household affairs. Georgiana follows after her, as does the four-footed slave, Galahad. When not so occupied, the ladies are to be heard practicing four-handed works and music fills much of the house, accompanied by the delightful sounds of feminine laughter, usually preceded by a *dreadful* chord, inevitably followed by a mournful howl, this followed by peals of laughter.

But now all is silent. E. has been called home to attend her ailing mother. I protested. No hope for it, Mary is away, Kitty is studying. I cannot join Elizabeth until tomorrow – another problem with poachers with which I must grapple. And I must attend to my work here. It is piling up, so burdensome that I am starting to have restless nights.

In Elizabeth's absence I have had the compensation of such a conversation with my sister as I have not hitherto experienced. Tonight at supper, in the middle of an entirely different subject, Georgiana asked suddenly if I remember Mother.

"I think of her often."

"What was she like?"

"Do you forget that she was your mother too?"

"I remember so very little. She was elegant. She smelled lovely. Her clothes were exquisite. She liked parties. I think of her as a beautiful painting – in fact, when I try to conjure her face it is her portrait which I see. I do remember that I used to just gaze and gaze as hard as ever I could."

"And?"

"That's all. I tried to "own" her with my eyes, but I could not remember her face when she was absent. I could remember everything she wore, her jewels, the sound of her voice – but not *her*. Did you ever see her and Aunt Catherine together? Were they like?"

I replied that I did not see much similarity, that Mother was always so cool and controlled, and Aunt Catherine was usually fussed and mussed. Then I asked her if she would like to accompany me into the gallery to study the portraits of our parents.

"Whyever, Darcy?"

"Do you never go to look at them?"

"No, I do not."

"May I inquire the reason?"

"I know not. I just know that the few times I have done so I start to cry. I have cried enough for a long lifetime."

"I dare say you have."

"And you, dear brother?"

"Ask me not."

※

26 AUGUST, 1813 PEMBERLEY

The tranquil bridegroom? Not this night. My wife and I are returned from Longbourn, and all is well there again. Not here. I had not expected to be delayed in returning to Pemberley, but Mrs. Bennet put on such a show of despair that my wife succumbed to her posturing and held our return. Too long, too long! I was not pleasant about this, as I am deeply concerned about getting so far behind in my work. Elizabeth urged me to return and tend to my affairs, and not worry about her. And how would she get home? She offered to take the coach back to the village. "This is beneath you!" I had shouted. She gave me such an angry look! At this moment Mother Bennet had let out one of her (too many!) pathetic cries for succor, and Elizabeth had run up to her.

Her coldness that night mattered not, since Elizabeth had found that she felt not at all romantic in her own home.

I stayed on, should not have.

Mr. Bennet saved my sanity. We embarked together upon Burke's *Reflections On The French Revolution*. We had discussed daring the same author's *Philosophical Inquiry Into The Origins Of Our Ideas Of The Sublime And Beautiful* (the title alone could take up a day's time) but Mary returned, and we departed hurriedly.

❦

27 AUGUST, 1813 PEMBERLEY

Something stands between us now, and I know not how to manage it. The work load at Pemberley seems insurmountable. What worries me the most is that I cannot seem to get to the account sheets. I start, but there are forever interruptions, too urgent to be put off. I am Sisyphus. No, I am Odysseus. I am a liege to love when I should be returning to my land and my passion for it. Am I chained? No, but I am enslaved and I cannot move. Does this make sense? No! But nothing does.

And Elizabeth? Is she then a siren, luring me from my steady ship? Will I ever be able again to steer my own course?

No. She is Calypso. And shall I be kept from my work for seven years? Indeed. I am her prisoner, whilst Ithaca falls to ruin. I must restore Ithaca, but it seems I cannot move.

I rose from the bed, found my way to the door, and descended to my study.

❦

28 AUGUST, 1813 PEMBERLEY

How can one fall from Paradise? So far, so fast, into such a desolation? How can one regain Paradise? How can I live in a place without the magic and beauty with which Elizabeth invests herself and her surroundings? – taking me into that place, from which I care not to exit? Not ever – not ever.

And yet I have managed to do that. To throw myself from that place.

It is late, D. I have not slept all night. I have paced the halls, I have paced what must be a thousand miles in these chambers. It is raining now, to make desolation even more desolate. Elizabeth is not here with me. Is she suffering as am I? Is she dry and safe?

I have taken Galahad into the room with me. He watches me pace, he does not sleep, from time to time he whines softly in his throat, a sound so *triste* that I am tempted to moan with him to the empty night.

How has this come about? Perhaps if I tell you *I* will begin to understand. Perhaps when I understand I will know where she has gone. I know she must be safe somewhere (WHERE?) – she would not risk herself nor the future of this benighted *bairn* into whose life she has so foolishly intervened.

Herewith I retrace the *farrago* – (will this help? – what can help?)

Yesterday? – the day before yesterday? (It is all so muddled in my tortured head) I received an urgent missive from one of our tenants, detailing the plight of a neighbor, a young farmer with a family of five – four little girls and an infant son. There was a mother. She had died in delivering the boy. The neighbor came to Pemberley and stood hat in hand, until I had left the breakfast table and come to him in the study. We were closeted a long time. Such a long time that Elizabeth knocked, and asked if there were aught wrong and could she be of assistance. I told her no, but the neighbor in one long desperate plea told her of the tragedy, and the problem with the newborn.

"This baby must be found a wet nurse. I will come with you."

"I will arrange this, Elizabeth. Do you not have a singing lesson this morning?"

As I think back, she gave me a strange look, but did take her leave, not without asking the good samaritan to relay her condolences. When our visitor left and I was about to go to the family, I was interrupted by yet another emergency matter . . . Finally quitted the study to find, to my astonishment, Elizabeth, dressed for riding, descending the stairs in haste.

"This is the appropriate costume for a singing lesson?"

"I am on my way to help with that babe. Too much time has passed already."

"I have told you, Elizabeth, this is my responsibility."

"And I am suggesting herewith that you detail it to me."

"No."

"Yes."

And so saying she shook off my hand and hurried from the house. I was about to go after her when yet another emergency intervened.

One could hear the sound of galloping hooves growing fainter and fainter, until the sound was gone o'er the horizon. I was furious! Shouted at all within earshot to avert these fiendish interruptions, to let no one else in the house, to leave me alone. Ran out, almost knocking down Rose in my haste, saddled Champêtre without waiting for help, had him in a gallop before I was in the saddle. Almost my undoing as I had been careless with the cinch and the saddle slipped at the moment I swung into it. I had to leap to the ground, spilled (of course), rolled in a backward somersault and found myself unhurt, but by now in a towering rage. (And filthy). And the angrier because several grooms, racing to my aid, had seen this stupidity. Lucky for me the horse had known to stop at the instant the saddle came loose.

More time had escaped me. By the time I came to the home of the bereaved family the place was deserted. I could detect from the clouds of dust spiraling into the sky that there was action off to the north, and we flew in that direction.

Good observation, Darcy. (I remember that feeling, because it was the only decent feeling I have had in all this miserable time. Ah yes, one other – I did perform a most astute tumble in the spill from the horse.)

There was a large assemblage in front of a small cottage; from the distance I could discern a diverse group, several wagons, men and standing horses, and one figure I knew to be my wife. She was holding a small bundle against her shoulder.

I drew up in a shower of pebbles, and leaped to the ground. If Elizabeth recognized that I was in a fury she did not acknowledge it, but asked sweetly if I were all right.

"Why do you ask that?"

"Because it does appear that you have had a tumble."

"I am fine, give up that child and come home with me."

She demurred, saying that she would return when the problem was settled.

What idiocy possessed me at that moment, I know not. I demanded she hand me the child. She did. I have never held an infant, but did fumble it from her. At which moment the babe started up a howling that could have waked the dead. I do not know what made my wife laugh, but laugh she did, nor did she offer to help me in my plight.

Everyone was gawking, including a houseful of new witnesses who were standing in the doorway – a nursing mother, a covey of children, some of whom were giggling.

One of the farmers took the screaming creature from me. I wanted to thrash Elizabeth for causing me this loss of face, and most particularly for making me a subject of ridicule. Turned on my heel, calling back to her, "Return when you will. I care not."

Her reply was cold, "It is quite obvious, Mr. Darcy, that you care not. Fair riddance to you."

She went into the house, I rode off more angry than ever I knew I could be.

She has not returned. I ate supper alone. That is to say, I sat at the table with my book. The household was hushed, as if there had been a personal death. No one, not even Reynolds, ventured to address me. Even the kitchen, usually so full of the sound of voices and banging pots, was silent.

And then, of course, it started to rain. I cursed the elements, I cursed the ill fortune of the death of the mother, I cursed the baby, I cursed myself. Elizabeth? How dare she laugh at such a moment? And at me! Did I curse her? No, not Elizabeth.

⁂

29 August, 1813 Pemberley

I could write no more last night, D. I paced through the house, I went outside, returned inside.

There was nothing else for it. I dressed, took my candle, and went to the stables. Inky black skies, the wind moaning through the trees. Still raining. Set the candle down, saddled up, rode off (having taken good care, this time, to set the saddle correctly,) then had to ride back, because I had forgot to blow out the candle. (All I needed now was the burning down of my own stables!) And what was I doing? I had no idea where to look. What clue was there, who could find her?

Of course! The dog! I headed back to the house, which by now was stirring. Nielson peered out the rear door. "Get me Galahad. And an article of the mistress' clothing. Hurry!"

How many false starts! How great this torment! Hurry, Nielson!

At last the door opened, the dog bounded out, Nielson came with a tippet oft worn by Elizabeth. He had Galahad sniff the garment. Now another dash to the stables, where I leaped from Champêtre, located Dulcie's blanket, offered same to the dog, same process of recognition. FINALLY we were off, Galahad running in wild circles, nose to the ground. Indeed he did lead us in a variety of directions. Hours (it seemed) of false leads. And finally – FINALLY – we were led to a trail which I knew would take us to the home of young Crowley. Why had I not thought of this myself? So logical. (Did the dog do this by logic, or did his nose lead us thither?) No matter, within moments we heard a neighing, and Champêtre replied. Dulcie! Elizabeth would be within. Now, an equine colloquy which stirred up every owl in the forest, a twittering of disgruntled song birds, and a cacophony of neighboring dogs.

Champêtre was fairly prancing in anticipation, my own heart was beating fast. We came to the cottage, only too well heralded. Young Crowley stood in the door, holding a candle. Behind him I could discern Elizabeth. I knew 'twas only the candlelight, but about her head there shimmered the appearance of a halo.

I apologized for waking the family and was reassured that no harm was done. I asked my wife if she would do me the honor of coming home with me. She assented gravely.

Dulcie, it seems, had a lame foot and could not be ridden. Crowley brought her to me and handed me a lead. Placed my lady on Champêtre, swung up in front of her, asked her to put her arms around me, if she would do that.

She did so, saying, "We have much to discuss, Darcy, but I have no mind to fall to the ground, apparently as you did yesterday."

And off we rode.

By then the sky was becoming lighter, and soon the sun would be rising. The birds were beginning to waken, the rain had blown away, there was the breathable hint of a warmth to come. I inhaled deeply, content in the knowledge that she was there with me, that my anger had subsided, leaving me with something of the contentment which had moved into my life when Elizabeth had done so.

Harold heard us approaching and was there to help Elizabeth down. I was sorry for that. I would like to have been the one to hold her. Would this not have saved us the discussion which would follow and which I would like to have avoided? My arms around her, a long look into her eyes, a murmured something or other – why not "I love you"? Would that not have done it?

We approached the house in silence. Always I hold a door for her, always I receive a smile of thanks. *Frustré* again; Nielson was there, and it was he who received the smile. He informed Elizabeth that a bath had been readied for her. She thanked him. Nielson's responsibilities end there. It is my prerogative to carry her up the stairs. *My* prerogative.

"Let me carry you up the stairs."

"No thank you."

"Please."

She assented. As I tried to lift her I knew at once that my shoulder was hurt. "I fear I cannot manage it." As I set her down, I was afraid that she would laugh at me again.

"Did you then hurt yourself when you were thrown?"

"I was not thrown. I fell. And yes, it seems that I have wrenched my shoulder."

She looked concerned and I was glad for my injury.

When she emerged from the bath I was sitting in front of the fireplace. I rose and offered her the sofa. She sat, still silent. I looked at her, but could not speak, and then I fell to my knees and buried my head in her lap. All I could say, into the warm softness of her, was, "It was all wrong without you."

She spoke not, but began to toy with my hair. I did not stop this. It felt nice. And then she spoke,

"Such lovely curls; how your mother must have loved this wonderful mop of yours."

I shook my head.

"No one, Darcy? No one ever said that? Who was there to love you and to console you? No one?"

A muffled, "There was Mrs. Reynolds."

"No one to laugh at you when you were acting foolish? No one to help you through such times? Darcy, look at me."

I could not, D. Luckily she did not press the request.

And then she said, "I am sorry, Darcy, that I caused you such displeasure, but I am not sorry for what I did. It needed to be done. I am truly sorry that I laughed at you. It did – at the time – seem a felicitous way of making everyone's travails easier, but 'twas not easier for you."

"I was foolish, Elizabeth. I ask your forgiveness. And pray, do not stop laughing, even if it must be at me."

She bent her head to me, kissed my "mop," put her head back, and so help me, she went to sleep. And so did I.

Many hours later I awakened to discover that we were both in the bed.

❧

30 AUGUST, 1813 PEMBERLEY

And so it goes – or does it? Are we reconciled? Yes. Are we as we were? No. Is this better? No!

What can be done? Perhaps Elizabeth can answer it, but I dare not ask. I must be staring at her as I did when I was so tormented, because tonight she rose from her chair, put down her book, turned the chair around and reseated herself, her back to me. Not a word said, but how eloquent!

And how foolish I am. I left the room and went to my study. Could not concentrate. Accomplished NOTHING. Soon I returned to our chambers, but Elizabeth was in bed, lying far off to the side. I was certain that she was not asleep, but I did not dare to approach her.

Deep into the night I gave up the attempt to sleep and rose. I went to the fire, stirred it, threw on more logs, and sat me down on the couch. Then I moved to my desk, and here I am, old friend, and I am not feeling at all right about my world, my self, my foolishness. If only you could talk to me!

❧

31 AUGUST, 1813 PEMBERLEY

I fell asleep there at the desk as I was writing to you last night. I awakened to Elizabeth's hand on my brow.

"What is it, Darcy? You have no fever. But you are so strange – so strange."

"Sometimes I know not who I am."

"Who are you?"

"I first thought Sisyphus. Now I believe it is Odysseus."

"And I?"

D., how could I answer that? She did it for me.

"Am I, then, Calypso?"

Thunderation! How comes she to these revelations? I could say naught.

"Darcy, it is cold here. Stir up the fire, and do let us sit there." And so I did, and so, we sat. Then she said,

"Darcy, I am not trying to bind you to me with female wiles. I am of no mind to lure you away from your work, your passion for Pemberley. I am not here spinning out enchantments to lure you into my power, I am not designing magic spells to keep you bound. Trickeries are for other women. I know naught of their schemes. I know naught of schemes to keep you from your true course."

"You are my true course, Elizabeth."

"No. It is more complicated than that, as all this proves. When I have been in your arms, Darcy, I had thought we were of one mind. I had thought we came together as equals."

She rose, went into her dressing room, and shut the door. Good God! What have I done!

* * *

2 SEPTEMBER, 1813 PEMBERLEY

Let the day begin. I have summoned to Pemberley the bereaved family. Sent Mrs. Reynolds to the village for a variety of purchases. By now she will have assembled a hamper of clothes for the children, garments and napkins for the babe, and enough food to fill the family larder for a good spell.

A young lady who can nurse the bairn has been located. She has no known attachments, and will move in with the family. I do not know this lass or anything about her, but one does feel sad that she is in such a plight. What happened to *her* child? Dare one ask?

I have asked Elizabeth to share in the planning conference with me and the father. She gave me such a look of gratitude that my heart sings again. The day is glorious! I know I should not feel exultant where there is such travail for others, but I cannot help myself.

LATER

Conference ended, chores attended, cup upended. (I am entitled to make the rhyme because I knocked over my cup at tea.)

Now a pause, and time to finish out the day for you. Elizabeth was most helpful, and I realize that it is to everyone's advantage that she become a full partner, especially in the management of the tenants' domestic details, so urgent, and of which there are so many.

I keep thinking of her expression as she looked at the motherless babe. I keep thinking of how gorgeous she is when she is angry. Furious as I was, I never had desired her more. It takes me back to the first days when I met her at Netherfield. What liked I the best? Her beauty? Not at first. I am not even certain that I found her beautiful. Not at first.

At first I enjoyed her wit, admired her brilliance, respected her courage and self-possession, and was enchanted with her high spirits and spirited defense of what she held true. In addition, I was touched by her sweetness and concern for her sister, and later I admired her loyalty to her family, troublesome as I found them in those days. Above all – *above all* – I was taken with the ways in which she challenged *me*.

Why was I not "taken" with her in her defiance of the matter of the last few days? I know not. I only know now that I was bone-headed and foolish, and I am sorry for it. She is thoughtful and kind, she has sent to Mother Bennett for a balm to be applied to my shoulder which, she promises, will relieve the pain.

And yet – and yet, something stands between us. That easy surrender to me which was so enthralling – will that return?

In the meantime I am plowing ahead with my work, trying to catch it up. Elizabeth has suggested that I employ a steward to assist me. Never! Not until the son who will someday be here – (but not too soon, I pray.) Someday he will grow into the position of my assistant, and beyond that he will take the reins from me. A long way ahead.

In the meantime, a steward? When my father succumbed to that, it brought the Wickhams. And it foreshadowed father's death. A steward? NEVER.

3 SEPTEMBER, 1813 PEMBERLEY

I have been awakening before cocks' crow, dressing and going quietly downstairs to work. I can do all this in the dark; find the tinder, locate the candles and the wax jack, and set myself to work. What I cannot do, always, is to stay awake. This morning Elizabeth found me slumped onto the desk, with the candles guttering, my pen still in my hand. I felt her hand on my brow and roused. She was dressed for riding.

"Are you quite well?"

"I am quite well."

"Go to bed, Darcy. You are working too hard."

"I cannot, Elizabeth. I have let the account records fall far behind."

"I shall bring you some coffee." So saying, she left, but returned soon, handed me the cup and sat herself down. Across from me.

"Darcy, I have a fine penmanship. Let me help you." She put her elbows on the desk, cupped her face in her hands and stared at me.

"I would like the pleasure of your company, Elizabeth."

"Only if you will allow me to help in some way. Meantime, better than sleep, I think you need some sport, and I invite you to teach me and my good Dulcie how to take the jumps." She held out her hand. I let her lead me out.

⁂

4 SEPTEMBER, 1813 PEMBERLEY

Even from the first day when I rode Dulcie to make certain of her, I found her to be fleet, deft footed, intelligent, interested, and affectionate. When we came to the stables this day she did her usual – snorts, soft neighs, nuzzles. This made Elizabeth laugh, and I joined. Suddenly it all began to feel right again.

I held out my hand, Elizabeth put her foot there and mounted. Once she is astride, the horse picks up her feet, arches her neck, and is the personification of pride.

I mounted Champêtre, who moved to greet Dulcie. First he put on a capital display for his friend – he reared, straight up, front hooves flailing the air. He insisted then on trotting over to greet her by placing his head across the mare's neck. Elizabeth leaned over and gave him a kiss. (I much doubt that this gesture would be approved in any training manual.)

We rode out to the pasture and over to a ground where there are low barriers . . . I asked Elizabeth to dismount.

"I am not to ride?"

"Later."

We then led our horses across these logs. Several times. Now Elizabeth asked, "Why did I get dressed in these clothes?"

"Patience, madam."

Finally I allowed her to remount, and did the same.

"Now we can jump, Elizabeth. But you may not use the stirrups."

A protest, but she accepted the stricture. We reapproached the barriers, I reminded her to grip with her knees, and then slowly and steadily we cantered to the barrier and took it together. "Slow, steady, lean into it – BRAVO!" We worked for an hour, and then I called a halt. She protested, I insisted. As we were dismounting, Briarley came to me with a summons from the house. He is new at Pemberley. I greeted him, "How are you getting on, Briarley? Are you comfortable at Pemberley?" Positive assurances.

Sometime later my wife entered in response to the announcement for dinner. She washed, then came to the table, started to sit down, and let out a groan. "What now, Mrs. Darcy?"

"I disobeyed you, my lord."

"Elizabeth! You have been at it all this time?"

"I have. I deserve to be punished."

"Do not look to me. I suspect that indeed you will be."

She excused herself and limped away from the table. When I arrived upstairs she was on the bed, and Mrs. Reynolds was tending her with a mustard plaster to the back. I suggested that we remove the plaster and that I be permitted to help with a massage. Mrs. Reynolds excused herself from the room.

"And what know you of such a procedure?"

"I know only too well. We often have need of massage after a fencing bout. I know full well what I must do."

She asked, "Is this pain the punishment to which you referred?"

"I dare say."

What I did not realize, D., is the difference between a burly fencing opponent and the supple body of one's adored mistress, especially when there has been a bad spell between the two. I did start with the noblest of intentions, but within a short while I felt a quickening in my body that forced me to discontinue my ministrations.

"Do not stop, Mr. Darcy. Please – it is wonderfully soothing."

"Foolish lady! Now I am in worse trouble than you." (I think that is what I said.) Then I threw all caution to the winds and kissed her on the nape of her neck. She rolled over (not without a groan of pain), I covered her face with kisses. I then said, "Each time is as special as the first time," and received a tremulous smile. Then I added, "Even though you do smell vaguely of the breakfast Hunt table."

Then her laughter. And what then? I can not write of it, D. There were copious tears, tears of a deep sadness, tears of pain, (these made her laugh, and that caused me to laugh – at *such* a moment!)

"Of all times to make love, Elizabeth! When you are in pain!"

She said, "I think it may have been the best time."

<hr>

15 SEPTEMBER, 1813 LONDON

In London again. I was not wrong. We were, indeed, laden with luggage. As we were about to depart, Elizabeth suddenly remembered her new bonnet, darted back into the house, declined all assistance and ran up the stairs to rescue the band box. I exited the carriage, leaned against it, and watched her flight with amusement. Mrs. Reynolds, at the door, was also watching. "Bless me! The mistress runs like a gazelle." Then she looked at me and clasped her hands in prayer. "She is right for you, Mr. Darcy. Your union is blessed in Heaven. And might there soon – ?"

"Do not say it, Mrs. Reynolds. Later will do."

We arrived in Mayfair in time for a chat with Georgiana, who looks prettier every day. Elizabeth attempted in every tactful way to ascertain if any of her plans had included the young musician whom she seems to have in mind for Georgiana, but she was artfully dodged.

What a delicious dilemma for me, D.! My two favorite ladies attempting to outwit one another, all the while simulating an air of such innocence! Where should I place my bets? For whom do I cheer? At one point Elizabeth looked in my direction, seemed to catch the sense of my thoughts and smiled. Soon after that she quit the game. I decided it had ended in a draw, but I am pleased that my sister is emerging with a mind of her own, and with a fine wit to boot.

Now Georgiana played some new Beethoven pieces for us. Her skill is beyond perfect! Elizabeth seated herself to try out the instrument with a few exercises, exclaiming at its splendid properties. She looked up, caught my glance, rose promptly and kissed Georgiana. We excused ourselves.

All of London was abustle with carriages racing back and forth bearing various ladies to various chambers of beauty for various transformations. Meanwhile the Darcys were lost in their own "transformations."

At length E. announced that she must perform her ablutions and disappeared. She reemerged, toweling her locks and perfuming the air with the tonic smell of chamomile leaves. She disappeared into her dressing room, and when she reappeared she was wrapped in her warm cloak.

"May I not see the gown?"

"You shall see it later." She gave me a lingering look, noting my white tie and new dinner jacket and all such nonsense.

"Oh, Darcy! You are such a beautiful man! I hope that I shall make you proud!"

I felt inches taller as we left for the evening.

The scene we entered was not unlike the usual festive party in London, but many times magnified. Such a bustle of carriages and grooms and escorts and elegant couples ascending the marble steps! We entered, were announced, and Elizabeth ascended the massive staircase with the glittering chattering ladies to deposit her cloak.

Men do not chatter, but there was a steady hum of conversation, into which even I entered. I was introduced to my host, Lord Egremont. Chap about my age, squat and rather egg-shaped. Actually beginning to lose his hair. Vague memories of having known him, but remaining at 'the vague.' Harrow? Cambridge?

Of a sudden there was a hush, and I turned. Elizabeth was descending. Shock waves went through my body, and I dare say a few others.

It was not the gown *without* which caused the sensation.

It was the form *within*. I am not proficient at describing women's fashions, and I was certainly in no condition to do justice to this case. But let me assay it –

This *Athena* was sheer liquefaction. "The material" you ask? I think she says it is slipper satin from Paris. The color? Grey, to be sure. The style? Ever so simple – not a ruffle or a bow or furbelow in sight.

The cut? Ah! Some new form of draping that, while revealing nothing, somehow reveals everything. I will not dwell on that shape, (or I shall write on forever) only to mention the firmness and lean lines of this body.

So here we have subtle cloth over a supple, graceful form. But hold! Below the knee there was some kind of fold over a long slice which is cut from the knee to the floor. As my lady moved, the skirt moved with her just enough to reveal one slim gleaming leg, the delicate foot encased in a gray satin slipper. And then the cloth would slip back until the next (eagerly awaited!) step. The only jewels in sight were a diamond ornament pulling her soft gleaming hair back from her face and the pearls, to be sure.

When she stepped down onto the floor she stood most demure, waiting for me to claim her. As I did so, I had a sudden vision of this same Goddess aloft in a peach tree. Enchantment! Enchantress! How she has wrapped my very soul within her spell.

We admired the house, we danced, took refreshment, danced again, and did not stop dancing until the musicians had stolen away. What a delight with such a partner, and such fine music!

It seems our dancing was not unremarked. Lord Egremont made a special approach to engage us in comments about the addition we had made to the evening, tried to engage us to return at the next event, etcetera, etcetera. Now he was eyeing me closely, wrinkling his lofty brow.

"By Jove, I know you, Mr. Darcy. I have some scattery thoughts which keep sliding, but by Jove, we have met." We went through the usuals – schools, cricket, fencing (no! not fencing) – by now he had turned his attention from me and was scrutinizing Elizabeth with relish. I could come to no conclusion as to previous encounters. Made our farewells.

❦

16 September, 1813 London

What is the hour? Not quite dawn, I venture.

"Age cannot wither her, nor custom stale. Her infinite variety . . . "

I shall give Elizabeth these words shortly when she awakens. Now I have a confession to make to you – Elizabeth denounced me at one time for my wicked pride, thus changing the course of my thoughts about myself, and – to be sure – changing my life. Nevertheless, this night – nay, morning, I must confess to *pride*. I dare say no one in Great Britain has ever felt a larger portion of such than I did last night. I will confess it again and again!

LATER

We were awakened by the chime of the bell. The sun was high, and when I checked my timepiece I was startled to find that we were past noon.

At breakfast we were delivered a tray with several invitations.

Elizabeth remarked, "Perchance 'twould be better for our sanity if you were not such a fine dancer, Mr. Darcy."

I replied that it takes a fine partner to make me appear to be such a fine dancer. Then I became reflective, and she asked for the reason. I had been thinking of Elizabeth in the gown, and of the progress she had made throughout the evening, with all eyes turned upon her, and all ladies whispering to one another behind their fans. I will not even remark upon the consternation she aroused among the gentlemen.

"You are very modest, my dear. You are quite the stellar attraction of London, and I dare say that Mrs. Crowley can look forward to a lustrous and successful career."

"If I am the 'stellar attraction,' Mr. Darcy, I am not aware. I am only aware of you when we are together."

I put down my fork and looked hard at her. I cannot think of many wives who would put it thus. Moreover, I know that she is too truthful for artifice and flattery. What could I say in response to such a compliment? I kept looking at her, smiling a bit. Then said, "What can I say?"

She smiled back. "No need for words, milord."

※

24 SEPTEMBER, 1813 PEMBERLEY

Georgiana is at Pemberley and has been joining us for breakfast. This morning Elizabeth inquired if she knew the alphabet game.

Georgiana did not, and Elizabeth explained the rules. G. clapped her hands and asked if we could play.

Elizabeth assented, "Start with "A," use a proper name, and connect it with a fitting noun beginning with the same letter, for instance, 'Addison; Author.'"

Georgiana immediately offered "Bach; Bassoon."

"Bully, Georgiana!" I then added, "Caroline, Charlotte; Cousins."

Georgiana said, "Don't forget 'Catherine.'"

Elizabeth added "Clementi," and then scolded us for changing the rules of the game.

Georgiana said, "That's changing more than the rules of the game."

There was a silence, then I said, "That's the girl, Georgiana." She looked pleased.

Elizabeth suggested that we start anew, doing objects in words of three or more syllables, starting with 'A.' Georgiana quickly contributed "antimacassar," to our applause, and we were off again.

"Manservant!" "Nursery!" "Ormolu!" "Omnibus!"

"Postillion!" "Preferment!" "Poulterer!"

"I said, "Peach tree!"

As Georgiana protested that this was but two syllables. Elizabeth laughed, tried valiantly to suppress it and said,

"You are expelled, Darcy."

Georgiana asked immediately, "Elizabeth, is that what you call a 'secret language word?'"

I gazed at my sister with the greatest delight. "Bravo, Georgiana."

"Peach tree?"

I felt a sudden urge to kiss her on the brow, rose, and did exactly that. When I did, it drew tears. She fumbled for her serviette, found it, wiped her eyes, and fled the room. I would have followed her, but Elizabeth restrained me. "Let her be, Darcy. She has much to overcome, and she is doing splendidly. I think you realize not how much in need of affection she has been. What you did just then must mean more to her than ever you will know."

I sat down, but could eat no more. We were both silent. Then I said, "Is there a three syllable word to describe Georgiana's mood just now?"

Elizabeth could not answer then, but later came behind me as I was fastening my neckband and cravat. She watched a moment, commenting on how well they become me. Then added, *"Herzenleid."*

"And the meaning?"

"It is the German word for 'heartache.'"

"Capital! I did not know that you know German!"

"I do not know German. I know music."

We then discussed her plans, my plans, and bid one another *au revoir.* As I ran down the stairs and off to the stable I was thinking of that word, 'heartache.' How well I once knew such feelings. Is Georgiana to be rescued from *hers?*

Proper subject for nightly prayers!

26 SEPTEMBER, 1813 PEMBERLEY

I awaited Elizabeth in my study this morning. She has become such a splendid ally that I await her arrival in order to start the day's work. I looked around the room, at the objects so identified with father – his table globe whereon he had showed me the continents and oceans of our world; his wire spectacles, still in the cubby hole of the desk; his favorite books; a black Wedgwood vase –

I do, indeed, remember his stern lectures with their stern strictures, all delivered in this room.

I remember my father telling me of the arrival of my first horse and taking me to meet the animal when he arrived at the stables. (Number One Champêtre!) Just now I recall one morning when he awakened me at dawn to watch the breech birth of a colt. I remember how he had to fight to get that creature into the world. And how, when I asked my questions later, he answered me with evasions.

I remembered Elizabeth coming in the morning when I fell asleep at this desk, feeling my forehead, and offering to bring me coffee. My mother? Would she have done that for Father? I do not remember such a gesture.

I remember her closed door. I remember her descending, aglow, on the nights when my father was home and there were guests, or when they were to attend a social. I remember listening at the door of the drawing room one night and hearing my mother laugh, and how surprised I was to hear it.

I wonder what would they say now if they were to return and see the changes wrought by the young Mrs. Darcy. Above all, would they recognize the once silent and subdued Georgiana?

Finally, I do wonder this one thing; in planning so assiduously for my marriage did they ever consider aught beyond *position or possession?* – Was that *their* consideration when they married?

And one thing more; if my parents were so misguided in their advice, and I now know this to be a fact, why did I take it so to heart and try so valiantly to fulfill their wishes for me?

Strange, as I sit here I am feeling no sense of anything but sorrow for them. Would that their lives together had been more joyous.

As I muse thusly, D, I would go to my knees, here in my study, bend my head and send up a prayer of Thanksgiving to my Maker.

I shall do just that. No, later. I hear Elizabeth's light footsteps approaching.

5 OCTOBER, 1813 PEMBERLEY

Dear D. Georgiana and I are planning a surprise for Elizabeth's birthday. A special function at Pemberley in honor of the occasion. The big surprise will be a theatrical – more of that anon.

The study these days is a place quite different from *autretemps*. Tables are piled high with lists of guests, and of things to do, (quickly whisked away when necessary), frequent meetings with the staff. Rose looked terrified at her first summons to a meeting, and needed reassurance that her position was not in peril. Now everyone is as excited as we.

My plan is to take Elizabeth off to London, where, indeed, I have affairs to tend. Before we leave I must take care of a gift which I am eager to present her (in addition to a jewel from my mother.) I do think she would dearly enjoy a dog. I remember vividly her happy relationship at Netherfield with Beau. I remember her attachment to the recently departed Galahad, and I know how much she misses him. (As do I!) It is time to fill the breach he has left. Tomorrow I go to select a pup at the farm of a tenant who is a good breeder of pedigreed Pointers. A hunting dog, but I rather suspect it will become part of the household.

I plan for us to return the day before the party, with the pup established and there to greet us, thus giving Elizabeth time to get acquainted. And time to do the necessaries in connection with entertaining. As always, she will want to see to the flowers when first we return. How can we divert her? Aha! "Affairs of business." I will find a problem, and ask her to listen as I read a letter, and consult with her. Now I have to think of an appropriate problem. Dealing with Pemberley? No, that is my domain. Something to do with the household! Reynolds will know the answer. Whatever, Elizabeth will start to get ready for supper at the last minute, wash her hair, brush it, add a dab of powder to her nose, slip into a gown, which will, of course, not be a party gown, but still she will be lovely. Breathe not a word of any of this. It is easily suppressed until our return from London. Past that time? We shall have trouble keeping the secret from her!

8 OCTOBER, 1813 PEMBERLEY

Chose "our" dog today. What a lovable armful! I held him for longer than I intended, studying his silly fuzzy face with the black, black eyes. He is a round fur ball, although when grown he will be short haired. It was not difficult to make the selection. Farmer E. put all the males onto the ground and this one crawled right to me and onto my boot, where he snuffled busily at all the good horse smells. Of course I bent to pick him up, and he licked at my face with his warm sticky tongue.

D., I cannot tell you of my reaction. Of a sudden there were tears in my eyes, the source of which I cannot fathom. I wanted to take the dog with me right then and there, but that of course is out of the question. He will not be weaned for a good four weeks. I kissed him right on his silly muzzle, and promised I would soon return to take him to a happy home and a loving mother.

I rather think that I am more excited than Elizabeth will be!

As I approached Pemberley, Champêtre began to neigh, and soon I espied Elizabeth astride Dulcie, cantering towards us. She sits the horse so well! She handles the horse so beautifully. She looks like a young Greek athlete in her slim trousers. What training had she? She is a fine equestrienne, and I cannot believe she learned this in Hertsfordshire. She appears to use *haute école* horsemanship. Where did it originate? So far I have not dared to ask. We approached one another, both horses prancing with pleasure.

"Shall we try a taller jump?"

"Perhaps not"

"Still in pain?"

"No, but perhaps I should not jump."

※

10 NOVEMBER, 1813 LONDON

Have removed the unsuspecting Elizabeth to London for a week in order to let events take their course at Pemberley. The party will be arranged, the dog will be in quarters, the house will be made festive, and then we shall return.

I am having trouble keeping from her the fact that there are frequent dispatches from Georgiana and Reynolds, (including an acceptance from my Aunt Catherine.) I assume that this will please E. As for myself, I am not so certain. How much did my mother tell Aunt of my infatuation with the stage? And did she tell her of the parental mandate to renounce the theatre? Just how will Aunt react to Darcy's theatrical presentation?

I care not for myself – I do care that she could throw a *sabot* into the pleasure of my wife, possibly into the success of the evening itself.

The table in our London hallway is again deep in invitations. Word went around quickly that the Darcys were in town. It seems we are celebrated for our dancing, and I dare say that the town is agog to see again the wearer of the famous (or should I say "*infamous*"?) gown.

Elizabeth has been reading about royal functions in the *New Monthly Magazine* – some folderol about presentations at Court. She remarked something to the effect, "All this fuss about feathers and a train, all prescribed in agonizing detail. In backing away from Her Majesty, might not one step back right on to the train and topple into it?"

I asked her if she would like to be presented. She wrinkled her nose and said that having made the remark she had just made she could not possibly want to be presented, even if she *wanted* to be presented.

"A rather prolix statement, that."

"True. I am trying to be fair. I know you can arrange it. I am not certain that you care to arrange it. And the more I think on it, the less it seems the appropriate course for me. When we have a daughter –"

I gave a start. "Elizabeth! You are not –?"

"No, I am not. But there will be children, Darcy. Many years from now it may seem a good thing for a daughter."

Just as I sat back, relieved, she said,

"Daughters."

We have been to Covent Garden; saw *The Hypocrite* at the Lyceum. This is an adaptation of *Tartuffe* and brought back some pleasant memories, as well as several very unpleasant ones. These latter were racing in my head and Elizabeth looked quizzically at me when I failed to respond to one of the great comic scenes (one which I had once played so well!) Should I tell her of my wrecked career? No, best left alone. She will be seeing me in action soon enough!

We did have a discussion about the character of Tartuffe which I found stimulating. "He is such a fool and such a hypocrite!," said my wife. "How can people be deceived by such a one? And yet, it seems they never fail to be gulled, no matter how broad the chicanery."

"Have you known such a personality?"

"Truthfully, no. Have you?"

"Have you ever watched a session of Parliament?"

She laughed aloud and gave me a hug.

I showed her the Liverpool Museum, took her to an exhibit of portraiture at Spring Gardens. We walked in Hyde Park. She wanted to take a boat ride on the Thames, and we did that. It was raining, but we bundled up, huddled together, and did not mind. At one point she lifted her head and made as if to drink down the rain, in so doing exposing her graceful throat. I kissed her there, pulled her scarf around and tucked it in, then kissed her again.

We had boarded near Westminster Bridge and were rowed down 'the silver stream' – under Blackfriars, under London Bridge. We disembarked just before the Tower. My carriage awaited us there. I ordered a halt at the first tavern I espied, and we went in to warm ourselves with a hot rum drink.

A roaring fire in our room and a hot bath for each ended the day. I requested our supper to be served upstairs.

Hot bricks had been placed in the bed. As I was bending over my love she asked," Which glorious city is next, my love?" I told her I believed we were scheduled for Siena, or was it Avila?"

She is asleep now, and I am writing at length to you, D., when I should be studying my part. I doubt that Elizabeth has any suspicion of our plans. She knows *not* that Mary has been chez Bingley for these past weeks, nor that I was not always on my rounds at Pemberley, but engaged in rehearsals with my two sisters-in-law.

※

18 NOVEMBER, 1813 PEMBERLEY

Returned to Pemberley this morning somewhat fearful that someone in the household would give the plans away, but so far all was unruffled and there was nary a sign of the intense activities which were underway. The only change apparent would be the presence of the new pup, but so far there was no evidence.

Just as I had assured myself that all was concealed, we heard a yelp from the servants' quarters. Elizabeth stopped and inquired if she had heard a dog, but we assured her that the sound came from the stables. We ascended to our quarters with those members of the staff who were carrying our valises. As always, the room had been readied for us and was aglow with a welcome fire and great vases of autumn foliage. I studied the letters which were on the desk upstairs, was assured by Reynolds that the stacks in the study would be sufficient to keep me occupied for several months, washed, and exited the room for our noontime dinner.

Elizabeth paused in the hallway to admire a vase of tall autumn leaves on the sideboard in the upper hall. Suddenly we heard a loud shout, a louder yelp, sounds of a scuffle, then the light sound of pounding paws and into our view flew the newest member of the household, *Sultan* himself, followed by a panting Nielson. As he tried to scoop up the pup, the latter literally flew at Elizabeth, who caught him in her arms. The expression on her face as this flying object hit her was a joy to see. Within seconds these two were hugging and kissing, as Nielson, wringing his hands, was apologizing. Elizabeth reassured him that there was no cause for such, and turned to me with a radiant face, "Mr. Darcy! I sense your fine hand in the introduction of this new character. Am I correct?"

I assured her that she had surmised aright, and that the pup was for her birthday.

She became even more radiant, "How wonderful! And I had been so sure that you would have forgot the event."

I then told her that I would not dare forget her nameday, told her the name of the dog and other significant details. By now she had put him on the floor and was kneeling in front of him. He kept flying at her and trying to recover his station in her arms, she deftly (but hopelessly) attempting to curb his exuberance. Now ascended a puffing Mrs. Reynolds, who stopped and dabbed at her eyes with the corner of her apron. I inquired was she weeping, and was there aught amiss."

She replied, "On my faith, no, Sir, but this is so like the moment when I first met Mrs. Darcy and Galahad rushed her in just the same manner and you were such a sad and lonely man and it all came over me and I am sorry to distress you –"

At this moment Georgiana came from her room carrying a rag doll from her childhood. She, too, knelt and ceremoniously handed the doll to the frolicking pup. He took it and tore through the halls with the object in his mouth, the loose cotton limbs flailing wildly. We all watched in amusement. Finally he returned to us, dropped the doll at Elizabeth's feet, and fell beside it, his tongue lolling and his fat sides heaving for breath. I heard snuffling and turned to see Mrs. Reynolds at it again, this time even more moist (if possible.) I put my arm around her shoulder, and patted her, inquiring should I fetch a towel. This made her laugh, and soon she was recovered sufficiently to explain that the cause of her *deliquescence* (my word, not hers) was for Georgiana and her memories of what a sad lonely little girl *she* was.

By now the pup was on his back, all four paws waving in the air, and both ladies were rubbing his stomach.

Mrs. Reynolds apologized profusely and we assured her that there was no cause for contrition, that we all agreed that the Darcy "children" were a happier duo than ever before, and that we were hungry.

Nielson moved to take the dog. Sultan made sure to regain the doll. Last glimpsed he was being carried down the stairs by our most formal Nielson in his most elegant butler's outfit, doll's arms and legs flopping in all directions. Elizabeth took my arm, gave me an enraptured look, murmured a thank you, and down we went.

☙

21 November, 1813 Pemberley

And so came the evening of the birthday fête for Elizabeth. If it were not for Georgiana I am not certain we could have overcome the many moments when the truth was close to being revealed, but her quick wits and tactful explanations saved all the quirky moments and our lady was surprised indeed. My sister and I worked out a massive deception.

We three sat down to supper in our informal dining room as if it were an ordinary family evening. We had our glass of wine and a light bouillon. Then Nielson came in to inform us that there had been a disaster with the roast, and that cook was substituting a soufflé which would take some time. I suggested that we move into the drawing room whilst we waited. Would Georgiana play for us? She most gracefully assented.

We entered, and therein were assembled all the guests. A united shout stunned Mrs. Darcy, who collapsed into her husband's arms, and therein broke into tears. Quickly recovered and greeted one and all. Sultan was brought in and exclaimed over. He was then put to bed (or so I thought.)

Dinner was announced and we entered the grand dining salon, which looked handsome indeed, with tall tapers the length of the table, epergnes filled (but not overfull) with red berries from our grounds and pink tulips ordered from Holland, grown by Crowley. I know Elizabeth well enough to know that her first chore in the morning will be to find Crowley and ascertain how he was able to accomplish this miracle.

There were champagne toasts all around, honoring every person and every detail; a toast from Elizabeth acknowledging me, which quite caused my ears to ring and my heart to sing.

We went into the drawing room for coffee and dinner wine and more toasts. Opening of gifts – sachets, shawls, books – etcetera! Then I, with ceremony, invited our guests into the grand hall. Chairs had been arranged, a trio was present (harpsichord, harp, flute). I announced our surprise – a theatrical – scenes from *Henry the Fifth* to be played by myself, Miss Jane as Alice, and Miss Mary as Katherine. The expression on E.'s face almost broke my solemnity, but I held to my graveness, excused myself and went behind a screen to don the cloak and crown, whilst we had diversion of Handel's *Largo* from *Xerxes*.

The ladies were splendid! The play was splendid! I felt splendid. All my love of the drama returned full force. Ovation! Cries for "Encore!" Graciously agreed to. A reprise of a part of the scene (Act III, iv) which we played in French. The ladies were as excellent in French as in their own language. Mary, bless her, rose to impressive heights, emerging as the star of the performance. Cheers and bravos, for her, for all three, encoring of "Encore."

I acknowledged Mr. Bennet for his excellent skill in the education of his daughters. He could not rise. Why? Because he was holding the pup, who was sleeping soundly in his arms.

"Our critic?" I asked.

"Encore now *insisted* upon. (Planned.) Mary and I performed part of the courtship scene from the same play, starting with "Now fie upon my false French," and ending with, "Here comes your Father." It is fortunate that she had few lines after I declared, "Then I will kiss your lips, Kate," and moved as if to do so. She lost her queenly air, her poise, and looked as if she would flee the scene. I stopped this, gave her a brotherly hug, and a kiss upon the brow. More cheers.

So ended the theatrical, with everyone rushing to offer congratulations. Among the first was my Aunt, who advanced upon me, assuring me that my talent stems from her. "I was a star in all the tableaux we staged when I was your age. I would have been a fine dramatic actress if these had not been silent performances, and if I had been allowed." I searched out Elizabeth. She had not moved, so I went to her. All she did was to say my name. Mrs. Siddons could not have given it a better reading.

The evening ended very late. We will reconvene at Highlands for dinner on the morrow. Aunt Catherine was all warnings to the ladies to be sure to wear sturdy shoes, that we were to be "hauled out" to the Grecian temple for our aperitifs, weather permitting.

Family members are guests of the Bingleys, for which I bless the entire pantheon of Greek gods. Charles and I had sparred for this. He lost.

When we retired to our rooms (it was late indeed) I threw myself onto the couch in front of the blazing fire. Elizabeth joined me and looked at me with such ardor and gratitude that I scarce knew how to respond. I kissed both her hands but could say not a word. Not that I needed to! She commenced to describe her joy, missing not one detail. She particularly dwelled on the play and the casting of Mary, she could not refrain from discussing the skill, the air, the spirit, the self-possession of all three of us.

I dare say she would yet be enumerating all the minutiae if I had not found my own voice and embarked upon, "d'hand, de fingre, de nayles, d'arm, d'elbow, de nick, de sin, de foot" – (in the best manner of a French aristocrat pronouncing newly learned English words, and all the while touching each enumerated zone.) When I reached for her foot and cupped it in my hand – the high arch, the narrow heel – she laughed, but of a sudden she was not laughing, and she clung to me.

What a night for me, D. To have had my two loves – my lady, and the stage. And (finally) to achieve that perfect silence. (A few murmurs yes, the sound of our breathing – these tell me all I need to know – and is there aught more eloquent than a beloved's soft cries?)

22 November, 1813 Pemberley

I awoke this morning and reached for Elizabeth. Her side of the bed was empty. "She has indeed gone to find Crowley" was my first thought. Then I heard the scratching of a pen. Sat up quickly. Elizabeth! Sitting at my desk! Writing with *my pen!* I roared, "Woman, what are you doing?"

She looked up from her labors and said so sweetly, "Good morning, my marvelous Mr. Darcy. In answer to your dulcet question, I am writing you a thank you note for my most wonderful party." She came to the bed, sat on the edge and said, "Think me not offended, Mr. Darcy, but I am quizzical. What distresses you so? I but borrowed your pen."

What could I tell her, D.? No matter what I said, it would not come out right. Writing and the art of penmanship have been of paramount importance to me since first you came into my ken. Often the mere act of dipping my quill into the ink and commencing to tell you of my thoughts and experiences has taken from me the weight of my cares. As for the quills, they are to me as the brush is to the artist. Sharpening a quill pen is an act of devotion. Like any delicate tool, such a pen does not pass easily from hand to hand. If someone has used my pen, I can tell the difference in a trice.

What to tell Elizabeth? I said, "You had better dress. We are due for dinner at Jane and Charles' and we dare not be late. As for my seeming childishness, I have decided to atone by ordering for you a desk which will be placed near my own. Near the window, good light, all that."

We arrived at Highlands at a seemly hour, and found the party assembled outside, as warned by my aunt. A warm, soft wind was blowing, the grounds looked splendid in the clear light. As we approached the structure I admired the tableau, a scene of grace and felicity. From a distance it appeared as an elegant ballet, the men, dressed in their black coats and faun breeches, bending to the ladies, whose gowns and bonnet ribbons were rippling in the gentle breezes. Wine and appetizers were being passed.

We were greeted with exclamations of enthusiasm regarding the surprise of the previous evening, with emphasis upon our theatrical. I observed Mary. She was enjoying her new celebrity, and I swear, D., she showed a different look. As for our hostess! It all agrees with her, even her "condition." Subtle! One cannot define it. Is it possible she could be even more beautiful? She is. It is clear that Charles has not been oblivious to the glory of her. His glance rarely leaves her, and he fairly shines with joy.

Miss Jane tried to greet us individually, but my aunt would not leave off. Lacking Elizabeth's presence she had been (it seems) concentrating her attention on Miss Jane and hectoring her about the hardness of the bed, the slowness of the servants in bringing water for the bath, etcetera, etcetera. Mrs. Bennet was reassuring her about how very helpful the staff had been, but my aunt continued on as if Mrs. Bennet were not there. Now, looking haughtily about her, she moved on to the landscaping, the condition of the lawns, the positioning of the ha-ha fences, the temperature of the wine, the validity of design of the temple – I could see that her attentions were beginning to disconcert our hostess, and it was not long after our arrival that Miss Jane excused herself 'to see to the meal' and left us. Elizabeth quickly followed her, and they stood in deep conversation for some moments. Elizabeth gave me a rueful half smile when she returned to us.

As we were driving home to Pemberley she leaned to confide in me. I was certain that she would comment on my aunt's deportment. Could I defend the lady? No possible way. Instead, God bless her, she murmured that she had a request to make of me. "Say it, Elizabeth."

"My slightest wish is a command to you?"

"You know that. It does seem, however, that you could not have much to ask after all your surprises."

"But I do, Mr. Darcy."

"Say it."

"Will you assign a pen to me for my very own?"

And then, soon! (How rapidly the days do go!) It was night and she in my arms, and we in one of the ardent kisses which she has learned to accept – and, nay, to return. I pulled away, and in a conversational manner said her name. I could feel her ardor abate – the breathing slows, the body temperature cools. (Now I know what the phrase means, 'Playing with fire.')

Her eyes opened wide. "What is it, Mr. Darcy?"

"I have been thinking, Elizabeth. I have decided you may indeed use my pen. But you may not touch the ink."

Laughter, low and like music. Warm embrace. Started *da capo,* finished the symphony.

❦

1 December, 1813 Pemberley

Elizabeth dotes on Sultan. And vice versa. When in her presence he follows her every move. She is training him slowly and steadily. So far he sleeps in the scullery, but I would like him outside our door when he is house trained. Why? I have always wanted a faithful dog to be sleeping outside my door.

These have been busy days for me, old friend. The weather is relentlessly a'drip, and all kinds of problems come with it. Leaking roofs (not ours, *grace à dieu*), flooded floors, etcetera, bedeviling many of our tenants. Wagons have slid off the road, supplies cannot be delivered. Name it! It occurs! In going about my rounds I have many an occasion to enter into the home of a tenant, and I am finding some interesting chaps. Their hobbies astonish me, so various, so expertly crafted, and involving so much patience and care. Some carve, some fashion objects from clay, some build miniature toys for the children. The women sew, and some make dolls and doll clothes, which I find also interesting. They create the dolls from knobby branches, grasses, corn cobs, simple rags.

It does occur to me that the Almighty has fashioned many of his children with many diverse talents.

The weather being what it is, one does think of Noah's Ark. If board we must, I am convinced that there will be a person expert in caring for each human and creature need, and that there will be harmony and comfort.

Meantime I go about my work, and return fairly soaked to the bone. By now it is evening, and not only wet but *cold*. The steam rises from my trusty steed. I turn him into the stable (he is not reluctant for this!) and rub him dry after we take the saddle from him. He fairly talks his pleasure and gratitude.

Then the master takes his cold soaked self into the manor where there is awaiting a roaring fire, a hot bath for a delicious immersion, a hot tea, and Madame Venus.

⁂

26 December, 1813 Pemberley

Keep warm, D., there is sleet pounding down on us. To look out the window is to look upon a world delineated entirely in whites and greys, with an occasional shading of lavender. Not a creature to be seen. Pemberley is quiet; we have given leave to whomsoever of the staff has requested it. Those who remain are not allowed to help with the preparation of meals, an occupation which Elizabeth enjoys, and to which she is training Georgiana.

It is a good thing I do not believe that spirits return. I can well imagine my mother's dismay at seeing her daughter hard at work in the lower regions of her house, scrubbing the dirt from garden vegetables. As for the mistress, what *would* my mother say? (Best leave that alone, eh?)

Our Christmas was a wonderful one. I take no credit for it; it was a plan brought forth months ago by the two ladies. A plan so pleasant that I am certain it will become a tradition here at Pemberley. Moreover, it is most practical. I take credit in that I initiated the earliest stages of it by discovering that one of my tenants is a splendid carver, and had accomplished a sturdy rocking horse from wood scraps. I asked him to bring it over and called Elizabeth to come to see it. She reacted with enthusiasm. Within hours she and Georgiana had hatched the scheme to invite all tenants and their families to a Christmas noon dinner, and to have such a horse for each home with children. What an assignment! Could it be managed? "Of course!," said Elizabeth.

Actually, the project became a delight to me (memories tug at me but are elusive) and I came to be involved in the assembling of many of the objects.

Actually, the project became a delight to me (memories tug at me but are elusive) and I came to be involved in the assembling of many of the objects.

The affair was enormous, but ran smoothly. Because of the cold, the party was held in the long gallery which Crowley decorated with aromatic fir boughs. A long trestle table was heaped high with wondrous vittles – Christmas goose, tongue with red currant sauce, roast game hens, sweetbreads and chicken fricassee, salad, asparagus, peas, beetroot, plovers' eggs in aspic jelly, French and English mustards, mayonnaise, confitures. Desserts – macédoine of fruit, meringues à la crème, fresh cherry jelly (made last summer by Elizabeth and cook), roundabouts (a round sweet biscuit with indents all around the rim), ice and cheeses. For the children – twelfth cakes recreated into Christmas biscuits, each containing a coin and a bean, distributed with verbal warnings to nibble with care. (Be not impressed by my listing, D., I have in front of me my wife's menu.)

Carols were sung by the church choir and several of our tenants provided music. This led to my swinging Elizabeth out to dance, and soon the adults and many of the children joined. We put them through "Sir Roger de Coverley" to shouts of pleasure.

The horses were presented. As the children of each family came forward shyly for the offering from the two ladies, I had a strange experience. Tears filled my eyes. *Whyever?* I turned away, so E. would not see.

🙰

6 JANUARY, 1814 PEMBERLEY

Aunt Catherine came to visit us last week on her way home from London. She stayed a fortnight, kept the household in an uproar, enjoyed *herself* thoroughly, caused not a few verbal skirmishes, on which she, (but not we) thrived. Within days we two were flatter than the *crêpes* which cook served as a sweet on Aunt's last evening. Actually Aunt did not reach her full stride until that very evening, when she demanded to know of me what had happened to the hunting print which had hung above the mantle in the London house.

("Good lord," thought I, "the poker!")

When Elizabeth queried her, she silenced her, wrathfully demanding to know what would she, Elizabeth, know of Darcy family holdings. Elizabeth was amazingly calm in view of the dreadfulness of such a remark.

I cannot say the same for myself. I needed to protest such an offensive remark, but how could I explain the replacement of the picture without retelling the events of the dreadful night on which the poker had been won? And how could I explain the childish act of hanging such an instrument on the wall?

Finally I inquired of Aunt if she were referring to the hunting print which had hung in the salon. (Not the most brilliant sally of my life.)

Scorching me, in turn, she demanded what other object had hung there over these many years, and did I not know of the value of this particular *objet*, and did I not know that she herself had given it to my parents on the occasion of an important anniversary?

Then she turned on Elizabeth again, "You sold it!"

We both gasped. I quickly told the servants they were no longer needed. They left hastily.

Elizabeth colored, stood quickly and remarked in the iciest tone I have heard yet, "Madam, you have insulted me in the past in every possible way, but this time you have overreached yourself."

She was not easy to quiet and at last I had to say, in my coldest possible voice, "Mrs. Darcy, say no more. This is an order."

Then I turned to Aunt, "The print, Madam, is in the study, and if you had taken the trouble to look through the London house for yourself I think you could have spared this family a good deal of grief. Now I insist you apologize to my wife."

"You may accept my apology, Mrs. Darcy. It is herewith tendered as ordered."

Elizabeth said, "Your graciousness, Lady de Bourgh, is accepted, as ordered." She sat down, but glared *at me*.

Well, at least we, who both had been well wilted before the clash, now had our spirits restored to working order.

Aunt was not to be deterred, "And what, Mr. Darcy, have you managed to hang in place of that glorious work? A POKER! Not even a fine poker; certainly not one from the Darcy household. A beaten, filthy, scurvy thing. How do you explain yourself, Sir?"

Foolish Darcy! How was I to explain the circumstances of how I came to acquire the blasted poker? By now Elizabeth was looking at me keenly and frowning. I could see that fine-tuned brain of hers going to work.

As suddenly as she had started the battle my aunt announced that she was feeling poorly and would retire, and acted immediately upon her decision.

Dead silence in the room. We stared at one another. Finally E. asked softly, "Mr. Darcy, when did you acquire this object which I can only assume is some kind of trophy?"

I told her that I was not to be questioned.

"Allow me one question."

"Allowed."

"Darcy, has this object anything to do with your trip to London in quest of the vagrant Wickhams?"

Great thundering Jupiter! How came she to such a conclusion!?

I stared at her long and hard, thinking, thinking, what could I tell her? It was clear to me that I could tell her naught. And that is what I told her.

She was silent, put the room to rights, snuffed the candles, went to the door and held it for me. We proceeded up the stairs, into our chambers, undressed, and got into bed, all in the same dread silence.

She turned her back to me, and I dared not touch her. I could tell by her breathing she was not asleep. And then in one quick movement she turned and was in my arms, asking over and over, "What did you *do* for me? What did you DO for me?" And then she started to cry.

When I finally quieted her she said, "All the time after you had left me at Lambton I was thinking that you had walked away never to return. Now it seems possible that you never might have, that you might have lost your life. Oh Darcy, *what did you do for me?*" And then (again!) she wept.

I cradled her for a long time before she quieted. Then came the low throaty laugh. "Well, my dear Mr. Darcy, your Aunt Catherine has opened Pandora's Box. What in the name of heaven can we expect next?"

෴

10 JANUARY, 1814 PEMBERLEY

Dear D., As I started to write this afternoon, Elizabeth called out to me, "You are writing to D.?"

"I am about to start. Have you any objection to this overly zealous habit of mine?"

"I could well be somewhat jealous of D., but I am not. However I have something I would like to say to D."

"I shall be your scribe. Tell me."

She sat on the edge of the bed, "Dear D., This is Mrs. Darcy inform-
ing you that Mrs. Darcy is expecting and –"

That is as far as she got. I almost overturned the inkstand as I leaped
to my feet and hastened to her side. I am to be a father! The baby is due in
August. A son?

I gave her the hug for which I knew she would be waiting, returned
to the desk and for a while I sat there resting my head on you, D. Such
strange thoughts came to mind; the fencing lessons can be discontinued.
Luigi will be relieved. So am I. But what chaff to be considering now. Elizabeth is with child! There will be an heir to Pemberley. And yet, and yet – it
might be a girl. No matter . . . Whether boy or girl, I am overcome with
happiness – and yet, and yet surely this will be the end of the paradise in
which I have dwelt. E. will nevermore be mine alone. Everything will change.
She will want the bedroom door open, as was her mother's. I know full well
that this will mean Sultan dashing into the room forthwith. How can we be
intimate with a dog ranging the room?

There will be hordes of workmen and WORSE – decorators –
bringing – pink and white? Blue and white? A son and heir?

My thoughts run wild, D.

Would that there were some way to have our fill of the women we
adore without getting them with child! Eventually, yes. But so soon!

I am happy – I am distraught – And she sits there so calmly with a
happy smile on her face. My thoughts return to *The Annunciation*. The image I doted on was by Mantegna? Or was it Giotto? A girl might it be? –
followed by four more like the Bennet family?

Perhaps I shall have my horse saddled and go for a ride? That is
what I shall do!

❧

15 JANUARY, 1814 PEMBERLEY

Today after our tea, Elizabeth returned to her reading of *Self Control*,
the latest best seller by one Mary Brunton. I had determined to write in you,
D., but her bubbling laughter, interspersed with many exclamations of vexation kept me from my concentration. For a moment I was annoyed by this,
and was about to chide her, when I realized that *I was not being distracted,*

but that I did not have the desire (or the need!) to write in you, my oldest and, formerly, only friend. Not this afternoon, and not in the future. I threw down the pen with a clatter, and Elizabeth looked up.

"What is it, Darcy? Why the furrowed brow?"

"I seem to have reached the end of the road in my relationship with this Diary."

"The habit of almost a lifetime? The long hours you spend with your friend, Mr. D.?"

"That is precisely the rub – 'the long hours.' It is a habit I no longer need. I have you now, and I find you somewhat more satisfying as a confidant than D. D. is too silent for my taste."

"I? I *somewhat* more satisfying?'"

"Sometimes you say too much, often you say too little, but always you are the most alive spirit I have ever known, and I could go on, but then I might turn your head, and how can I feast on your beauty when your head is on backward?"

And so I shall write "Adieu" to you, D., a fervent thank you for being my friend for all these years. Without you I am not at all certain that I would have ended sane, sensible, (well – reasonably so), happily married, and with a potential for being a good father (which I am soon to become, God save us).

I have in mind that I shall take your key and have it melted to make a locket for my lady. I fancy that I shall put a snippet from my "mop" therein, and perhaps an inscription – what shall it be?

Perhaps, "For Elizabeth, best friend and best confidante, with pride in who and what you are, and prejudice, all in your favor."

Will there be room for all that?

There is in my heart.

THE END

ACKNOWLEDGMENTS

With Thanks

I have not written seriously for fifty years. In 1945 I ended my work as a screen writer and went back to family responsibilities. I have been writing – yes – light verse, poems to friends, and song parodies for every occasion – but, when I assayed prose, a deep anger emerged which, in my judgement, spoiled the writing.

Then came, in 1996, the BBC production of *Pride and Prejudice*, and into my thoughts came a cascade of questions about Fitzwilliam Darcy (so elegantly played by Colin Firth). I could not get the character out of my head, so I started listening to those thoughts and this book is the result.

The writing came easily, in a rush – two months, to be exact – but I had written, in effect, a screen treatment, with all the visuals still in my head and not on the page. Good dialogue to be sure, and of course I had Jane Austen's characters to play with, but where was it all taking place?

The diary would never have been fleshed out if it were not for the amazing role that friends and new acquaintances have played all these months. I say "new acquaintances" because people with information I needed have come out of nowhere and freely given me of their time and professional knowledge. And my friends have been a source of wonderment to me for their generosity with their time, for their enthusiasm, encouragement, good criticism, and for infusing me with a confidence which I lacked.

I list the names of all these people without defining the role each has played, except for:

MY FAMILY, with especial gratitude and love to my stalwart husband Michael, and to my daughters, Fay Abrams, Betty Rauch and Bunni Zimberoff for their invaluable helpfulness and expertise; and to the entire family for their enthusiasm and shared passion (well, most of them) for *Pride and Prejudice.*

ALLEGRA AND LARRY YUST for their unstinting help in choreographing and shepherding Darcy's Diary from first draft into publication.

And to everybody for their many ways of helping, for their largesse, their laughter in response to my words, and, yes, in some cases for their tears – my grateful thanks.

FAY ABRAMS
WALTER ARLEN
SALLY BENNETT
MAGNOLO "MAX" BUGARIN
LUCRETIA COLE
THE COMPUTER PLACE
SHELBY CRAFT
DUTTON'S BRENTWOOD
MICHAEL FASMAN
RON GOTTESMAN
CAROLE HAMNER
THELMA AND AL HERZIG
HENRY HILTON
THE HORMOZI FAMILY
DAVID KANINI
ANNETTE KAUFMANN
KAREN KAYE
ELAINE KENDALL
BERNICE KERT
DAVID KNIGHT
PAUL KUSSEROW
DAVID LESSER
STEPHEN LESSER
DR. PAUL MALIN
BETTY RAUCH
THE REVEREND GEORGE F. REGAS
JOYCE REED ROSENBERG
LEO SIGMAN
RUBIN M. TURNER, ESQ.
ELEANOR WASSON
JANETTE WEBB
MILTON WEXLER
JAMIE WOLF
DIGBY WOLFE
THE YUST FAMILY: LARRY, CLARA, VICTORIA, ALEXANDER AND ALLEGRA
BUNNI ZIMBEROFF